BLOOD RUNS COLD

A Detective Jim DeLong Thriller

Angela Kay

Join Angela's Facebook reader's group, Author Angela Kay's Crime Book Club! Lots of surprises, bonus material, contests, games, and giveaways at https://www.facebook.com/groups/authorangelakayscrimebookclub

For Manny Grimes, after seven years, your murder is finally solved.

For those who supported me and had faith in me during the long years of writing and rewriting.

For my readers.

Chapter 1

THE SKY WAS STILL murky from the heavy storm the night before, the dew lingering in the early morning air. The leaves on the trees sagged toward the ground, droplets of water rolling to the earth. The crisp spring air brought enough of a chill to require a light jacket. It seemed almost perfect for the occasion for which Detective Jim DeLong parked his car.

He released an inward groan when his new dress shoes sank in a soft spot on the grass, then scraped off the mud as he stepped onto the concrete. He drew in a breath and pushed it out, letting the smoke from his cigarette evaporate into the air. DeLong tossed it onto the ground, thinking it was time he quit. Lately, his wife had been hounding him about it, and in all honesty, smoking was a nasty habit.

Surveying the premises, he noticed the police cars scattered in the area, lights glistening against the puddles.

One officer searched the inside of a mustard-yellow Kia, dusting for fingerprints. Another pulled a light blue dress with frills on the bottom from a Dillard's bag. He made a comment that his daughter would love the dress. When he spotted DeLong nearby, he cleared his throat and returned the dress to the bag.

DeLong paid little attention to him as he noticed the caution tape blocking off the back of the building leading to the river.

He made a beeline in that direction, pushing through a small crowd of bystanders trying to see what was happening. A man was taking videos with his cell phone. As he neared, DeLong heard an officer request that he put the phone away. Reluctantly, the onlooker muttered something underneath his breath, slipped the phone into his pocket, and took a small step backward, frowning at his companion by his side. When the officer focused his attention on another onlooker, the young man retrieved his cell for more videos.

Slipping underneath the tape, DeLong scanned the area. To his left was an officer standing near the building's entrance, speaking to a young couple. The woman's breathing was erratic, her face white. Her long, dirty blonde hair clung to her skin and her velour outfit. The man kept his right arm wrapped around her waist, drawing her near to his chest as he responded to the officer's questions.

"Hey, Jim."

DeLong glanced sideways to see Jeffrey Newman, his lead Crime Scene Investigator, walking his way.

It had been a while since DeLong last saw Newman. His wife had given birth to a premature baby girl, so he had taken his leave to take care of his family. Three weeks ago, DeLong received a text that they were expecting a second baby.

"Jeff," DeLong acknowledged, "how's Christina and the baby doing?"

"They're good," Newman said, his expression stoic. "Her sister came into town a few days ago to help while I'm working. Christina's worried about this pregnancy since we almost lost Sara during labor."

"Sam's available if you need anything," DeLong offered.

Newman smiled. "Thanks. Remind me to show off photos later."

The gleam in his eyes was unmistakable. DeLong was happy for his friend, but still envious. After months of trying and running tests, he and his wife realized a second child wouldn't happen. He found it frustrating that a couple like the Newmans could try for so long to no avail, and then it happened back-to-back. And then there was Samantha, getting frustrated at her own infertility. As an only child, she wanted their daughter to have a brother or sister to enjoy.

But the doctors informed them last week it wouldn't happen.

"What do we have?" DeLong forced himself out of his daydream.

"The couple over there," Newman nodded toward the man and woman DeLong saw earlier, "were running along the trail. They spotted something in the water, went to check, and found the body."

"Any ID?"

"No. No ID, no purse, no phone."

"Could it have been a robbery gone wrong?" DeLong asked as they made their way to where the crime scene was sectioned off.

Newman sighed. "I don't think so, Jim. You'll see why."

The body was discovered at the Savannah Rapids Pavilion. Depending on the time of day, the trail was busy with runners and walkers.

The trees were full of luscious green leaves, the creek to the side, whispering, showing its white teeth as it powered against the rocks.

All-in-all, it was a peaceful area, and now murder only darkened it.

DeLong took notice of the building he'd walked by before meeting with Newman. Reporters had arrived, forcing their way through the crowd of bystanders. He was sure cameras were rolling, but the officers were doing well in keeping anyone from crossing the tape.

The building was out of view of where DeLong and Newman were heading. If anyone saw anything, then they were likely running or walking along the trail.

As they neared, DeLong observed the body of a woman lying in the water. She was roughly five foot six, wearing a black t-shirt. Her arms and legs had deep gashes and bruises. It appeared as though she had put up a good fight.

Her jeans were ripped, but DeLong wasn't sure whether it was a fashion statement or a result of the struggle. Since she still wore her jeans, he assumed she wasn't sexually assaulted, but he wouldn't know for sure until the coroner performed the autopsy.

DeLong made his way toward the water and kneeled by the body, taking in the strong fragrance of sunflower and mud. She lay on the ground, her legs and arms askew, a red handkerchief placed over her face.

No, it likely wasn't a robbery. If the murder was random, they wouldn't have bothered covering her face. It was always possible the couple who found the body did. He made a mental note to find out.

Hand marks were visible on her arms, telling him someone had grabbed onto her tight. Her neck had discoloration as though her killer had strangled her.

After slipping on latex gloves, DeLong removed the cloth and found his victim's head facing the dry land. Dried blood clung to her skin from a deep wound on the side of her head. He glanced around, wondering if the weapon remained at the scene.

He inspected the handkerchief, noting the gold flowers design and the words "love always." With care, DeLong folded the handkerchief and placed it in an evidence bag.

During his time on the police force, he had seen many ways for a murderer to kill his victims. It always troubled DeLong, knowing human beings had such disrespect for life. A part of him thought he needed to get out of the game. But when he analyzed crime scenes, he wanted nothing more than to find justice for the victims.

DeLong brushed the wet blonde hair with care from the woman's face. He let out an angry curse.

He angled his head to the side, snapping his eyes shut, then forced himself to turn back with a daunting sigh.

Her too-familiar face was pale and bruised, almost to the point of being unrecognizable. Her eyes closed to the world.

"You know her?" Newman's quiet concern was clear.

Pulling back, DeLong rose, finding himself unable to take his eyes away.

"Yeah," he said, his voice dry. "I know her."

Newman waited a few beats before he opened his mouth to speak. However, DeLong wasn't in the mood for questions he didn't want to answer. So he turned away and headed to where the witnesses stood.

As they walked toward the couple, the coroner went down the steps to retrieve the body.

The young woman had stopped crying, though her lips quivered and her eyes gleamed with tears. She still clung to her friend for support.

"I'm Detective Jim DeLong," he said. "Can you tell me what you saw?"

"We were running on the trail when we saw her." The man's face revealed no angst, yet his voice betrayed him.

"Do you come here often?"

He nodded. "Every morning, we run five miles."

"Did you see anything or anyone out of the ordinary? Maybe someone seemed nervous, angry?"

"No. We didn't see anything until we saw her."

"Who spotted her first?" Newman asked.

"I-I did." The woman's voice was timid, her eyes hollow. "She was just laying there. So still." She shivered and leaned in closer to her companion, who wrapped his arms tighter around her body. A small sob escaped her lips.

"Did you put this handkerchief over her face?" DeLong held the evidence bag for the couple to see.

"No," they said in unison.

"Can we go now?" he asked. "I should get her home."

DeLong nodded as he reached into his jacket pocket for his business card. "We'll contact you if we have any more questions. In the meantime, if you need anything, or remember anything, call me. It doesn't matter how big or small."

As the couple walked away, one of Newman's investigators called out from the wooded area.

"I think I've found something!"

DeLong and Newman jogged to where the investigator kneeled. Overgrown tree branches partially hid him. The investigator donned a pair of latex gloves and reached underneath a shrub for a large gray rock.

DeLong made his way over, Newman following close behind.

"Look at this. Could be a murder weapon."

The rock was smooth and covered with a dried red substance. The investigator opened the kit he had placed next to him and pulled out the Luminol and a cotton swab. He rubbed the dark stain and dropped the clear liquid onto the swab. They watched as the color turned pink.

Next, the investigator dusted the rock and captured a partial print. After gathering all he could from the evidence he found, he packed it away.

DeLong looked around the canal, deep in thought. They still had to confirm the blood on the rock belonged to the victim, and a partial print wouldn't reveal much. But, it seemed they already got lucky. Most other evidence would likely have been destroyed because of the heavy overnight rain.

As he glanced around the premises, DeLong felt a slight surge of hope amid his churning stomach.

Newman cleared his throat to get DeLong's attention.

"You wanna tell me how you know the victim?"

A few heads bobbed their way, and DeLong motioned for Newman to follow him. What he wanted to say, he wanted to keep private.

Even though he'd eventually have to come forward and tell the whole story.

But until then, it'd be a secret among friends.

Chapter 2

DeLong paced his office, dreading to make the phone call. He'd prefer to take a dive in acid than open old sores, but he knew it had to be done. Newman offered to do it for him, but DeLong didn't feel right passing off the responsibility.

"Do it, Jim," he ordered himself. "The sooner you call, the sooner you can hang up."

Before he could convince himself to change his mind, DeLong found the name in his contact list and pressed *send*. His heart rose in his chest as he paced faster. He was sure he'd burn a hole in the carpet.

"Jim?"

The voice on the other line was cold, yet indifferent.

Considering how long it had been, the reaction wasn't surprising. DeLong froze in place, trying to think of something to say. His mind was swirling, and his hands clammed up. He scolded himself for feeling childish. There was a reason he needed to call.

He cleared his throat, wishing he had poured himself something to drink so it wouldn't feel so dry.

"Hi, Sullivan."

No reply.

"Been a long time, brother," he continued. DeLong ran a hand through his hair as his long-forgotten past whispered to him. He wished his old friend, Russ Calhoun, was still around. He'd always been the one who could silence the voices of his past.

Not his wife.

Not his mother...or anyone else, for that matter.

Just because Calhoun *knew*.

"What do you want?"

DeLong heard faint footsteps over the phone line.

To the point. He understood that.

"I'm afraid I have something to tell you. Something..." DeLong trailed off, trying to find the words. The movements had stopped short, and Sullivan sucked in a deep, shaky breath.

"What? What are you trying to say? Is it Mom?" he asked. "Did something happen to her?"

DeLong shook his head as he braced himself.

"No, she's fine," he said, clearing his throat. "It's Bree."

Silence.

"Sully?"

"What about Bree? What do you want, Jim?"

"This morning, some runners found her at the Savannah Rapids Pavilion. By the canal. She's...dead."

"No. It can't be."

DeLong's heart felt heavy. He clutched his cell phone tighter in his hand. The breathing on the other line became unsteady. Unsure of what to say, DeLong fell into his chair.

"I'm so sorry," DeLong continued after a moment of silence.

"What happened?" Sullivan's voice croaked. He cleared his throat.

"We're not sure yet," DeLong said. "But it appears she put up a fight with her attacker."

He heard a sound as though Sullivan punched a wall.

"She didn't come home last night. I thought..." he trailed off. "Are you certain it's her? I mean, maybe it's someone that looks like—."

"It's Bree, Sully." DeLong closed his eyes and pushed out a deep breath. "Are you in town? I'll need you to come identify her body. I'm the lead investigator in this case," he continued, "but if you don't want to see me, I-I'll understand. I can send someone in my place."

"No, um..." Sullivan paused. For a second, DeLong thought he'd lost him. Then he said, "I'll be there. Let me, um...sorry, I have to go. Just text me when and where to meet you."

With that, Sullivan ended the call.

DeLong didn't know what to expect from the conversation, nor did he know what to feel. He sat in deep thought, paying little attention to the knock at the door. Newman stuck his head in the office.

"I take it from the look on your face that you called him."

"Yeah. I called him."

Newman stepped inside, clicked the door shut and sat in a chair across from DeLong's desk. He crossed one leg over his knee, clamping his hands together. Newman narrowed his eyes as he studied DeLong.

"How'd he take the news?"

DeLong waited a few beats before responding. "As well as you can expect."

"Yeah, I can only imagine." Newman leaned back in the chair. "How long ago was it since you last spoke to him?"

DeLong pushed out a heavy sigh as he remembered his parting with his brother. No matter how he tried, he still couldn't shake the memories loose, even after all these years. He swallowed and looked at Newman, hoping his face didn't betray his thoughts. "I saw him once at his wedding almost ten years ago when he married Bree. Honestly, other than family stuff, it was the first time we'd spoken since we were kids. He didn't even want to invite me. Dad made him."

DeLong frowned, then scoffed, shaking his head.

"Things didn't go well for us because back then I cared about nothing but getting my next drink. The next time I saw him was at my dad's funeral four years ago. I'd been sober for a few years, but I'd screwed things up enough for Sullivan to not want anything to do with me. Over the years, we've become masters at avoiding each other."

"Man," Newman whistled. "I can't even imagine what it's like to be estranged from your own blood."

Before he could respond, his cell phone rang, and DeLong answered, thankful for the break from unwanted memories.

"DeLong."

"Detective, it's Dr. Harmon. I've finished the autopsy."

"We're on our way." He motioned to Newman as he rose to his feet. "Tell me what you found."

"She died approximately nine hours ago. There was no sign of sexual assault. The cause of death was hemorrhaging in her brain. It appears she was beaten several times with a blunt object. Her skull was crushed, and after a while, she bled out."

DeLong stepped into the warming morning, Newman hot at his heels. "You're telling me she was still alive when her killer left the scene? For how long?"

"My best guess? An hour. But chances of her surviving her injuries if someone *had* called an ambulance are very slim. It was a miracle she lasted that long. Even if she'd made it to the hospital..." the doctor hesitated before continuing, "...she would have been comatose."

DeLong rubbed his eyes with a sigh. "Thank you, Doctor. Newman and I will be there shortly. Her husband will also meet us to identify the body."

As they climbed into DeLong's truck, he sent his brother a text asking him to meet them at the coroner's. Once the message went through, he relayed to Newman the results of the autopsy. After he finished listening, Newman pushed out a breath. He opened his mouth as though to say something, then changed his mind. DeLong turned the ignition and pulled out of the parking lot. He glanced over at Newman, noticing the tense silence that had befallen him.

"What?"

Newman released another sigh. "I want you to be prepared, that's all. I also think you should one of your guys take over."

"I'm perfectly capable of being objective," DeLong snapped. "And I don't need preparing. It's my brother, for goodness' sake."

"Your brother with whom you haven't had a friendly conversation in years," Newman pointed out with a frown. "And that's not what you need to prepare yourself for."

At a stop sign, DeLong twisted his body so he could glare at Newman.

"My brother didn't kill his wife, if that's what you're saying."

"With all due respect, Jim, you don't know him anymore," Newman reminded him. "Remember, usually, the killer is someone the victim knows. And a good many of those are committed by the spouse."

DeLong gripped the steering wheel, causing his knuckles to turn white. No.

He refused to believe what Newman was saying.

Even though he realized Newman was right.

But how could Sullivan murder his own wife? He wouldn't hurt another human being...not unless they proposed a threat to him, anyway.

He sniffed and shook his head free of the thoughts.

At the sound of a horn blowing, he put the car back in motion, his mind reeling. DeLong argued with himself that it wasn't possible his brother would murder anyone, let alone his wife. He also sent up a prayer that the meeting with Sullivan would go smoothly. The thought of seeing his brother always brought butterflies to his stomach.

Chapter 3

SULLIVAN LOOKED THE SAME as he did the last time DeLong saw him, except for the salt and pepper hair and goatee. Wrinkles circled his eyes, but the handsome elder brother still had the youthfulness of the DeLong genes. He was an inch shorter than DeLong and wore small, rectangle eyeglasses. The muscles in his arms showed he still worked out regularly.

He sat on a bench outside the room where his wife lay on a slab. Sullivan bounced his knees and clutched his hands into a tight fist. His breathing was heavy, eyes wide. He was muttering underneath his breath, "It won't be her."

"Sully," DeLong said as he and Newman walked up.

His brother looked up, eyes wide and dark. Sullivan rose, trying to mask his trembling legs.

He only nodded at DeLong, then glanced over at Newman.

DeLong introduced his brother to the investigator, forcing himself to ignore the knots in his stomach. DeLong felt heat rush to his head as he watched Sullivan. There were many things he wanted to say to him. But he wasn't sure where to start. It was hard to find anything valid when Sullivan kept his gaze on Newman.

"I'm sorry for your loss," Newman said. He extended his hand to shake Sullivan's. "We'll do everything in our power to find out who did this to your wife." Glancing toward DeLong, then back to Sullivan, he said, "Are you ready? Or do you need a second?"

Sullivan cleared his throat, tugging at his tie as though it was strangling him. "I just want to get this over with."

DeLong nodded, and they led him into the small autopsy room. Dr. Harmon stood over the table with a clipboard in his hand, jotting something on its pages. He looked up and offered a small smile, setting the clipboard aside.

"This is the husband," DeLong stated. "Sullivan DeLong."

Dr. Harmon's left eyebrow rose with curiosity, but he chose not to say anything when the detective shook his head.

Sullivan remained quiet, his eyes glued to the outlined sheet on the gray slab.

Dr. Harmon prepared to remove the sheet. "Are you ready?"

Sullivan swallowed hard. "Yes."

Pulling the sheet to her shoulders, Dr. Harmon stepped back.

Sullivan stared at the motionless body. Tears formed in his eyes. "Oh, Bree." Sullivan had a catch in his voice. He reached his hand for her face but didn't touch her. His breath rose and fell in quick gasps, on the verge of hyperventilating. His hands shook, and Sullivan jerked around, face pale. "That's her. That's my wife."

DeLong followed his brother out of the room, trying to get a read on him, but it was almost impossible.

"When was the last time you saw her? Or spoke to her?"

"I don't know. I don't—I can't think. I can't..."

DeLong took Sullivan's elbow, intending to lead his brother to the bench, but was shrugged off.

"Don't touch me," he snapped, throwing out a round of curses.

DeLong ignored the gesture. Instead, he crossed his arms and asked, "Do you know of anyone who would want to hurt her?"

"No," Sullivan said, his voice distant.

"Any reason why she would have been at the pavilion?"

"She loved it there," Sullivan said. He closed his eyes and pressed his fingertips against his lids. "She'd go there whenever she wanted time alone. I can't believe this is happening. This is all surreal."

"I know," DeLong agreed, matching his brother's tone. "Do you need any help with Ally? I'm sure Sam would be happy to help."

Sullivan shook his head, but DeLong wondered if he was paying him any attention.

Newman held out the evidence bag with the red handkerchief. "Have you ever seen this before?"

Sullivan glanced at it, blinking his eyes several times. "Yeah, it used to be hers. Haven't seen it for a while though."

"When we spoke on the phone, you said she didn't come home last night," DeLong reminded him. "Do you have a reason why she wouldn't come home?"

Sullivan didn't answer. Instead, he put his hand on his forehead. "I can't think right now. I need—I need to be with Ally."

"Okay," DeLong said. He exchanged a quick glance with Newman. "But the sooner we talk to you, the better it'll be."

Sullivan nodded. He staggered a few steps back. "I know." With that, he turned and scampered away.

Chapter 4

DeLong learned of a wedding which took place during the time frame of Bree's death. He had investigators talk with the wedding participants.

They learned the rain had begun shortly before the ceremony, around six thirty in the evening. After the wedding was over forty-five minutes later, the party had gone inside to the reception. By that time, the rain had come down in sheets. In their rush for cover, no one took notice of anything out of the ordinary.

Reflecting on his first conversation with his brother, DeLong considered the options of why Bree hadn't returned home last night. Were they having a fight? Was that why Bree was at the pavilion? Did she need time to think things through?

He didn't want to think his own blood could have killed his wife. However, he had to admit Newman was right: he didn't know Sullivan. And he knew nothing of his marriage to Bree. It wasn't uncommon that the spouse was the killer.

DeLong thumbed through the crime scene photos, inspecting his sister-in-law's body. She lay in the water, her head crushed, arms bruised.

This wasn't random.

That much DeLong knew.

She'd been bludgeoned in a way that seemed to be out of anger. He was assuming whoever killed her placed the handkerchief over her head. It was a sign of remorse.

DeLong tried to picture what had happened to her. The markings on her body showed she didn't give up without a fight. He knew Newman's investigative team found fibers underneath her nails. With any luck, Bree would have gotten a piece of her killer.

He couldn't imagine the pain and fear brought on her. He didn't want to imagine. Grotesque pictures like these were bad enough with complete strangers. But for someone you knew, there were no words. And seeing her dead, assaulted—it made things personal. No matter how things were between him and his brother, they were still family.

Still blood.

And that alone made it personal to him.

Having had enough of staring at his dead sister-in-law, DeLong flipped the file closed. He lowered his head to the desk to gather his thoughts. He tried to remain collected.

DeLong reached for his cell phone and punched his wife's name from the recent calls list.

"Hey, honey," Samantha said, a smile in her voice.

DeLong didn't answer. He opened his mouth to speak, but no words came out.

"Jim? Are you there? Is something wrong?" Samantha's voice grew with concern and wonder.

"There's something I need to tell you," he said when he found his voice. "Are you sitting?"

When she said she was, DeLong informed her of what he could, without giving away too much detail of the investigation. As he did so, his mind wandered. He imagined how he'd feel if it was Sam instead of Bree. The thought alone wasn't bearable. He couldn't fathom what his brother was feeling. He and Samantha had come a long way in their marriage, fought many battles that nearly destroyed them. Through it all, he knew it'd kill him if he ever lost her in that manner.

"Oh my goodness," Samantha said, her words above a whisper. "I saw her and Ally a few days ago. How's Sully dealing with it?"

"Not well. If I had to guess, I'd say he hasn't processed it all yet."

"Do you have any leads?"

"Not yet. So far, no one's come forward, and we haven't had a conversation with him. Sully..." he trailed off, not wanting to tell his wife about the air of tension between them. "He left to go get Ally."

"When you see him, will you give him my condolences?"

"Of course." After a knock at the door, Newman stuck his head in. DeLong waved him in. "I've got to go. I wanted to tell you the news before you heard it somewhere else." DeLong hesitated. "And I wanted to let you know how much I love you."

"I love you too, baby."

"How do Sully and Sam get along?" Newman asked as DeLong set his phone on the table. He lowered himself to a chair. "If you don't mind me prying."

"Sullivan prefers to keep himself out of my family's business," DeLong said. "Bree and Sam had become good friends over the years. They made sure to have playdates with the girls." He paused with a heavy sigh. "Sullivan never wanted Ally to be around me. I think as far as he's concerned, I'm nothing but a drunk." DeLong let out a nervous scoff. "But Bree wouldn't accept that. She was always the family keeper. She insisted on us being a part of Ally's life."

Newman ran a hand through his hair, eyeing DeLong. He seemed to try to read his thoughts. To keep himself busy and avoid the investigator's gaze, DeLong opened his drawer, pretending to search for something.

"Are you going to tell me why you and your brother are on the outs?" Newman asked.

DeLong continued thumbing through files in his drawer. Without looking up, he said, "I told you. He doesn't like having an alcoholic for a brother."

"Is that all?"

DeLong felt the heat from Newman's glare burning into him.

"I know you," Newman added. "There's something about this so-called brotherly rivalry you're not telling me."

It was obvious Newman wasn't going to let it slide.

Yes, there was something beneath the surface, but only a few people knew about it. He hadn't even been able to tell Samantha his deepest, darkest secrets. He wanted to keep it that way. He'd spent too long forgetting that chapter of his life.

Even now, sometimes the memories gave him nightmares. He'd wake up in night sweats, his breathing erratic. DeLong closed his eyes as the images and sounds filled his mind.

The crying. The laughing. The taunting.

Always taunting.

"Jim?"

DeLong opened his eyes again to see Newman gazing at him with curiosity. He was still waiting for an answer.

"Well," DeLong hesitated. He slid his drawer shut and leaned back in his chair with a sigh. "Let's just say events in our childhood wedged us apart. It's not something I like to talk about."

"I understand," Newman said. "But if you want my help, you're going to have to trust me. I need to know more about your brother. And about your relationship with him. I need to know you can remain objective." Newman leaned forward, his eyes narrowed. "I promise whatever you tell me will never leave this office. So talk to me, Jim. Not as your investigator. But as your friend."

DeLong hesitated once more before letting out another sigh. He still wasn't sure whether he wanted to go into detail, but gave Newman enough to satisfy his curiosity.

"When we were kids," he began, his voice above a whisper, "Sullivan and I were best friends. He's seven years older than I am. Still, he never minded me hanging out with him. Neither did his friends.

"One day, we met this new kid in the neighborhood. His name was Drake. He was nineteen, and he had trouble written all over him. But even so, he was a charmer. He charmed Sully and our friends into hanging out with him. I never liked him. There was something off. Something in his smile. He made my skin crawl. Drake liked to push me around. Tell me to get him a beer or whatever he wanted. My brother and his friends got into a lot of trouble. It was strange how fast Sully changed. He was always the quiet type. Doing nothing without permission. But when he met Drake, Sully became a whole other person."

DeLong paused as he reflected on the moment. "One night, Sully had a major fight with our dad. I don't know what it was about. But Sully was angry and sneaked out. I begged him not to. I didn't have a good feeling about it. But he told me he needed to get out. He asked me to stay home and cover for him."

DeLong stopped speaking as the memories of his childhood came flooding back.

"Hold on," Newman said, his voice soft. "I'll get you some water."

DeLong didn't respond. He leaned back in his chair as the memories spilled. He'd forgotten how it affected him.

When Newman returned, he handed him a water bottle. DeLong opened it, taking a long swig of water before continuing.

"Anyway," he resumed, "Sully left. His friends were waiting in another car for him. But instead of staying home, I followed them on my bike. I guess I thought I'd try to convince him to come back home. I followed them a few miles away from the house to a gas station. They tried..." he trailed off, shaking his head.

"They robbed it?" Newman guessed after a pause.

"They tried to," DeLong said. "But things went downhill fast. The gas station attendant had a shotgun behind the counter. Cliché, right? Anyway, he shot Drake first because he was the one with a weapon. I'd never seen such force impact a body so hard." DeLong paused before continuing, his blood running cold as he remembered the look of horror on the young man's face. "He died immediately. My brother was just standing there. I'll never forget the look on his face. He was near Drake when he was shot, so the blood splashed on him. Sully didn't move. I don't think he could. Then he noticed I had come into the station. He screamed at me to get back. The attendant shot Sully in the shoulder. There was blood everywhere. He kept shouting at me to get out of there. To run. Instead, I ran to his side, saying I wasn't going to leave him."

"Where were the other kids?"

"By the time the police arrived, they'd already scattered. Sully was arrested and taken to the hospital for treatment. They'd already booked me. Long story short, we were sentenced to juvie for twelve months."

"But if you didn't do anything," Newman said. "If you arrived after it all happened, why were *you* sent there?"

"The gas station attendant said I did." DeLong took another sip of water. "There was only his word. The cameras in the station were only for show. His word against two kids. You know how it goes."

"Okay," Newman said, deep in thought. "So you were in juvie for twelve months? How can you be a cop now? That's on your record forever."

DeLong gave his friend a faint smile.

"One day, after two months of me being on the inside, they released me. They said the gas station attendant admitted that I had told the truth during the trial. That I had entered the building after everything went down."

"Why did he finally tell the truth?"

"Because there was this investigator," DeLong said. "He was on leave from the Navy. Heard about the incident, heard about the trial results. Well, he was a well-respected man. One of the best. He thought something was off during the trial. It had taken him only two days to get the truth of my innocence out. I was released."

"This investigator," Newman said. "I don't suppose his name was Russell Calhoun?"

DeLong lifted the corner of his lips to a smile. "He was my mentor from day one." DeLong let his words sink in as he reflected on the memory of his old friend. "He got me out, and we were good friends ever since."

A tear threatened to fall from his eyes. He rubbed them with his knuckles, realizing his hands had shaken. He hoped Newman didn't notice.

"When Sully got out, he'd changed. He couldn't even look at me. Our friendship ended the night my brother climbed out the window. As soon as he turned eighteen, which was a month and a half after his release, Sullivan left. And I wouldn't see him again unless it was for special occasions. Even then, it was rare. He made sure of that."

DeLong straightened files on his desk to keep his emotions at bay. He was well aware of Newman watching him.

"You blamed yourself," Newman concluded.

DeLong let his shoulder rise and fall. "Although I was only in there for two months, I couldn't handle the things that went on in there. And the way Sullivan changed afterward didn't help my morale. All I wanted was to forget. I'd started drinking just to forget. It worked for a while, then the nightmares came. I was unhinged, drinking even more. Desperate for the memory to go away."

He realized his voice had softened.

"That's tough. Did you try to fix things with Sullivan?"

"Yeah," DeLong frowned. "But he wouldn't hear it. There are times when you have to realize some things aren't fixable. Some things are just too dark. And neither of us are good at handling certain things."

"Man, I'm sorry," Newman said. He leaned forward, his eyes full of concern. "Listen, Jim. People make mistakes. I've watched you over the last year. You've come a long way to overcome your addiction, your fears. But you need to learn to forgive yourself. Take what happened during the Manny Grimes investigation, for example. Calhoun, your wife, the drinking. You won't be able to move forward otherwise."

Newman leaned back to study DeLong.

DeLong looked away, trying to hide the tears threatening to fall.

"Is that all to your story?" Newman asked.

DeLong couldn't seem to forget the things that happened inside the detention center. He thought back to the promise his brother made him make just before his release. DeLong decided he had spoken enough about his past. He looked back at Newman, who waited with patience for an answer.

"Yeah," DeLong assured him. "That's all."

"All right. Are you sure you'll be able to get through this, okay?"

DeLong gave him a half-smile, wondering the same thing. But instead of admitting so, he told Newman he'd be fine.

"Let me tell you what," DeLong said. "If you believe I'm becoming anything less than objective, tell the captain and I'll remove myself. No questions asked, no complaining."

"And no off-the-clock investigations?"

DeLong laughed. Jeff Newman did know him too well.

"No off-the-clock investigations," DeLong confirmed.

"Deal."

"Great. So tell me what you got from the lab."

"Fingerprints were lifted from the eyelids but didn't reveal any hits in CODIS—neither did the fiber we found underneath her nails. My guys bagged hair samples, but we couldn't get anything other than brown hair. None of the samples had follicles attached."

DeLong frowned, grabbing a pen from the desk to rap it along the side. "Anything else at the crime scene?"

"No. Rain likely washed most everything away. Or the offender cleaned up after himself."

"It's a horrible way to go," DeLong said to himself. He flipped open the file which rested on his desk and stared again at the lifeless body of his brother's wife.

A text sounded from his phone, and DeLong looked to see that it was Samantha. Frowning at the text, he said, "Sam wants me home as soon as possible."

"Is everything okay?" Newman asked.

"I don't know," DeLong said. "Why don't we break for lunch? I'll run home, and we'll touch base later."

"Okay," Newman agreed as he rose. He paused before stepping out of the office. "Everything will be fine. You'll be able to get through this. You're Jim DeLong. You can get through just about anything."

DeLong was gathering his things and looked over at Newman. "That's because I have good friends I can count on."

"Hold on," Newman said as he grabbed his phone from its clip. "I need you to say that again, so I can have it on record."

"Go home, Jeff," DeLong said with a smirk.

Newman let his shoulder rise and fall as he slipped the phone back into its place and turned to leave.

"See you in the morning," he called over his shoulder.

DeLong hesitated before gathering the rest of his things. Placing his hands on his desk, he leaned over, taking in deep breaths, trying to erase memories of the past. He wished his brother hadn't breezed back into his life. Things were so much simpler when he didn't have to reflect on things that had happened when they were kids.

Closing his eyes tight, he sucked in a heavy breath and pushed it out.

But Sullivan *was* back in his life, even if only for a moment. DeLong wasn't sure how things would end after the investigation was over. Would they come to a middle ground? Would they go their separate ways as they always did?

He didn't know, but what he did know was that his family needed him. No matter how things ended, the most important thing was finding justice for Bree.

Grabbing his things, DeLong locked his office to go home to his wife.

Chapter 5

DELONG CLOSED THE GARAGE door and made his way inside the house. He heard soft murmurs floating from the living room. He knew his six-year-old daughter, Bella, was in school, so he guessed Samantha was likely watching television.

After coming onto the scene and finding his brother's wife's lifeless shell, he wanted to hold his wife for as long as he could. It was nothing but a harsh reminder that in the blink of an eye, everything can go wrong. With the memory of Bree etched in his mind, she haunted him. Seeing her in the water left him feeling empty.

Samantha liked to tell him everything happened for a reason.

But for what reason could someone such as Bree DeLong to be murdered?

He couldn't fathom a viable answer.

She was a kindhearted young woman who wanted nothing more than to help those less fortunate—particularly children.

"Honey, I'm home," DeLong said. Draping his jacket on the back of the kitchen chair, he released a long yawn. His eyes felt heavy, and his stomach rumbled. But despite his hunger, he didn't feel like eating. He would opt for a quick nap, but he wasn't sure that would happen either.

"Jim, we're in here, honey."

We?

Was someone here?

Remembering the urgency in Samantha's text resulted in his stomach churning.

DeLong grabbed a Coke can from the refrigerator and stepped into the living room.

Though deep down it didn't come as a surprise to him, DeLong almost dropped the can when he saw his brother sitting on the couch next to his wife.

"Sully." He blinked a few times as if he were trying to stop imagining things. "What are you doing here?"

"I'm sorry to come here like this." Sullivan glanced over at Samantha, then back at DeLong. He looked as though he wanted to say something, but instead, he shook his head, pushing to his feet. "Sorry, Sam, I can't do this. I should go."

Samantha put a hand on his wrist to keep him from moving away. "You're always welcome here, Sully. Right, Jim?" She shot her husband a look of warning.

"Of course," he stammered.

Samantha pulled Sullivan back to the cushions.

DeLong studied his older brother, taking in every sadness, every anger. He seemed to have aged a few more years since DeLong had seen him at the morgue. His eyes were hollow, and he looked as though he hadn't slept for a week.

He wanted to say something consoling to him, but what could he say? There were no words to ease someone in this time of grief. If there were, he wasn't aware of them.

"How are you doing?" He sat on the edge of the coffee table.

Sullivan only shook his head. His eyes watered, a single tear sliding down the corner of his eye. He bounced his knees and set his head in his hands.

"I had nowhere else to go," Sullivan mumbled. "Ally's in school. I-I went there to tell her what happened, but I couldn't."

"We'll figure this out. I promise." DeLong cleared his throat, pressed his fingertips to his eyelids, and leaned in toward his brother. "Why don't you tell me everything you know? Start from the last time you spoke to or saw Bree. What she was doing, where she went, who she spoke to...don't leave anything out."

Sullivan looked at DeLong, then at Samantha and back again. "The last time we spoke was yesterday morning. I think around six or so. It was before she took Ally to school."

"How did she seem?" DeLong asked.

Sullivan shrugged. "Normal."

"Do you know what her plans for the day were?"

"I think she was going to that ministry she runs—Protecting the Lord's Children. After that..." Sullivan trailed off. Finally, he said, "After that, she was supposed to go home."

"But she didn't go home?" DeLong pressed.

"I don't know. I went fishing with an old friend."

"From what time to what time?"

Sullivan narrowed his eyes at DeLong. "What does that matter?"

"I need to build a timeline," DeLong explained. "That's all."

Sullivan squared his jaw, reminding DeLong of how their father always looked when he was forcing himself to remain calm.

"Ten that morning to five in the evening. We went to Clarks Hill Lake."

"What's your friend's name?"

"James Simmons. We used to work together."

"Where did you go after fishing?" DeLong asked. He motioned for Samantha to hand him a pad from the end table. He wrote the information down.

"Are you implying I killed her?" Sullivan snapped.

DeLong saw the hot anger flash in Sullivan's eyes. He opened his mouth to say something else, but before he did, DeLong held up his palm. He was used to spouses getting flustered by the police as they attempted to weed out suspects.

His brother was no different.

"I have to ask these questions, Sully."

"I wouldn't hurt her. I loved my wife. We had a good marriage. I can't...I can't believe you'd actually think I'd..." Sullivan trailed off and rose to pace the room.

DeLong remained silent, well aware his wife was glaring at him. DeLong shook his head to warn her to stay out of it.

"We were happy," Sullivan continued, speaking through his teeth. "She didn't leave me, and she wasn't having an affair. We were happy."

"Good. Did she have any friends who wanted something more from her? Something she wasn't willing to give him?"

Sullivan shook his head with conviction. "No. I mean, everybody loved her. You know that. That goes without saying. People loved her, but not in any romantic sense."

"Did she seem upset over the last few days? Like she was worried about something?"

"No. I mean, I don't think so."

"And you? Is everything good with you? You don't have anything to worry about? Anything that's upsetting you?"

DeLong watched as his brother gazed at him. It looked as though he wanted to say something, but couldn't decide what it would be. He put his head in his hands, sighed and looked back at DeLong.

"Why don't you say it, Jim?"

"What are you talking about?" DeLong shook his head with frustration. "I need to ask you these questions. I'm only covering all the bases, Sully."

"These questions are pointless!" Sullivan sliced his hands in the air. "How is whatever it was I did going to help me find my wife's killer?"

"Why don't you just answer my questions, Sullivan? Let me do my job." The words came out gruffer than he intended, which resulted in his wife hissing his name.

Sullivan gaped at his brother, frowning, arms crossed over his chest. He shook his head in agitation.

"No. I was wrong to come here. What was I thinking? I mean, I need someone capable enough to find out who murdered my wife." A mixture of undeniable anger and pain flashed in Sullivan's eyes. "I need someone I can trust."

"You can trust Jim, Sully," Samantha interjected, eyes wide, glistening with tears and worry.

Sullivan let out a scoff. "Him? Jim DeLong? Are you kidding me? No offense, but my drunk little brother could fly off the rails at any moment. You, of all people, should know that."

DeLong squared his jaw to remain calm. He kept quiet as Samantha stammered.

Sullivan shook his head and cursed. "Forget it. This was a mistake, and I'm out of here."

Before anyone could respond, Sullivan flew out the door.

DeLong frowned, well aware Samantha was glaring at him.

"Go stop him!" she hissed through her teeth, jabbing her index finger toward the door.

Obliging, DeLong chased after his brother, calling his name. He knew it was a fruitless effort, even before he saw Sullivan climbing into his car and pulling away, tires spinning hotly on the cement.

Chapter 6

"HE JUST LEFT?" NEWMAN stood in DeLong's office, arms crossed, watching his friend with curious eyes. He'd listened to DeLong's recount of his brother's visit, and the shock was evident on his face.

"I can't blame him," DeLong muttered. "But how can I help him if he won't trust me to do my job?" He leaned back in his chair to stare at a crooked picture of a dog on the wall.

"It's hard for siblings to lean on one another," Newman said with a sigh. "Especially when you've been estranged for so long."

"Maybe it is too personal." DeLong rose to straighten the picture frame. "Maybe I should recuse myself from the investigation after all."

"Or maybe you let me talk to your brother," Newman suggested. He took a seat and crossed his legs. "If things stay heated between you and Sully, then that's the best alternative. I'll deal with him. But you need to stay on this investigation. There's no one better than Jim DeLong to find Bree's killer."

DeLong moved toward the window and opened the blinds. He saw an eagle perched on the tree limbs in the distance.

"The Grimes investigation proved it," Newman continued. "You were so stubborn. Even when Captain Stewart threw you off the case, you kept at it. Nothing would stop you. Now that it's family, you can't just throw in the towel. You wouldn't want to. It's not who you are."

DeLong reflected to almost two years ago, when he had investigated the murder of a man named Manny Grimes. It was true he didn't stop his investigating. Not when he fell back into his drinking habits. And not when Captain Stewart found a reason to throw him off the case. During the investigation, his long-time friend and mentor, Russell Calhoun, and Newman's partner, Taryn Elliott, were killed in the line of duty. It was protocol for him to step away, even then. However, it was DeLong who had figured out the truth.

It was DeLong who had uncovered the fifteen-year-old conspiracy.

He'd been able to bring justice to all the victims.

And now, whenever he thought of Calhoun, he couldn't help but see Calhoun's and Elliott's body, the blood splattered throughout his old friend's apartment.

DeLong shook his head, took a sip of water and glanced at Newman.

"If Calhoun were here, what do you think he'd say?"

DeLong lifted the corner of his mouth in a smile. "He'd insist on talking to Sully himself and I continue to 'do what I do.'"

"Exactly." Newman gave a single, confirming nod. "And that's exactly what I'm going to tell you."

DeLong considered the pros and cons of handing the investigation over to one of his other men. The pro was that others would be more objective to do what they had to do once the investigation progressed. Things De-Long felt would make him hesitate.

Such as arresting his brother if it should come to that.

But that was why he had Newman, right?

As much as he trusted his men, DeLong wanted to lead the investigation. How could he sit by and watch while someone else investigated a family member's murder?

Jeff Newman was good at keeping him in line. He would make sure DeLong doesn't falter from the task at hand. His captain had already given him the okay to be the lead investigator in Bree's murder as long as he focused on his job.

His captain trusted him.

As did Newman.

So he needed to learn to trust himself.

"Fine," DeLong said. "You give Sully a call and interview him. I suggest you do it somewhere other than here. He'll be more comfortable that way."

"Consider it done."

"Have you learned anything new from the lab?"

Newman nodded. "We went through Bree's car. The fingerprints be-longed to your brother's family. There were unknown partials. We're trying to track them down, but it doesn't look as though anything was out of the ordinary there."

"Okay, so the medical examiner said Bree died nine hours ago," DeLong mused. He tried to imagine the struggle. "That puts her death around ten. Because Dr. Harmon believes she bled out for about an hour, the killer was likely with her a little before nine. The wedding party was inside at the reception by seven thirty."

"That leaves a gap between seven thirty and nine," Newman interjected.

"Yeah," DeLong agreed. "Let's start at the beginning. I want to know everything we can find out about Bree's day, right up until she was killed."

Newman nodded as he rose. "I'll call your brother right now."

"Hey, Jeff," DeLong said as the investigator pulled the door open. He waited until his friend turned back. "Thanks."

"You'd do the same for me," was the reply.

Chapter 7

THE COFFEE SHOP WAS slow for the late afternoon and still blended with the aroma of freshly brewed beans and pastries.

Two baristas were whispering amongst themselves, occasionally glancing toward a young man sitting near the door, staring at his laptop. It was obvious he was pretending not to notice. A coy smile played on his lips when one of the girls giggled.

Newman chose a table in the back corner so they would have more privacy.

"It's been a while since I've had Starbucks."

Sullivan pulled his chair from under the table and sat. He gripped the cup with both hands as if he were trying to warm himself despite the warmth of the coffee shop.

"I'm more of a Dunkin' Donuts guy," Sullivan said.

"Yeah? My wife and I used to come here all the time," Newman continued. "It's kind of our place. But for some reason, this pregnancy makes her sick every time she has coffee. She doesn't like the idea of me coming here alone."

Sullivan's lips curved into a slight smile. "How far along is she?"

"Fourteen weeks," Newman said. "It's truly a blessing. We never thought we'd have one child, let alone two. Especially after we came close to losing our first."

Sullivan nodded with a frown. "I never thought I'd want a child."

Newman detected something in his eyes, but couldn't decide what it was. He made a mental note to mention it to DeLong.

"But it's the best thing to have happened, right?" Newman said, taking another sip of his Iced Caramel Macchiato.

Sullivan gave a quick nod and cleared his throat.

"How's Ally doing?" Newman asked.

Sullivan shook his head, focusing on his cup. "I, uh, I haven't told her yet. She's still in school. I'm trying to pull myself together before I have to tell her." He scoffed. "I guess a part of me thinks she's going to come home any second."

"I'm sorry you're going through all this," Newman said.

Instead of answering, Sullivan asked, "Can we just get this over with, please?"

"Of course," Newman said, setting his drink on the table. He reached into the bag he carried for a small notebook. "Okay, well, first off, Jim told me about your conversation earlier." Newman kept a close eye on DeLong's older brother. "I want you assured that he's one of the best investigators I know. There's no one better than your brother to be working this case."

Sullivan scoffed, then reached his fingers underneath his glasses and rubbed his eyes. "No offense, Mr. Newman, but I know my brother better than anyone. I know him better than he knows himself."

"Then why did you go to him in the first place if you didn't want to talk to him?"

Newman asked the question before he could think better of it. Sullivan didn't seem to notice, or maybe he didn't care about the bluntness.

"Honestly, I didn't. Sam called me, so I went over there to talk to her. I couldn't bring myself to tell Ally, and I didn't know where else to go. She was friends with Bree, so I thought she may know something I didn't. At least help me figure something out. Instead of helping me think, she insisted on bringing Jim home."

Newman sipped his drink as he listened.

Sullivan let out a soft snicker, tearing his napkin into small pieces. "Sam and Bree had always been so pushy about us having a relationship."

"Can I ask why?"

"Let's just say there are things only three people in the world know about us as kids," Sullivan said. "Things happen that drives people apart, and we all react to the situations differently. I ended up leaving and Jim drank."

"I know you and Jim were in juvie." Newman studied the elder brother's reaction. Sullivan's eyes skirted around the coffee shop, a faint frown playing on his lips.

"Yeah? What'd he tell you?"

"Only that you made a mistake with a guy named Drake. That both of you ended up in juvenile detention. But Calhoun got Jim out."

"That's all he told you?" Sullivan asked.

Newman took a sip of his drink before replying. He wanted to gauge Sullivan's reaction.

"Yes. I'd known Calhoun for a couple of years. He was a good man. His friendship with your brother was...special."

Sullivan flashed a ghost of a smile before frowning into his cup. "The night we tried robbing that gas station was something I've always regretted. Especially since Jimmy got caught in the middle of it all. I never wanted that to happen. I will always be thankful for Calhoun. He got Jimmy out of that place." Sullivan swallowed, then cleared his throat. "But his drinking changed him. It got worse over the years, and I wanted nothing to do with it."

"According to Jim, you stopped speaking to him before he began drinking."

Sullivan narrowed his eyes and kept his face unreadable, but his eyes clouded over. "What does it matter?"

It was obvious there was something deeper at play in the brothers' relationship, but Newman didn't want to force the issue. Now wasn't the time or the place. And forcing secrets out had a way of destroying even the best of friends.

Newman pushed his curiosity aside for the time being.

"Well, whatever happened in your past," Newman said as he took another sip of his drink, "the Jim DeLong you knew growing up isn't the same Jim DeLong today. He's a good man."

"Are you sure about that?" The edge in Sullivan's voice created a rise in Newman. Sullivan leaned back in his chair and took a sip of his coffee. "Samantha mentioned he's sober again. For how long did she say?"

Newman saw where he was going, but refused to take the bait. Instead, he flipped open his notebook.

"Let's get started, okay? You're an accountant?"

"Actually, I'm a tax auditor. I work from home."

"What about Bree? What did she do?"

"Bree worked at a nonprofit organization called Protecting the Lord's Children. Or PLC for short. Ever since she was young, she wanted to help kids that didn't have anyone. She wanted them to feel like they were part of a family."

"Did she ever bring any of them home with her?" Newman asked.

"Yes. She did often." Sullivan frowned. "I didn't always like that. Some of the kids she mentored were a little sketchy."

"How so?"

"Well, most, as I'm sure you can imagine, come from broken families, and some are orphans. It doesn't take much for them to be broken inside. She'd found paraphernalia hidden away before. We don't know who they belonged to. They're smart enough to keep from being caught, but some of them seemed the type. Bree always liked to look for the best in people. She liked to say, 'if you don't give someone a chance, you both can miss out.'" Sullivan scoffed. "I certainly heard that enough times in my life." Sullivan took another sip of his coffee. When he set it back on the table, his eyes watered. "But right now, I'd give anything to hear it again."

Newman remained silent as Sullivan turned to glance out the window.

"I'm sorry. I'm emotional right now. I keep having to remind myself that she's gone. Still, I don't believe it."

"I empathize with you," Newman said. He didn't know how he'd react if Christina was murdered. The thought was unsettling.

A tear slid down the corner of Sullivan's eye and he wiped it away as he cleared his throat.

"Can you think of anybody who may have wanted to hurt her? One of those kids, maybe?"

Sullivan paused as he considered the question, staring at the table.

"I don't—I don't know. I mean, Bree wasn't the type to start trouble. Most of those kids loved her."

"Tell me about the ones that didn't."

Sullivan bit his lip. "Well, J.J. was in a gang before Bree met him."

"What's this gang called?" Newman pressed.

Shaking his head, Sullivan said, "I don't know. Or I don't remember. I only know he was in a gang. I didn't...didn't want to know too much about those kids. It was easier not to worry."

"Do you think this J.J. can overpower her?"

"I don't know." Sullivan pressed his fingers to his eyes. "Maybe."

"Anybody else you can think of?"

"Uh, well, most of the big kids can. They're in their early teens. So they act like teenagers. Mostly, they seem to care about Bree. If you want to know which one would hurt my wife, I can't tell you. All I can say is either any of them or none."

Newman scribbled on his notepad.

"Last week at school," Sullivan began, "Ally had gotten into a fight with a friend of hers. Principal Kelley called the parents in to discuss it because the girl had hit her head. He wanted to be sure nothing like that happened again. The mother of the girl accused Bree of being an unfit mother because of the children at the ministry. She even threatened Bree. Said if anything happened to her daughter again, she'd kill her. I had to drag Bree away."

"Did you think she was serious?"

Sullivan shook his head. "I didn't think so at the time. My wife was always kind of a risk taker. When she found someone hopeless of being saved, she'd do whatever she could to turn their lives around. It scared me because she'd been in dangerous situations." He pushed out a breath. "If I'd tell her about my concerns, her response would be, 'Jesus would do it.'" He lifted the corner of his lips to a crooked smile. "She had a way of scaring me, but I couldn't help but admire her."

"She seemed like quite a woman," Newman commended.

Sullivan let out a soft curse. "Makes you wonder how she ended up with a messed up guy like me."

"What's the name of the girl Ally fought with? And her parents."

"Dawn and Blake Parsons. Their daughter is Josie."

Sullivan frowned and glanced toward the window until he sucked in a heavy breath and pushed it out. "There may be someone else. Benjamin Beaumont. He's our neighbor."

"Tell me more about him," Newman requested as he jotted the information on his pad.

"He's in his early twenties. His father's a good friend of mine. I don't want to think his son would actually kill anyone. Especially my wife. But he's...he throws tantrums for no reason at all. One minute, Ben's fine, then the next he's throwing things, yelling. I asked his dad about it once. He claimed it was stress from his classes. But I think Bree knew more about what was going on with Ben than what she would let on."

"Did she ever seem uneasy toward him?"

"To a point," Sullivan said. "I think he had developed some kind of romantic feelings for her. There was a time when I overheard her say 'just take a breath and calm down. Nothing is happening.'"

"What did he say?"

"I'm not sure. She was on her cell. I didn't ask her about her conversation."

"And you're positive she was speaking to Ben?" Newman asked as he scribbled on his pad.

"Yeah, she said his name. Something like 'look, Ben...' And then I stopped listening in. My cell rang or something."

"Tell me more about your wife's relationship with him."

"When he and his family moved here, for the longest time, Benjamin would keep to himself."

Sullivan took a sip of his coffee.

"He opened up when he got to know Bree. He liked her. I think she made him feel safe. But the anger issues have always been there. He lives with his parents while he finishes school. He used to help Bree out at the ministry until she told him his time there was over. I guess his own problems made things worse. She wouldn't discuss it. She told me she'd promised to not tell anyone about his issues."

Newman noticed the single tear that escaped the corner of Sullivan's eyes. He commended his strength during the interview. He tried to read what the elder DeLong was thinking but came up empty.

"When can I collect her things?" Sullivan asked.

"After we've completed the investigation," Newman answered. "Her clothes and wedding band are evidence now."

As he took another sip of his iced coffee, Newman considered what he needed to ask him next. He knew it wouldn't go over well with Sullivan.

"What I'm about to discuss now, I have to ask," he began. Sullivan eyed him, and Newman guessed he knew where the conversation was going. "Jim said you went fishing with a friend, is that right?"

"Yes, James Simmons. We were together from ten to five o'clock."

"Where did you go after that? We need to figure out your timeline from after five."

"Home," Sullivan said. He sniffed.

"And Bree wasn't there at all?" Newman asked.

Sullivan shook his head. "I hadn't heard from her. I was waiting for her to come home."

"You didn't think to look for her?"

Sullivan shook his head. "It's not unusual for her to be late, so I didn't worry. Ally spent the night with a friend of hers, so I went to bed early, around seven."

"Okay," Newman said. He paused before continuing, looking down at his notes. "Can anyone verify that?"

He glanced up to see the elder DeLong shaking his head.

"I'm going to need a list of Bree's friend," Newman said. "Will you be able to provide that?"

Sullivan replied that he'd have to find Bree's address book with the information. He promised to bring it to the sheriff's office when he did.

"Thanks. That'll be a help." Newman closed his pad, concluding the interview. He tucked it away in his bag. "We'll keep you updated as much as we're able."

Sullivan nodded, glancing outside, watching cars drive by.

"This isn't real. I mean, Bree never hurt anybody. She only wanted to help others. Why would anyone want to hurt her?"

"We'll do everything we can to find out," Newman assured him. "In the meantime, I need you to do something you're not going to want to do."

"What's that?" Sullivan said.

"Trust your brother," Newman said matter-of-factly. "If anyone can sort this out, he can. And he will. Believe me."

Sullivan didn't respond other than to push his chair back and rise.

Newman followed suit, extending his hand toward Sullivan. "Thank you for taking the time to speak with me. I know it was difficult for you."

As Newman took his leave from Sullivan, he texted DeLong to inform him he was on his way back to the sheriff's office. A reply came when Newman pulled open his car door. DeLong would be waiting for him.

Newman climbed into his car and turned the key in the ignition. He looked up to see Sullivan open his own car door. Instead of climbing in, he retrieved his cell phone. It looked as though he was about to make a call, but changed his mind when he tossed the phone into the car. He slammed the door shut and smashed his palm on the hood.

He hesitated for a second before he raised his hand again, making contact with the hood.

Again.

And again.

A group of teenage girls walking by stopped, turned to gape at him, and then hurried away, still eyeing him.

Sullivan lowered his head to the hood of the car. Newman considered checking on him, but before he could move, Sullivan opened the door and climbed behind the wheel.

He watched, his mind swirling with questions, as DeLong's brother pulled away from the café.

Chapter 8

DELONG STARED THROUGH THE blinds at the comings and goings of the office, deep in thought. He'd already watched enough of the news raving about the body of thirty-nine-year-old Bree DeLong found by two runners by the Augusta Canal at the Savannah Rapids. After watching for so long, he had to turn off the news. Just the memory of pulling away the handkerchief churned his stomach.

The newscasters were requesting for anyone who may have known about the murder to contact the Piedmont County Sheriff's Office. DeLong also placed a request for Bree's cell phone records, but even with a court order, they claimed it would take a few days, per policy.

It had been a long, tiring day, but DeLong knew he wouldn't be able to sleep tonight. His mind raced around the idea of having to work with his brother, whom he tried hard over the years to forget. It was easier not having to go through his life thinking of the past, his brother and his short time in the detention center.

DeLong frowned with a slight shake of his head. He needed to lock his unwanted childhood memories away for good. It worked when he and his brother weren't on speaking terms. But now that they were forced back into each other's lives, how could he do anything but remember everything that happened to them?

He could always turn the investigation over to someone else, he considered. He could spend his days sitting behind the desk, pushing paperwork, which was more in his job description. As a detective, DeLong didn't have to go into the field.

He didn't need to spend day after day looking at real live murder scenes.

All he needed to do was lead his men. Tell them where to go, what to do next, and listen to what they've gathered so far. But he didn't want that for his career. He went out in the field because he enjoyed it. It challenged him. The thought of doing nothing but sit in the cool office didn't appeal to him.

But DeLong wasn't sure how well he could keep his head in the game. He and his brother had unresolved secrets that were better tucked away under almost twenty-four years of living.

The past was already baring its teeth.

Should he turn over the investigation?

DeLong sighed and reached for the knob intending to head for the break room to get a cup of coffee. But a low, harsh voice stopped him.

Help me.

At the sound of the words, DeLong held his breath. The nape of his neck tingled. His heart beat quicker than normal, skipping a few beats. He looked around his quiet office as though he'd find one of his men playing a joke on him.

No one was around.

But why would they be?

He'd heard the words one time before. A year and a half ago, in fact. But he didn't want to believe it was happening again.

It couldn't be.

Could it?

"Hello?"

DeLong's own voice sounded even deeper than was normal. He stood still, listening for any sound. He only heard the soft whirring of the computer.

DeLong let out a slight chuckle as he walked around his desk and sat in his chair. Rubbing his eyelids, he cursed.

Help me.

He saw the monitor flicker off, then on again. A hooded figure flashed on the screen, then disappeared as a knock simultaneously sounded at the door.

Startled, DeLong cursed, then scowled when Newman entered the office.

"Hi."

"Shouldn't you wait until I invite you in?" DeLong ran a hand through his hair, trying to steady his nerves.

Newman stepped into the room, shutting the door behind him.

"Why? You weren't doing anything."

"I was thinking."

"About?"

DeLong glanced at the blank computer screen, then back at the investigator.

"I was thinking Jeff Newman's the nosiest person I've known."

Newman smirked. "Right."

"What'd he say?" DeLong asked.

Newman spent the next few minutes going into detail about his conversation with Sullivan.

"Okay, so our next stop will be at Ally's school," DeLong muttered.

"I also got confirmation the blood on the rock belongs to your sister-in-law," Newman added, "However, the fingerprint didn't reveal anything, but we expected as much."

"Okay," DeLong muttered. He fell into his chair, running his hand over his face. "Let's head out."

Chapter 9

B Y THE TIME DeLong and Newman arrived at Ally's school, vehicles were piled at the parents' pickup line.

As DeLong led the way to the main door, Newman nudged him with his elbow. Following his gaze, DeLong stopped to watch his brother.

Sullivan hung his head, focusing on the ground, arms linked across his chest. The bell rang, and Sullivan lifted his head, lowering his arms. He ran a hand through his hair, then leaned over to the side mirror, checking his reflection.

"Want to go over there?" Newman asked.

DeLong shook his head.

A few minutes later, he spotted Ally walking out the double doors. She paused halfway to the car, then ran to where her father stood. Sullivan kneeled and wrapped the child in his arms. The embrace lasted for a few minutes until Ally pulled away. It appeared they were speaking.

Sullivan pushed to his feet and opened the back door for Ally.

He glanced in DeLong's direction, then did a double take. Their eyes interlocked for a few seconds before Sullivan shook his head and shut the door. He hurried to the driver's side, climbed in and pulled away from the curb.

DeLong watched as they disappeared onto the road.

"You okay?" Newman asked.

"Yeah, I'm fine." DeLong shook his head to clear it as he continued to make his way into the building.

He'd been to Ally's school once a few years ago when she wanted to bring him for career day. But it was a long time ago. Being here today felt different.

They made their way to the front office.

"Excuse me, ma'am," DeLong said to the lady behind the counter. "I'm Detective Jim DeLong of the Piedmont County Sheriff's Office, and this is Jeff Newman from the crime lab. Do you have a few minutes to answer a few questions?"

The woman frowned. "Is there something wrong?"

"Earlier this morning, the mother of one of your students was found dead," DeLong explained. "We're in the process of retracing her steps. Her name was Bree DeLong."

"I don't know who that is," the woman said.

"Okay, is Principal Kelley available?" DeLong asked.

"Sure. Give me a second and I'll ring him."

They waited as she spoke into the phone, telling the principal he had visitors from the sheriff's office. After she replaced the phone on its cradle, she informed them Principal Kelley would be a second.

On cue, the principal emerged from his office.

"Detective DeLong, come on in."

DeLong made his way around the counter with Newman following. He accepted Principal Kelley's waiting hand and shook it.

DeLong introduced Newman as they took their seats.

Principal Kelley sat back in his chair, crossing one leg over the other. "What brings you here?"

"I don't know if you've been notified," DeLong began, "but this morning, my sis—Ally's mother—was found. She was murdered."

Principal Kelley's eyes widened, and he leaned forward, linking his hands over the surface of the desk. "I'm sorry to hear that, Detective. I had no idea."

"Her dad informed us Ally and a friend of hers got into a fight last week."

The principal bobbed his head with a sigh. "Ally pushed the girl during recess, causing her head to hit the pavement. Thankfully, she didn't get injured. But the mother of the girl wasn't happy. We asked the parents to come in after the school day was over so we could assess the situation. Toward the end, Mrs. Parsons said that Mrs. DeLong was only causing trouble by allowing her daughter to be around danger."

"Danger?" Newman echoed. "Are we talking about the ministry?"

The principal nodded. "The mother was saying Ally was becoming just like those kids." He shook his head. "I'm afraid some people just don't have a heart like Ally's mother. Sad, really. This world is just getting worse."

"Do you know why the girls were fighting?" DeLong asked.

Principal Kelley shrugged. "Neither girl would say. Everything went back to normal by the end of the day. Ally had even apologized later. Children fight every day. But it was unlike Ally to be so aggressive. When Josie hit her head, the teachers, and I thought it best to discuss the situation with their parents, so they could be aware."

"Okay, thank you for your time, Principal Kelley," DeLong said as he scribbled the names in his notepad. After he finished, he retrieved his business card and passed it over. "If something else comes to mind, please give me a call."

"Will do," the principal agreed.

After they left the office, DeLong said, "We'll have to question the Parsons."

"Agreed," Newman said. "People get all bent out of shape when it comes to their children."

DeLong glanced at his watch to see time was fleeing. "Why don't we break for now? We'll begin the interviewing tomorrow morning."

"Want to go grab something to eat before we call it a day?"

As DeLong pulled away from the school, he contemplated the idea, thinking a night out with a friend would be good for him.

"Nah, not tonight," he said, contradicting his thoughts. His mind studied the blank screen of the monitor. "I just want to go on home. It's been a long day."

"Okay," Newman said, watching the detective.

"What?" DeLong asked, rubbing the back of his neck.

Newman seemed to consider whether he wanted to say anything more until DeLong looked over to see him shrug.

"Nothing. Let me know if there's anything I can do to help. I can understand you're feeling anxiety...you know, having to deal with your older brother like this."

DeLong let out a breathy scoff. "What—you're a shrink now?"

"I'm a friend," Newman said.

DeLong hesitated, and before he could respond, they were interrupted by the shrill of the cell phone.

He answered to find it was Nancy, the desk sergeant. She informed him that his brother was waiting for him.

"Thanks, we're almost there now," DeLong said. After he ended the call, he said to Newman, "Sully's there now."

They rode the rest of the way in silence.

When they walked through the double doors, he found Sullivan sitting in a chair in the small waiting area. Nancy was eyeing him, but when she spotted DeLong heading their way, her cheeks reddened, and she resumed her work.

Sullivan had his head in his hands, knees bouncing.

"Hey, Sully," DeLong said to his brother as they neared.

Sullivan looked up and rose from the chair, eyes bloodshot and glassy. "Here. I wanted to give you Bree's address book."

DeLong accepted the leather brown book. "Thanks."

He skimmed through the contents as a silence fell over the men.

Sullivan cleared his throat. "What are you going to do now?"

"Tomorrow we're going to start interviewing," DeLong informed him. "Beginning with Benjamin Beaumont. After that, we have a few more people on our list. We're also going to contact Bree's friends. Maybe one of them knows something, but haven't come forward yet."

"If they knew something, don't you think they would have by now? I mean, they're her friends. They would have said something."

"Not necessarily," Newman interjected. "There are many reasons they may not have come forward. Quite often, they don't think what they knew could have been what got her killed."

Sullivan frowned. Instinct had DeLong wanting to put a reassuring hand on his brother's shoulder, but he refrained from doing so. Almost as though Newman was reading DeLong's mind, he put a hand on Sullivan's elbow. "Listen, it's been a rough day for you. You should go home and rest."

"Okay," Sullivan said, his voice worn. He nodded, scanning the vast room. "Is there anything else I need to do?"

"Besides go home?" DeLong asked, raising his eyebrow. "No. Just be with Ally. We'll let you know if we need anything else."

"I guess I'll see you soon then."

"Or, if you want to, Sully, you're more than welcome to spend the night with us. Sam would love to have you. Bella as well. If not tonight, then any night. Just know you guys don't have to be alone."

"We'll be fine." Sullivan paused. "Just do whatever it is you need to do to find out who killed my wife. Don't worry about us."

"Sully..." DeLong began, unsure of what to say. He didn't want to let his brother walk away without coming to some kind of understanding. He realized now wasn't the time to mend family issues.

"Don't, all right?" Sullivan said, holding up a palm. "I'm not ready for this right now."

DeLong nodded in understanding.

"I'll stop by first thing in the morning," DeLong said.

With a shrug, Sullivan muttered "goodnight" and walked away, leaving DeLong and Newman staring in his wake.

DeLong met Newman's gaze.

"Welcome to the life of the DeLong brothers," he grumbled.

"You okay?" Newman asked as they headed for DeLong's office.

"I'm fine," DeLong said. His mind had drifted, and the sound of his voice seemed far away.

When they stepped into the office, Newman closed the door, then turned with hesitation to face DeLong.

"Sully mentioned not wanting a kid," Newman said. "Why's that?"

"A lot of people don't want kids, and then change their minds after having them," DeLong pointed out. He forced himself to focus on the conversation but wanted Newman to leave him alone with his thoughts.

"Yeah, I know," Newman said. "But there was something in his eyes."

DeLong shrugged. "I don't know what you're talking about."

Newman opened his mouth as if to say something more, but was interrupted.

"Goodnight, Jeff," DeLong said. He closed his eyes, took a couple of deep breaths, and then reopened them. "Go get some rest. Then in the morning, we'll head over to Sully's neighborhood."

Newman hesitated a beat, and then in answer, put a consoling hand on his shoulder before he left for the night.

Sullivan sat in his car in front of the house and called his mother. It was a conversation he wasn't looking forward to, but something he needed to do. He hadn't watched the news yet, but he assumed they were all over Bree's death. He didn't want his mother to find out from anyone else.

"Hello?"

"Mom," Sullivan said. He tried to control the tears in his voice.

"Hey, honey." His mother's voice sounded cheerful. "You didn't call me yesterday. How are you?"

"Mom, something's happened."

"What is it?" he heard the sudden apprehension in her voice. He imagined her eyes were knitted together as they usually were when she worried. "What's happened?"

"Bree-Bree," Sullivan stammered. With his free hand, he gripped the steering wheel. "Bree's dead."

There was a brief silence.

"Oh, honey," his mother said. "I'm so sorry. What happened?"

Sullivan told her everything he could. As he spoke, he noticed the blinds in the upstairs window opening. Ally's face filled the glass.

Sullivan checked the dashboard clock, which told him it was seven o'clock. She'd have to be in bed in an hour, but he didn't feel as though either one of them would find sleep.

His mother said something on the other end of the line, but the words didn't register.

"What did you say?"

"I'm coming to you, okay? I'll get a flight out tonight. I'll—"

"No, Mom, I don't want you to do that. I only needed to tell you before you heard it on the news."

There was a silence on the other end before he heard a heavy sigh.

"Jim?" she asked.

Sullivan didn't answer.

"I know your brother won't rest until he's gotten to the bottom of this, Sullivan."

"I've got to go, Mom," he said. "I just needed you to know before you heard it any other way. I love you. I'll keep you updated." Sullivan pressed *end call* and dropped the phone to his lap. He lowered his head to the steering wheel and sobbed quietly.

His cell phone rang. When he saw it was his brother, he tapped *decline* and replaced the phone in his lap. The last thing he wanted to deal with was his younger brother.

His mind, as it often did, drifted to his days in juvenile detention. He wouldn't admit it, but it haunted him every time he thought of those two months his brother stayed there. He tried to ignore the memories, but they were there to stay. He couldn't pretend it never happened.

Because it did.

Sullivan shook his head clear of his thoughts. He knew he was prolonging going inside his house. It was the first time he'd be home knowing Bree would never return.

Sullivan opened the car door and stepped into the humidity. He slammed the door in agitation, following an angry curse. Before he moved, he took a long look at his quiet house, wishing his wife would walk out and kiss him the way she used to.

The way she never would again.

He went up the walkway and unlocked the knob. Sullivan entered, shutting the door with a soft click.

He relieved the neighbor who had agreed to watch Ally while he was away. After she left, he gazed up the stairs. All the rooms were dark.

Sullivan listened to the silence.

Nothing but dead silence.

Chapter 10

DELONG DIDN'T LOOK AT the clock, but he was sure he'd been staring through the darkness for at least two hours. He felt sleep drawing him, but DeLong refused to rest. When he arrived home earlier in the evening, he had asked Samantha if she knew whether Bree was in any trouble, or if she seemed upset. His wife replied Bree never confided anything to her.

DeLong had tried at least three times to call Sullivan, but each time it went to voicemail. Sullivan wasn't willing to let him in, and DeLong understood that. But he wasn't willing to give up either. Despite his brother's outlook toward him, DeLong believed Sullivan should be around family.

Their mother lived a few states away with her new husband, so all Sullivan had right now was his younger brother, whether he liked it. He considered calling his mother to ask her if she'd come to town for a few days but decided not to overstep his boundaries. Sullivan was an adult, and if he wanted his mother, he'd ask for her. Besides, knowing Felicity DeLong, she'd be on the next plane to Augusta the minute she heard the news.

A rush of heat swallowed his body, and he felt as though the covers would suffocate him. DeLong rolled out of his bed—slowly so as not to wake his wife—and crept out of the room. He peeked into Bella's room to watch her sleep. Her breathing was steady, face peaceful.

They hadn't told her yet about her aunt, but DeLong knew they needed to do so soon. He wasn't sure how to break the news that her Aunt Bree was dead. How would she react once she found out?

After watching Bella sleep for a few more minutes, DeLong pulled the door, leaving it ajar to let a small amount of light seep in. Walking down the steps to the kitchen, DeLong grabbed a can of Coke from the fridge.

He popped the top and chugged half of it, then entered the living room, pressing the cool can to his sweating face.

His mind continued drifting to the state of Bree lying motionless in the water, her face bashed in. DeLong grabbed the remote and turned on the television. The news was still covering his sister-in-law's murder. A family photo flashed on the screen. DeLong studied the smiling faces in the picture. Ally wore a hot pink shirt with colorful polka dot tights and her head tilted back, mouth parted open as if caught in the middle of laughter. Her dad's arm wrapped around her small frame, an amused expression on his face. Bree stood next to him, looking over, a grin plastered on her lips.

It was the perfect family photo that wouldn't be recreated.

DeLong flicked the TV off and tossed the remote onto the couch.

Despite the sweat forming on his forehead, he felt a chill crawl up his back. Knowing he needed sleep, DeLong headed for his bedroom. Halfway up the stairs, he heard a faint sound in the night. His heart thrummed in his chest as he listened for the direction of the scream.

The shouting didn't sound like it was coming from Samantha and it wasn't a child's scream.

Was he imagining things again?

No!

The shout sounded as though it was coming from the backyard.

Sprinting for the kitchen window, he opened the blinds to look out.

He saw two people in the shadows. Everything seemed blurry, but he saw one trying to escape while the other held the first tight.

Help me!

DeLong rushed to the door and swung it open. The knob banged against the wall. The sound of splashing was distinct, but he didn't see water in his vision or hallucination or whatever it was he was seeing.

The hood of the killer fell back, but DeLong couldn't see the face. The one on the ground was Bree, and she was struggling against her attacker.

Her face turned in his direction, pale and bloodied. She moved her mouth, but the sound of thunder erupted in the sky.

DeLong was about to run toward the end of his yard where Bree was being killed until a voice from behind stopped him short.

"You're still up?"

DeLong spun to see Samantha standing in the kitchen, by the counter.

Heart beating against his rib cage, DeLong looked back to where the figures once were.

He pointed, his eyes still focused on the darkened space of the yard.

"They—they..." he trailed off and swallowed hard. Looking back at Samantha, he saw she was eyeing him.

She glanced toward where he was pointing for half a second and then she narrowed her eyes at him.

"Jim?" Concern etched in Samantha's voice. "Honey, what's wrong?"

DeLong reentered the kitchen and shut the door. He put his palms on the counter and leaned over. "Not again," he whispered.

"What 'not again?'" Samantha asked. Closing the door, she made a beeline to where her husband stood. She put her hands on his back and rubbed. "C'mon, honey, look at me."

With hesitation, DeLong turned to face her. She put her hands on either side of his face.

"Oh, Jim, you're burning up," Samantha said.

He grasped her hands in his.

"I'm fine, Sam. I'm sorry. I didn't mean to worry you."

"Come on, honey. It's late. You need to get some rest."

"I can't sleep." He realized his voice sounded groggy.

"You have to," Samantha said. "You won't be doing anyone any good if you're too tired to work. It's after two in the morning. Come to bed. I'll give you some medicine. Try to knock that fever down."

Too tired and frail to protest, DeLong allowed Samantha to guide him upstairs to their room.

He climbed into the bed. Chills crawled up his spine. He wasn't sure if it was from the fever or the memory of the shadows.

Samantha searched through the bathroom medicine cabinet and returned with two pills. Without protesting, he accepted the tablets and chased them with his Coke.

When Samantha climbed under the covers with him, he wrapped his arms around her waist. She sighed with content as he brought her closer to him.

"I love you, Sam," he whispered in her ear. "You know that, right? I don't know what I'd do if anything ever happened to you."

Samantha turned on the bed so she could see his face. She said nothing, only kissed him. He responded, wanting more, despite his fatigue. He never wanted to let her go. Moments like these were worth coming home to. He knew over the past year and a half, Samantha had a newfound love for him. He did for her as well.

And DeLong never wanted that love to slip away.

Pictures of Bree, her motionless, bruised body, continued to flash in his mind.

Sounds of his and Samantha's heated arguments when their marriage came close to an end almost two years ago flooded his ears.

He didn't want to let her go.

She had always been his anchor.

His doorway to sanity.

Trailing kisses across his face, Samantha whispered in his ear, silencing the voices. "You'll find who killed her. You always do. And nothing will happen to me. At the end of the day, I'll be here waiting."

She kissed him one more time and snuggled as close as she could. De-Long felt her heartbeat and heard her soft, rhythmic breathing. He listened and felt the curves of her body against his as he waited for sleep to take him.

When it did, he dreamed about Bree.

Sullivan lay in bed, unable to close his eyes. If he did, he'd only see his wife lying on that cold, hard table in the morgue.

It was a memory he didn't think would ever escape him. It'd haunt him until the day he died.

He wondered what she was thinking when she was dying.

Was she thinking of him?

Was she worried about what would happen to Ally?

Was she begging for the killer to let her go?

He turned to look at Ally, who slept next to him, her stuffed bunny rabbit tight in her arms. She'd come into the room a little while ago, unable to sleep. She didn't want to be alone.

Sullivan swung his feet over the edge of the bed and rubbed his tired, sleepless eyes. He walked through the darkness out of the bedroom and into the kitchen where he filled a glass with ice water.

Sullivan wet his throat and then entered the living room. His eyes focused on the family photo from last Christmas. He had to wait until his eyes became more adjusted to the darkness to see the dim faces. Bree wore a red velvet dress with black lace lining her neckline. Ally had on red leggings and a shirt with Mickey Mouse putting a star on a Christmas tree.

It was taken when they took Ally to New York so she could see *Disney on Ice*.

They were happy then.

Nothing could hurt them. They were together.

Whole.

Now, that happiness was gone.

In its place was a void.

A missing piece of a perfect puzzle.

"I'm sorry, Bree," Sullivan whispered to the portrait. "I'm so sorry I failed you." He gripped his glass tightly in his hand.

His heart beat faster, faster.

He leaned over, his free hand resting against his knee. His breathing became more erratic and he couldn't catch his breath. Tears spilled from his eyes.

Sullivan grabbed a fistful of his hair as if it would help him calm down. He felt dizzy, the room dancing in black and white blurs.

He threw the water glass through the air, screaming into the night as it crashed on impact. Water spewed across the wall and trickled onto the table beneath.

Sullivan fell to his knees, sobbing.

Chapter 11

THE NEXT DAY, DeLong's fever persisted, and Samantha had begged him to stay at home. He resisted, not wanting to feel as though he were out of the loop in the investigation. If worse came to worse, he'd only take part of the day to work, then return home to recuperate with Samantha aiding his every need.

The humidity didn't help how he felt. It only added more beads of sweat on his face. He found it harder to focus, and since he hadn't slept well the night before, he also felt irritable.

After a quick breakfast and a lot of caffeinated cups of coffee, DeLong and Newman stopped by Sullivan's house to check on him and Ally before scouring his neighbors.

He had put Officer Buckwheat and his partner outside the house last night as an extra precaution. He wanted a unit to be close to Sullivan and Ally should they need any help.

The air conditioning from Buckwheat's car must have gone out again because their faces were flushed, cheeks red.

DeLong handed them the takeout he'd ordered so they could eat breakfast and enjoy a cool drink. Buckwheat's partner, Officer Jones, put the wet cup to her cheek to cool off.

Resting his arm on the hood of the car, DeLong leaned into the window. "Did anything happen last night?"

Buckwheat shook his head as he took a bite of his sausage and cheese biscuit. "No, Detective. Well, that's not entirely true. We heard shouting coming from your brother's house. I went to check on him, but he insisted he was okay."

"Doesn't surprise me," DeLong said. "One thing I remember most about him when we were kids was that Sullivan would let things bottle up inside and fester. Then he'd have a tantrum. Throw things and scream until he couldn't speak anymore. His ears would turn bright red."

He looked over at the quiet house with a sigh.

"It's his way of dealing with things. Thank you, guys, for staying last night," he said.

"Not a problem, LT," Buckwheat said. "We'll stay here as long as we're needed."

Officer Jones narrowed her eyes. Setting her drink in the cup holder, she leaned across the driver's side. "Are you feeling okay, Detective? Your eyes are kinda glassy."

"Yeah," DeLong assured her. "I'll be fine."

He'd already had the conversation about his health with Newman and didn't feel like going through it again. DeLong thanked the officers and went up the walkway. He rapped his knuckles against the door and waited for Sullivan to answer.

When he did, DeLong saw his hair disheveled, and he wore the same navy blue Izod polo shirt and jeans as he did yesterday. Sullivan squinted his bloodshot eyes, trying to see without his glasses. His skin was clammy and had a pale yellow tint.

Sullivan leaned against the door frame for balance, rubbing his temple. The smell of liquor lingered on his breath.

"You look as bad as I feel," Sullivan mumbled.

"Couldn't sleep?" DeLong asked, his eyes narrowed. He crossed his arms over his chest. He wanted to say something about the drinking but remained quiet.

"No," Sullivan said, his voice heavy. "I just want it to go away. I want the pain to go away. I want to rewind the past. Make yesterday never happen. Or better yet, this whole week."

"Come on," DeLong said, "let's get you to lie down."

"Don't touch me," Sullivan muttered, though he didn't push him away, the way he did at the morgue.

DeLong assumed he didn't have the energy to do so.

He led his brother to his room and helped him into the bed.

"Try to sleep," he said. "I'll make you a pot of coffee so it'll be ready for when you're up. We need you to be alert today."

"I can't sleep. I can't feel."

"Have you talked to Mom yet?" DeLong asked.

Sullivan's eyes were closed, but he answered that he had.

"Is she going to come?"

"I told her not to."

"Are you sure about that?" DeLong pressed. "The company would do you good. And you won't have to worry about Ally."

He heard his brother let out a soft groan in answer and he chose let the discussion slide for the time being.

DeLong waited a few minutes until he was sure his brother drifted into sleep, then made a beeline to Ally's room. She lay on her bed, facing the wall so her back was to him. She must have heard the door creak open because she turned to face him.

"Hey, sweetheart." DeLong walked further into the room. He sat next to her on the bed and stroked her cheek. "How are you doing?"

She let her shoulders rise and fall.

"Did you get any sleep last night?"

"A little." Her voice came so soft, so timid. DeLong's heart broke because he had no idea how to fix her pain. He wanted to talk to her about her friend Josie Parsons, but he decided to wait until later. His niece wasn't in the mindset to answer questions.

"I'll be back to see you later, okay, honey?"

She nodded.

After offering a quick kiss on the top of her head, DeLong pushed to his feet and headed out the bedroom.

"Uncle Jim?"

He turned back to see Ally watching him, her eyes glassy.

"Are you going to find out who killed my mommy?" Ally's voice was thick with sleep.

"I have a lot of good men working on it," DeLong promised. "We're going to work really hard until we get some answers. Don't you worry." He offered her a slight smile. "Be sure to take good care of your dad, okay?"

Ally bobbed her head, with a long yawn, holding tight to the blue bunny she had since the day she was born.

"Get some sleep, okay?"

"Uh-huh," Ally mumbled, closing her eyes.

After another quick kiss, DeLong left the room to brew the coffee, then walked outside to find Newman leaning into the window in a conversation with Buckwheat and Jones.

They seemed to be talking about sports, but as he neared, the conversation ceased, and Newman straightened his body.

"How's your brother and Ally this morning?"

"Ally's asleep now and Sullivan is a bit hungover," DeLong looked back at the quiet house. He scratched his head. "He's sleeping it off."

"Hmmm," Newman said, "I can't say I wouldn't be tempted to do the same thing. Losing someone you love deeply in any way, can take a toll on anyone. It's very tragic."

"Yeah," he said with a frown. DeLong crossed his arms. He couldn't help but wonder if he'd stop caring about being sober if he were in Sullivan's shoes. Then he reminded himself it wasn't the case and cleared his throat. This was not something he wanted to reflect on.

He looked toward the house where Austin Beaumont and his family lived. He watched a slightly older man wearing a gray suit step out of the house, probably to leave for his job as a pharmacist.

"Come on. Let's get to work before he does," DeLong suggested, nodding toward the neighbor.

Obliging, Newman followed DeLong across the street.

As they neared, DeLong saw the reading glasses sitting on top of the man's head. He closed the door, slipped on the glasses and focused his attention to a sheet of paper.

"Excuse me," DeLong called.

Beaumont looked up and squinted through his lenses.

DeLong introduced himself and Newman. "Do you have a few minutes to answer some questions?"

"I'm running late for work," Beaumont said. "What's this about?"

"You're friendly with your neighbors, Bree and Sullivan, is that correct?"

Beaumont slid his glasses back to the top of his head. He nodded, looking past his visitors to Sullivan's house.

"Yes. It's a shame about what happened to Bree." He looked back at DeLong, studied him. "You in relation with them?"

"Sullivan's my brother," he explained.

"Yes, I can see the resemblance. But I've known them for years and didn't realize he had a brother."

DeLong cleared his throat, anxious to keep the focus on the investigation. "Listen, we have a few questions if you don't mind sparing the time. We'll try not to keep you."

Hesitating, Beaumont nodded in wary agreement. "Come on in."

They piled into the cool house and entered the living room.

Beaumont turned to DeLong. "Bree was a very nice lady. It's hard to think someone would want to harm her. She was the pillar of the community. But I'm sure you already know that." He motioned for the investigators to take a seat wherever they liked.

"How long have you known her and her husband?" DeLong lowered himself on the couch.

"About three years, I suppose," Beaumont said. "She was the first of the neighbors to introduce herself." He snickered. "Actually, she was the only one to come and welcome us to the area."

"Where did you move from?" Newman asked.

"North Carolina," Beaumont stated.

"I love North Carolina," Newman said. "I have family there. What made you leave?"

"My wife's parents lived here. When her mother got sick, we moved. She passed last year."

"I'm sorry to hear that," DeLong said.

"Bree and Sully were thoughtful enough to help take care of things around the house while we handled the funeral arrangements. I honestly don't know where we'd be without them."

"Where's your wife? We'd like to speak with her as well."

"She's at work." Beaumont paused, then added, "She's a nurse over at Doctor's Hospital."

"Okay. When was the last time you saw Bree?" DeLong asked.

"The other day," Beaumont answered. He looked above the mantle where his clock was. "She had just pulled up to her house."

"What time was that?"

"Around six. I didn't look at the clock."

"Was she alone?" Newman asked.

"Yes," Beaumont said. "She didn't stay for long. She came home, went inside, then left a few minutes later. And, no, I have no idea where she was headed."

"Has Bree ever mentioned to you about having issues with someone in particular?" DeLong asked.

Beaumont considered the question. "Not that I can think of."

"What about your son, Benjamin?" Newman asked. "Did Bree have problems with him?"

Beaumont's eyes flashed with anger. "What are you saying, Mr. Newman? My son's a suspect?"

"Not at all, Mr. Beaumont," DeLong said. "We have it on good authority your son and Bree were close, but at the same time, she seemed...worried...when it came to him."

Beaumont frowned. "Who said that? Sullivan?" He shook his head. "That accusation is preposterous. There was nothing going on between Bree and my son. They were friends. They cared about each other. He's heartbroken she's dead."

"Why did you assume Sully said something about Bree and your son?"

"Because he warned Benjamin to stay away from his wife," Beaumont squared his jaw. "But Benjamin tried to tell him there wasn't anything going on. Because there *was* nothing going on."

"So their relationship never progressed to more than friends? That you know of?"

Beaumont narrowed his eyes at Newman. His jaw clenched. "No. I ask again: is my son a suspect?"

"We're only making sure all bases are covered. It's procedure," DeLong said. "Where is your son now? As a friend of Bree's, we're entitled to question him."

"He should be in his classes at Augusta Regents." Beaumont leaned forward and looked DeLong in the eye. "You know, you should be questioning Sylvia Richardson about Bree. They have a long history. If anyone has reason to murder her, Sylvia does."

"Oh?" DeLong said. "Why is that?"

"Sullivan threatened Benjamin only a week ago that he needed to stay away from his wife. Sylvia was in the room, and it's no secret she's interested in Benjamin. She probably thought something was going on and decided to eliminate her competition."

"I see." DeLong exchanged glances with Newman. "Is there anything else you'd like to add?"

Beaumont shook his head.

"Thank you for your time, Mr. Beaumont," DeLong acknowledged. "If you think of anything else, don't hesitate to call us."

He handed him a business card as he rose.

DeLong and Newman left the house and walked the short distance back to Sullivan's.

They found him sitting at the kitchen table, frowning as he read the paper, an article about Bree. He had poured himself a cup of coffee and made an omelet which remained untouched.

"Did you get any rest?" DeLong asked, taking a seat across from him.

"Yeah." Sullivan's voice was low and muffled. He folded the paper and placed it next to his plate. "Did you find anything yet?"

"Depends," DeLong said. "Austin Beaumont claims you threatened his son, Benjamin. Is that true?"

Sullivan hesitated, looking as though he was about to protest. Then he let out a soft sigh. "Sort of. I warned Ben to keep away from Bree. But I meant nothing by it. I was only trying to protect my wife. She'd been acting paranoid. Because of his history, and the way he felt for her, I assumed Benjamin was the cause." He frowned. "But what does that have to do with Bree's murder?"

"Well, if he tried to form a romantic relationship with Bree, but she didn't like it, it's possible he killed her from rage. It wouldn't be the first time it's happened."

"So you think that kid killed my wife?" Sullivan balled his hands into a fist until his knuckles turned white. His teeth clenched. "Because she didn't want a relationship with him?"

DeLong shook his head. "I'm not going to jump to conclusions, Sully. We still need to question him. But you neglected to tell me any of this before. You *have* to be straight with us. No secrets."

Releasing his palms from the ball he'd formed, Sullivan lowered his head to his palms with a sigh. "I didn't think anything I said to someone else mattered."

"What you think doesn't matter, Sully. What matters is someone killed Bree. They beat her with a rock enough times to crush her skull. That shows rage. The fact they covered her face with the handkerchief—that's remorse. Whoever murdered her knew her. Even loved her. If you said something to Benjamin, it may have offset the chain of events. You know that."

Sullivan put his head in his hands, muttering something underneath his breath.

"We're going to need to take a look at Bree's computer. Yours as well. Maybe there's something useful on there."

Sullivan nodded in agreement.

DeLong paused as a thought came to him. "Have either of you seen or heard from Woo over the past few years?"

Sullivan shook his head, and then his eyes brightened with revelation. "No. You don't think he—"

DeLong held up a palm. "I don't think anything at this point. I told you. I'm not jumping to conclusions. I have to explore all options. Since she and Woo have history, we'll need to track him down. I'd say he's as good of a place to start as any."

"Someone want to tell me who this Woo guy is?" Newman inquired, leaning against the counter.

"Stephen Woo. He's Bree's stepbrother," Sullivan said. "A couple years older than her. He'd been arrested a few times for drugs and assault with a weapon. When Bree and I were dating, he'd try to make moves on her. Didn't like being turned down. He and I have shown hands pretty often."

Sullivan rose and paced.

"One day at a party," DeLong continued, "Woo slipped something in Bree's drink. When she got dazed, he helped her to a room. A friend of hers noticed she was missing. She went searching for her and found Woo on top of Bree. She was unconscious. The girl screamed at him and jumped him. A group nearby heard the commotion and ran to help. Woo was arrested on an attempted rape charge."

Sullivan looked at DeLong, eyes burning with hate. "If he did this, I will kill him."

DeLong put his hands on the table. "I promise whoever killed Bree, I will find him. I will find justice for her. Okay? I need you to be patient with us and trust me on this one."

Sullivan's eyes welled with tears. "Why? Why would he do that to her? She didn't deserve it, Jim. She was a good person. A great mother. She didn't deserve to die."

"I know," DeLong whispered. "Where's Ally?"

"Upstairs," Sullivan said with a sigh. "I didn't want her down here when you came back."

"Can I talk to her? I'd like to ask her about the fight with her friend."

Sullivan looked over at DeLong. For a second, he thought the elder brother would protest, but instead, Sullivan nodded.

DeLong pushed his chair back and rose. He made his way through the house until he reached the stairs. Ally was sitting on the top step holding on to her blue bunny.

"Hi there." DeLong smiled.

He lowered himself to the step below his niece.

"Hi, Uncle Jim," Ally said, her voice soft.

"Can I ask you something?"

She nodded her answer.

"I heard you got into an argument with a friend of yours. Um..." He paused as he tried to think of the girl's name without checking his notepad.

"Josie," Ally said. "But we made up."

"That's good," DeLong said. "It's not fun when you're fighting with a good friend, is it?"

Ally shook her head. "Guess it's like you and my daddy fightin'."

"Yeah, you're right about that," DeLong admitted. "What were you and Josie fighting about?"

Ally lifted her shoulders and let them fall again.

"Just kids being kids, I guess?" DeLong asked.

Ally nodded.

"I want you to know that if you ever need to talk," DeLong began, "I'll always be here for you. Aunt Sam, too. So if you need us, just say the word and we'll come running. All right?"

"I know, Uncle Jim," Ally said. She leaned over to hug his neck.

When they pulled apart, he kissed her cheek. "I've got to get going now. But I'll check on you a little bit later."

"Bye, Uncle Jim," Ally said.

"See you soon, kiddo." He ruffled her hair.

DeLong returned to the kitchen. After saying their goodbyes, he and Newman left the house.

Chapter 12

DeLong sent Newman off with Lieutenant Kane and paired himself with Sergeant Hunt. He instructed Newman to interview Sullivan's friend, James Simmons. After that, they would find Benjamin Beaumont and his mother. Alternatively, DeLong and Hunt would interview Stephen Woo, Sylvia Richardson, and the Parsons.

DeLong decided Dawn Parsons' recent quarrel with Bree provided him with a good motive for murder, so he decided to start there.

The Parsons family lived in a small ranch house on the edge of a cul-de-sac. Hunt pulled the car to the curb, and they stepped into the heat, making their way across the stone steps. DeLong rang the doorbell, and they waited.

He wiped his forehead, pleased to realize the fever seemed to be dying, albeit slowly. He was still experiencing discomfort, but it had become manageable.

The door opened after he rang the doorbell a second time, revealing a young woman. DeLong guessed her to be in her late twenties to early thirties.

"Sorry to bother you, ma'am," DeLong began. He held out his identification as he introduced himself. "We're investigating a death that happened at the Savannah Rapids Pavilion the other evening. We understand you knew her—Bree DeLong."

The young woman linked her arms across her chest and the ghost of a smirk came to her lips. It seemed to DeLong that she was trying not to smile.

"Yeah, I heard about that on the news. A shame." Mrs. Parsons narrowed her eyes. "But what does that have to do with us?"

"We heard you and she...exchanged words," DeLong said. He motioned to inside. "May we come in?"

Mrs. Parsons shrugged and pulled the door open wider. "Guess so, but I don't know what I can do to help. Bree DeLong and I didn't...you know...care much for one another." Her expression told DeLong she'd realized what she'd said. "I'm not surprised she's dead. But I didn't kill her."

DeLong and Hunt followed her into the kitchen, hearing the soft buzzing of the television.

"What was the argument about?"

Mrs. Parsons scoffed. "She's poisoning her daughter. Bringing that kind of trouble around? And Ally's best friends with my daughter. I don't like the idea of Josie being around screw ups and rejects."

"I see," Hunt muttered, "So you didn't like what she did for a living?"

"There's nothing wrong with helping other people. But she brought them home with her for dinner and whatever. I have to draw the line somewhere. I was already worried Ally might behave like them. After what happened between her and my Josie, I found my fears to have been valid."

"Had Josie and Ally fought like that before?" DeLong asked.

"Not that I know of," Mrs. Parsons admitted. "But things changed with that family. Ally would come over and I'd overhear her talk about her own parents fighting, and those little wretches. Even Bree's own husband didn't like the idea of bringing them around."

"Do you remember where you were from seven to nine-thirty the night she died?" DeLong asked.

"I was at a party for friends," Mrs. Parsons said. She placed a hand on her hip. "Look, Bree and I didn't see eye-to-eye. We never have. There is such a thing as being too nice. Those kids are high-strung on drugs. They probably killed her because she was trying to..." she put her fingers in the air to quote her next word, "...'help' them."

DeLong ignored the comment. "We'll need the contact information so we can verify that."

Mrs. Parsons offered a tight smile as she ripped a sheet of paper from a notepad resting on the mantel. She scribbled the information and passed it over.

"All right, thank you for your time," DeLong said. He handed over a business card. "If you think of something that may be of help, please call me."

"Sure. But, I'm telling you—those kids she put herself around are nothing but trouble."

"We'll keep that in mind," Hunt said, an edge in his voice.

They headed for the door, Mrs. Parsons following close behind. DeLong thanked her again and stepped outside, reaching for his cell phone from his pocket. He made a call, requesting for someone to interview Blake Parsons and check out his wife's alibi.

"I can't believe that woman," Hunt muttered as they made their way to the car. "Can you?"

"Some people are that way," DeLong said. "They prefer to keep to their own kind."

Hunt let out a curse. "That's prejudice."

"That's the world we live in, Hunt," DeLong countered. He pulled the passenger door open and climbed in.

As Hunt drove to Stephen Woo's place of employment, DeLong ran a background check on him.

"Geez," DeLong muttered, skimming the long rap sheet. "Some things never change." His latest charge was a year ago on an assault against his ex-boss. After being placed on notification twice for harassment, Woo was fired. It resulted in him attacking his boss with a sledgehammer.

Three times a charm, DeLong surmised.

Woo was now a mechanic at Johnny's Paint and Body. After DeLong and Hunt arrived, the manager led them to Woo while muttering underneath his breath about listening to his instincts.

They found Woo's head buried underneath the hood of a fiery red Mustang.

"Woo, these police officers want a word with you." The manager looked with accusation between his employee and guests.

Woo looked up from underneath the hood. He was a mixture of Chinese and American, slender, yet strong. He had a scar underneath his left eye and his hair was flat black with silver highlights. His fingernails were painted black.

Woo narrowed his eyes at DeLong. "I know you."

"Yeah?" DeLong said. "Been a long time since you and I've had a chat, Stephen."

"You Johnny Law now?"

"I have been for quite some time." DeLong linked his arms across his chest.

"Well, as you can see, I'm kinda busy here," Woo said with a laugh of ease.

"We won't take too much of your time," DeLong assured him. "But we would like a word with you. In private."

The manager seemed to take the hint. He huffed and shuffled toward his desk. DeLong noticed the manager occasionally glancing up from his paperwork, in their direction.

"A'ight," Woo sighed, wiping oil from his chin with an old cloth. "What can I do for you?"

"When was the last time you've seen Bree?" DeLong asked.

"Bree?" Woo laughed, then licked his lips.

"Yeah, Bree. You know, my sister-in-law." DeLong narrowed his eyes. "The woman you once tried to force yourself on."

Woo didn't flinch. Instead, he leaned against the car, hands on either side, legs crossed. "Last night. In my sweet dreams."

DeLong saw the twinkle in his eyes and had to fight the urge to throw a punch.

"I never could see what she saw in that brother of yours." Woo tossed his dirty rag between his hands. "Of course, I could see what he saw in her. I mean, that girl is fine. Have you seen her lately?" Woo whistled.

"That girl is dead," DeLong snapped, taking a step toward him.

"Detective." Hunt stepped up, putting a hand on DeLong's shoulder in warning.

In an instant, the look in Woo's eyes changed.

"Dead?" Woo stammered, shaking his head as though he couldn't believe it. "No, that's impossible."

For proof, DeLong shoved the crime scene photo under his nose. "Someone murdered her. They beat her with a rock until she was barely recognizable. Where were you, around seven to nine-thirty Tuesday night?"

"Wait." Woo pushed DeLong's hand away and stood nose-to-nose with him. "You think I killed her?"

"I think you had an erotic fixation on her," DeLong said, "hence the restraining order she had against you. It doesn't take much for dirt bags like you to lose their cool."

Woo looked as though he would make a retort. Instead, he took a step back toward the Mustang. "I was working." He tilted his head toward the small office. "You can ask the boss."

"Don't worry," Hunt said. "We will."

"Thank you for your time, Mr. Woo," DeLong snarled. "Let's hope I don't have to see you again."

"Sounds good to me, pig."

After a final glare, DeLong and Hunt walked to where the manager pretended to focus on the computer monitor in his office.

Rapping his knuckles on the doorframe, DeLong said, "Excuse me. Can you tell us whether Woo was working Tuesday night around seven to nine-thirty?"

The manager looked away from the screen with a frown. "Yeah, he was here. He closed the store for me, helping with the inventory."

"He was with you the entire time?"

The manager sighed and leaned in his chair. "Yeah. He was here from three in the afternoon until ten thirty that night."

"Thank you for your time," DeLong said.

The manager grunted in response.

"Should I be worried about having employed Woo? I mean, I wasn't so sure before—"

"Well, you gave him an alibi, proving he wasn't anywhere near our crime scene," Hunt informed him.

"Yeah, guess I did. No good deed goes unpunished," the manager muttered.

Instead of responding, DeLong left the office, Hunt trailing after him.

"Sorry," DeLong said to Hunt as they reached the car. "I was about to lose my head on the no good scumbag."

Hunt opened the driver's door and looked back to where Woo stood, having words with his boss. "Honestly, I think you handled it pretty well back there. If it were my family we were talking about, I'd have beaten him senseless."

They climbed into the car and Hunt turned the ignition.

DeLong looked out the window, deep in thought, as the vehicle was set in motion.

"What are you thinking, Detective?"

DeLong pulled his pad out of his shirt pocket and flipped it open, studying his notes.

Based on his brother's claim, Benjamin Beaumont had fallen for Bree, but she resisted. That's motive enough, whether the young man had anger issues.

Austin Beaumont tried to steer them away from his son, claiming Sylvia Richardson had a crush on Ben. Beaumont believed she may have been jealous. A weak motive at this point, but still a motive.

Dawn Parsons admitted to not liking her. If she believed Bree put her daughter at risk, then that was another motive. Parents wouldn't think twice about killing for their children's safety.

They still needed to verify the facts, but so far, DeLong had three motives and three suspects.

His mind whirled as he considered the possibilities.

"Detective," Hunt said, bringing him out of his thoughts. "Where to next?"

"Let's go visit Protecting the Lord's Children," DeLong murmured. He slipped the pad back in his shirt pocket. "We'll question the kids and the staff. Hopefully, we'll find Sylvia Richardson there as well. But regardless, maybe someone can shed a little light on what Bree did for them."

Chapter 13

W HEN LIEUTENANT KANE PULLED the car to the curb of James Simmons' lake house, Newman spotted an older man gathering fishing supplies. He wore a camouflaged cap, tan cargo shorts, and an open red plaid shirt. He had rolled his long sleeves up to his elbow and still seemed to be suffering from the heat.

"That could be him," Newman stated. He opened the car door and headed to the back of the house where the man was loading his boat.

"James Simmons?" Kane called out.

Hearing his name, the man turned his head. He used his forearm to wipe sweat from his brow. "Who's asking?"

Kane showed him his badge. "I'm Lieutenant Kane from the Piedmont County Sheriff's Office. This is Jeff Newman from the crime lab. Mind if we take a few minutes of your time to ask about Bree and Sullivan DeLong?"

Simmons looked across the lake, then back at Kane with a heavy sigh.

"What's this about? Are they in some kind of trouble?"

"I guess you didn't hear. Bree was found yesterday morning at the Savannah Rapids, by the canal," Newman answered. "She was beaten with a heavy rock."

"Goodness," Simmons whistled. "No, I didn't hear. I was out of town most of the day yesterday, visiting my daughter. Is Bree okay?"

"I'm afraid not," Kane said. "If you don't mind, why don't we go inside, away from this heat?"

Simmons cursed underneath his breath as he nodded and led the way into his house.

"Sorry about the mess," he said. "I wasn't expecting company."

Simmons cleared the magazines from the chairs, tossing them on the floor by the couch. He sat and motioned for Newman and Kane to do the same.

"How well did you know Mrs. DeLong?" Newman asked.

"Only through her husband," Simmons said. "I saw her four, maybe five, times over the last few years. Sully and I used to work together, then I retired. We fell out of touch for a while. When his daughter was born, he worked from home to help his wife out. We ran into each other a few months ago and started getting together for some fishing. He'd talk about Bree often." Simmons shook his head. "He must be out of his mind."

"Was he fishing with you Tuesday afternoon?" Kane asked.

"Yeah, he was here almost the entire day. They'd had an argument earlier that morning. He didn't want to be home when she was, so he hid out here. I'd convinced him he shouldn't run from the fight."

"What was the fight about?" Newman asked.

"He didn't say." Simmons looked at Newman, then Kane, his eyes glistening with curiosity. "Is he a suspect?"

"Should he be?"

Simmons laughed, holding onto his beer gut of a stomach. When he saw Kane was serious, he cleared his throat. "Of course not. Sullivan loved his wife. He just liked using me and fishing as a means to escape the family life every once in a while."

"Did he tell you where he planned on going after leaving you?"

Simmons shrugged. "Home, I suppose. He said he was going to try to talk to her. But he worried she wouldn't listen. Whatever they argued about, it must have been bad. When he got here, he was in bad shape. By the time he left, he'd cooled down, but seemed to be nervous."

"Okay," Kane said. "If you remember anything else, please call us at the sheriff's office."

"Will do," Simmons agreed.

He walked them to the door and shut it after they left.

"Sullivan DeLong still doesn't have an alibi," Newman stated as they made their way to the car. He frowned at the situation. "It's not looking too good."

"No," Kane agreed. He looked over the hood at Newman. "Something tells me despite whatever is going on between Detective DeLong and his brother, he's not going to take it very well if we need to arrest him."

"I know. That's why we need to tread carefully. He won't like it if we need to arrest his brother. Regardless, I don't have a doubt Jim will do whatever he needs to do."

They climbed into the car and Kane turned the ignition.

"And that's why if an investigation is personal, we shouldn't be allowed on the case," Kane grumbled.

He set the car in motion and drove.

"Normally, I'd agree with you," Newman said, "But this is Jim DeLong. He's one of the best we've got and he won't stop until he gets answers. No matter what it is. And he will do whatever he needs to do. The captain knows that. That's why he agreed to keep DeLong on this."

"If you say so," Kane muttered as he steered the car away from the lake.

Chapter 14

Though DeLong didn't know his sister-in-law well, he knew Bree had always wanted to help people. He remembered her telling him years ago the children's ministry was her passion. She'd built it from the ground up, a year before she and Sullivan were married. It had thrived since then.

A wooden sign sat in the front yard, reading *Protecting the Lord's Children: A Safe Refuge.* The grass was full and bright green, smelling as though it'd been recently mowed. She had planted a small flower garden on either side of the walkway. The stems were damp, showing someone gave the plants a drink.

"Nice place," Hunt observed. "I've never heard of this place."

"Yeah," DeLong said as they headed for the front door. "Bree spent a lot of time and effort creating this place. It had always been her dream."

"You admired her, didn't you?"

"I did. I do." DeLong stopped at the door and turned to Hunt. "I've always regretted not being more involved in her life. Now there's no chance to really get to know her."

Hunt didn't respond. DeLong guessed he didn't know how to react to the statement.

Just as well.

He turned the knob and was greeted by the smell of fresh lemon.

Bree's touch.

He felt her presence around him. Was she there with him? Was it his imagination?

Bree had created a memorial board on the wall above a couch. It listed the names and faces of a few teenagers who had felt they were beyond help and were now no longer around. Bree had the words *these things I have spoken to you, that in Me you may have peace. In the world you will have tribulation; but be of good cheer, I have overcome the world. John 16:33* framed on the wall across from the door.

It was one of Samantha's favorite Bible verses. DeLong had struggled with his own faith for years and still was. But because it was part of a deal he made with Samantha when they promised to work on their marriage, he'd been going to church regularly. He became stronger with each passing day, learning to lean on God as Samantha had. During his AA meetings, he was taught to trust in the Lord through all things, even overcoming his alcohol addiction.

They spoke with a young volunteer, Anna. She allowed them to speak with the children as long as she could remain present. As Anna led them through the house, DeLong spotted more Bible verses hanging on the walls.

He and Hunt sat in an upstairs room considered "The Safe Zone." It held a brown couch and two chairs. Pictures filled the wall, both professional and drawings some of the kids made. A wall art spread across the top, claiming "you can do it if you choose." A large Celtic cross hung above the couch.

They'd already questioned the staff, none of whom had anything new to add to the case. Bree's friend and partner, Sylvia Richardson, wasn't at the ministry house at the time. DeLong decided to pay her a visit at home.

For the past half hour, they'd been questioning the children.

As he expected, a variety of emotions was at play. A few cursed and screamed until the volunteers placed them in a timeout. Others cried, and some seemed to be at a loss with emotions with their hollow eyes and dark circles.

James Jordan, or J.J. as he preferred to be called, was sixteen years old. DeLong studied him, trying to get a feel for him. He paced the room, despite Anna's continuous requests that he sit. DeLong told the volunteer it was okay for J.J. to pace, as long as he answered all questions to the best of his knowledge.

J.J. was tall for his age. He was muscular and wore a tattoo of an eagle on his right shoulder. DeLong made a note that J.J. appeared capable of overpowering a woman of Bree's size, but then again, so did at least four of the other children he'd already questioned.

"How did you like Mrs. DeLong?" DeLong began. "Did you get along with her all right?"

J.J. nodded. "Yeah, we did. Everybody liked her. She was nice."

"Was there ever a time she made you mad?" Hunt asked.

"Sure," J.J. said with a loose shrug. "I mean, she was like a mom to us, I guess. Parents are there to get on your nerves, right?"

DeLong smiled. "I guess you're right about that one. Can you think of anyone who would have wanted to harm her?"

J.J. wavered his head that he didn't know.

"What about your former gang?"

J.J. blinked. "What about them?"

"Do you think someone from there would want to harm her?"

J.J. scoffed. "No. Can we talk about something else?"

"Why don't you want to talk about your former gang?" DeLong pressed.

J.J. frowned and didn't reply.

DeLong dropped it for now. "Okay, J.J. Where were you the other night? Tuesday?"

"Asleep. Bedtime's nine o'clock." He narrowed his eyes. "Why? You think I killed her?"

DeLong could tell anger was bubbling within him.

"These are standard questions," he said. "We're asking everyone the same things."

"Oh. Well, yeah, I was asleep."

"Do you know if anybody left the house?"

J.J. cursed underneath his breath. He rose and kicked the chair's leg, forcing DeLong to flinch. Arms crossed and his back to DeLong, J.J. said, "How should I know? I said I was sleeping."

DeLong hesitated before continuing.

After seconds ticked by, J.J. turned to face the detective and blinked. "We done?"

"Yeah," DeLong said. "If there's anything you think of, don't hesitate to give me a call. The volunteers have my card."

"Yeah, sure," he said.

DeLong nodded. Anna pushed herself off the wall and guided J.J. from the room. A few minutes later, she returned with a thirteen-year-old by the name of Zoe. She sported a nose ring and black lips. She wore a tight black shirt with a large red lip on the front and a pair of ripped black jeans.

Lowering herself to the couch, she leaned back, biting her lips. From the redness in her eyes, DeLong guessed she'd been crying.

DeLong remembered his brother mentioning that Zoe had babysat Ally. He assumed she must have been close with the family.

"How are you doing, Zoe?" DeLong asked.

For a long minute, she remained silent, her lips quivering.

"What am I supposed to do now?" she asked, her voice soft.

DeLong leaned forward. "I know this is a hard time for you, Zoe. I understand how you feel. We're doing everything in our power to find out who hurt Miss Bree."

Zoe met his gaze. Her eyes were glassy and clouded with deep sadness. "Your last name's DeLong, right?"

"Bree was married to my brother," he explained.

She frowned. "Then you do know. Bree was like a mother to me. She was my family." Zoe sniffled and swiped at the tears climbing down her face. "Now I have no one."

"You have the rest of us," Anna protested. "We'll get through this together."

Zoe shook her head. "It's not the same thing. With Miss Bree, I felt like I could be a part of something more. Something important. Now she's gone and I feel..."

"Lost," DeLong finished.

She nodded.

"You must have been pretty close. Did Bree ever confide in you?" DeLong asked. "Maybe she told you something that upset her?"

"Some jerk kept texting her. He kept telling her he loved her or something."

"She told you that?" Hunt asked.

"No," Zoe admitted. Then she added, "I wasn't supposed to look at her phone, but when I heard a message come through, I took a peek."

"Zoe," Anna said. "That's strictly—"

"Zoe, do you feel comfortable talking to us alone?" DeLong interjected.

She nodded, her eyes focused on the floor.

"Would you mind waiting outside?" DeLong requested of Anna.

"But—"

"Please," DeLong said. "As long as Zoe feels comfortable not having staff in the room, it's best we can talk to her alone."

Anna frowned but stepped into the hallway, closing the door behind her.

He turned back to the girl. "Do you remember anything about the text message?"

"Only that he was telling her he loved her and wanted to be with her," Zoe answered. She shook her head in thought. "I don't remember it word for word, but he kind of creeped me out. He said he couldn't live without her."

"Do you remember who it was that texted her?" Hunt asked.

Zoe stared at the floor as she thought. "No. Sorry, I wish I did."

"Did you ever ask her about it?"

"No. I thought I'd get in trouble," Zoe said. "We're supposed to respect other's privacies, and I didn't. I didn't want her to be mad at me."

"It's okay," DeLong said with a smile. He jotted the information in his notes. "Is there anything else you can remember? It can be something you thought was weird. Maybe something to do with one of the other kids, or staff, or someone else entirely."

She shook her head.

"All right, thank you, Zoe. You were a major help."

For the first time since he met her, Zoe's eyes widened with hope. "I was?"

"Yes, and I think you'll be fine. If Bree was helping you, then she must have seen something good in you."

She offered a sheepish smile, then frowned again. "Will you tell Mr. Sullivan I'm sorry?"

"I sure will," DeLong agreed. "I think we're done now. If you come up with anything else, don't hesitate to call me."

Before leaving the ministry, they interviewed one more teenager by the name of Petey but didn't get any new information.

However, reflecting on what Zoe had told him, DeLong felt satisfied that they may have gotten a lead.

The question now: who was obsessed with Bree?

Was it Benjamin Beaumont, as his brother claimed, or someone else?

As Hunt drove, DeLong took a few minutes to scan over his notes and try connecting the dots.

Breaking into his thoughts, Hunt said, "Are you hungry by any chance? I need to get something to eat. And check my blood sugar."

DeLong wasn't in the mood for food, but he knew Hunt was a diabetic. He nodded. "Sure, we can stop."

Hunt pulled into the nearby Burger King parking lot and parked.

DeLong ordered his usual Double Whopper, and as he ate, he slipped into deep thought.

He remembered Bree when they first. Her broad smile seemed to warm the soul. Despite Sullivan's wishes, she had wanted to meet his family. Sullivan had no choice but be in the same room as his brother.

DeLong still felt the residue of the tension that came over them.

Even then, Bree tried convincing them it was important for their own sake to forgive each other.

Does she know? DeLong had asked his brother.

No. And she'll never know. I'm telling you, you better shut your mouth about it, too.

The memory brought chills up his spine.

DeLong set half his Whopper on the wrapper it came in and sipped his Coke. He looked over to Hunt, who was scrolling through something on his phone. He had already finished his burger, leaving a few unsalted fries behind.

"You ready to go?"

Hunt glanced at DeLong through his reading glasses and watched him ball up the rest of his burger.

"You're not hungry?"

"Not really," DeLong muttered. "But to be perfectly honest, this entire investigation is giving me a sour stomach. The thought of eating, well, you know."

"I can understand," Hunt said. He placed his cell phone on its hook on the side of his jeans and removed his glasses, placing them in its case. "It's hard to think how I'd react if I were in your shoes, Detective. Trust me, I've tried."

"Just be glad you're not."

DeLong knew Hunt and his sister had been pretty close. He didn't get the chance to meet her before she died of breast cancer a few years ago, but Hunt often talked about her. Sometimes DeLong felt envious. He knew he'd never have that kind of relationship with his own brother.

They tossed their trash in the bin and walked out of Burger King in silence, DeLong's mind still churning with thoughts of his past and present.

Chapter 15

NEWMAN AND KANE MADE their way through Doctors Hospital in search of the Women's Center. They found someone to guide them to where Camille Beaumont worked.

She was found at the Nurses' Station, typing with fervor at the keyboard. One of her colleagues whispered something to her, and she laughed in response.

"Excuse me, Mrs. Beaumont?" Kane began. When she acknowledged, Kane made the introductions. "Is there someplace where we can talk in private?"

"Uh, I guess," Camille answered. She looked over at her colleague.

"Go ahead, I'll cover you," the petite woman said. She seemed to be trying to cover her curiosity.

"Thanks, Tammy," Camille said with a smile. She turned to her visitors. "We can go into the nurses' lounge for a little privacy."

She led the way and once they stepped into the lounge, she took a seat and crossed her legs with a low groan.

"My feet are killing me. I don't know what you're wanting from me, but I welcome the break."

Newman offered a half-smile as he sat opposite her.

"Have you heard about your neighbor...Bree DeLong?" Kane asked.

Camille nodded. "Yes, I did. I'm just beside myself. Do you know who killed her?"

"No one substantial is on our list yet. How close were you?"

"We were friends. Not best friends by any means, but friends enough. We were neighbors."

"Do you know of anyone that'd want to hurt her?" Newman asked.

"Goodness, no," Camille said. "Bree was a very nice woman. She was one of those that would be at your door in a New York minute if you needed her."

"How was her relationship with your son?"

"They were very close," Camille said. "Life has dealt Benjamin a tough hand. I'm afraid to think of where he'd be without her."

"So Benjamin and Bree didn't have problems with one another?" Kane asked.

"No," Camille said. She leaned forward. "What are you saying?"

Instead of answering, Kane said, "What about your son and Bree's husband? Did they get along?"

Camille frowned. "Most of the time they did. But..."

"Go on," Newman said when she'd hesitated a few beats.

"Well, over the past few weeks, it seems there was something going on with Benjamin and Sullivan. Then Sullivan and my husband."

"Can you elaborate?" Newman pressed.

Camille seemed to consider whether or not she should continue. "I had overheard Sullivan and my husband arguing about Ben and Bree. From what I gathered, Sullivan threatened Ben. I asked my son about it later, and he told me it was only a misunderstanding."

"What did your husband say about it?" Kane asked.

"Nothing. He kept muttering that Sully would pay if he ever threatened Ben again."

"Did he? Threaten Ben again?" Newman asked.

"Not that I know of," Camille said.

"Have you noticed anything out of the ordinary with Bree? Did she seem nervous, was she afraid someone may be following her?"

Camille shook her head as the loudspeaker erupted overhead.

"Nurse Beaumont, please report to the Nurses' Station."

"Is there anything else?" she asked as she rose.

"No," Kane said. He handed her his card. "But if something comes up, don't hesitate to give us a call."

"Of course," Camille said. She accepted the card and hurried out of the lounge.

Kane turned to face Newman. "If Sullivan threatened Benjamin Beaumont a second time to stay away from his wife, it's possible Austin Beaumont wanted to teach him a lesson."

"By killing Bree? I don't know about that," Newman said. "Sounds extreme."

"People have killed for less," Kane pointed out. "And besides, this takes the heat off Detective DeLong's brother."

Newman followed Kane out of the lounge, agreeing.

Chapter 16

"I STILL CAN'T BELIEVE she's gone." Sylvia Richardson sniffled, accepting the tissue DeLong handed her.

He studied her.

She was ten years younger than Bree and a former foster child. She met Bree when she was fifteen years old and had already been a ward of the state for three years. She was arrested for prostitution twice. After the second time, she was court ordered to do community service at Protecting the Lord's Children. Sylvia had since cleaned her act and grown passionate about helping others like her.

Sylvia's mother overdosed on prescription drugs three years ago and her father disappeared from her life. Bree was her only family.

"I know this is hard for you," DeLong said, keeping his voice soft.

"I saw her recently," Sylvia said with a sniffle. She blinked, a single tear sliding from the corner of her eye. "How can she be dead?"

"When was that?" Sergeant Hunt asked.

"Tuesday afternoon." Sylvia cleared her throat and dabbed her tissue at the corner of her red, puffy eyes. "We were together at the ministry, making plans for the next few months."

"Do you remember what time she left?" DeLong asked.

"Around five. She wanted to get home." Sylvia sniffled. "She and her husband had another argument, and she wanted to settle it."

"What was the argument about? Did she say?"

Sylvia shook her head. "I don't know. They've been having problems lately, and it seemed to have progressed. But she didn't want to talk about it."

"Did she mention she was planning to meet anyone at the pavilion?"

Sylvia shook her head. "No, but if things weren't going well with Sullivan, she probably wanted to go there to walk. It helped to clear her mind."

Sylvia blew her nose into the tissue and rose to toss it into the trashcan against the kitchen counter.

"Have you ever been present during any of their arguments?" Hunt asked.

Sylvia hesitated before speaking again. "I shouldn't say anything," she muttered, returning to her seat.

"Sylvia," DeLong said. He leaned over to get her attention. "Even if it is nothing, we need to know. If we don't get every detail of Bree's life, this guy could get away. You were friends with her, right? I'm sure you don't want that to happen."

Sylvia bit her trembling lip.

"They usually keep a lid on it, but lately, it had gotten worse. Especially the other day. The whole neighborhood probably heard them."

"Do you know what it was about?" Hunt pressed.

"I only heard the end of it. Bree and I were going out for lunch, so I went to their house to pick her up. She ran out, slammed the door. He followed, calling out to her. I could tell by the look on her face she was upset. She turned back to him and said she didn't want to speak to him."

"And she said nothing to you about the fight?"

"I didn't ask. I knew it wasn't my business, and she'd tell me if she wanted me to know. I asked if she was okay, but she crossed her arms and told me to get her out of there. Then she said she needed a drink."

"Okay." DeLong scribbled the information on his pad. Without looking up, he asked, "What about you? Did you have issues with Bree?"

Sylvia's eyes widened. "Wha-no, of course not! I loved her."

"We were told that if anyone had a reason to harm her, you might."

Sylvia scoffed, shaking her head as she wiped a tear with a finger. "I'd never hurt her. Bree was the closest thing I had to a sister."

"Where were you from seven to nine-thirty that night?" Hunt asked.

Sylvia frowned. "Am I a suspect or something?"

"We need to figure out everyone's alibis," DeLong said. "It's not a matter of you being a suspect. Yet."

"I was leaving the ministry," Sylvia said.

"Was anyone with you?" Hunt asked.

She shook her head.

"Okay, what about Bree's relationship with Benjamin Beaumont?" De-Long asked. "Do you know anything about their friendship? Was there something going on between them?"

Sylvia shook her head with fervor. "There wasn't anything to their relationship. They were friends. That's all."

"We were told you may have had a crush on Benjamin, while his feelings were directed toward Bree."

Sylvia gazed at DeLong and he waited, trying to figure out what she might be thinking.

"And we were also told you overheard Sullivan threaten Mr. Beaumont to stay away from Bree," he continued.

Sylvia shook her hair, her blonde ponytail flying behind her. "Nothing was going on between Ben and me, or Ben and Bree for that matter. Because of how we were involved with PLC, Bree insisted we not get into a relationship beyond friends. It's a good rule because it could get messy real fast. And anyway, she was married."

"So, Ben's involved with the ministry as well?" Hunt asked.

Sylvia nodded. "He helps out whenever he can between his classes."

DeLong could tell by the way the color rose in her cheeks she was flustered by their questioning.

"Just because rules are there, doesn't mean something can't happen," DeLong pressed, "So is it true you have feelings for Ben?"

"Do I love him? Yes," Sylvia said, squaring her jaw. "Ben and I are good friends. We both went through a lot in our lives. It helps to talk to...someone who understands what it means to be alone."

"When Bree was found, someone had put a red handkerchief over her face. It had gold flowers embroidered with the words 'love always.'" De-Long found the photo of the cloth in his files and passed it over. "Do you recognize this?"

Sylvia looked at the photo for a few seconds, then returned it. "No, I've never seen it before."

"All right. Thank you for your time, Miss Richardson," DeLong concluded. "If you remember anything else, give us a call."

Sylvia rose from her couch to lead them outside. "Do you have any suspects? You don't think it's her husband, do you? I mean, it's hard to imagine Sullivan would kill Bree."

DeLong opened his mouth to speak, but the words got caught in his throat. He considered the men who had the perfect family life and ended up killing their wives. There was no way to tell if a particular man was capable of killing. However, from all the crimes DeLong investigated throughout the years, he'd learned anyone was capable of killing. It was only a matter of opportunity.

"Unfortunately, we have more questions than answers right now," Hunt interjected.

DeLong shook his head to clear his thoughts. "Do you by chance know where Benjamin Beaumont is at the moment?"

"Um, today's Thursday, so..." she glanced at her watch, "...he should be in his Sociology class right about now."

"What room?"

"Hold on, I'll check the schedule."

DeLong and Hunt waited in silence while Sylvia disappeared into the house. A few seconds later, she returned with a sheet of paper and passed it over.

"Thank you again for your time," DeLong said. "We'll be in touch."

As DeLong walked to the car, he sent Newman a text, instructing him to go to the college and talk to Benjamin. In the meantime, he wanted to return to Sullivan's and check in.

Chapter 17

THE CAMPUS AT AUGUSTA Regents University was thriving with college students roaming across the grounds. Since the parking lot was packed, Newman and Kane parked a few buildings away and walked across the campus.

"Takes you back, doesn't it?" Kane stated, a grin plastered on his face. "College...the best years of my life."

"Really?" Newman shook his head. "I never cared much for school. I wanted nothing more than to get out and never look back."

They stopped at the building and Newman put his hand on the door handle and glanced at Kane.

"So much for that wish, huh?"

Kane chuckled as they stepped into the cold building. "I'd have thought you'd enjoy school."

"Let's say it was a struggle. Science and math came easy. It was all those filler subjects I needed that threatened my very existence," Newman said with a smirk.

"I was the first in my family to graduate college," Kane admitted as they continued through the halls in search of the room number DeLong texted them. "I always wanted to go to grad school, but as it turned out, life got in the way."

"It's never too late," Newman suggested, stopping by a closed door. "Here's the room."

Kane knocked and pushed open the door. "Excuse me, is there a Benjamin Beaumont in this class?"

Newman scanned the small room filled with approximately twenty people. Every head turned with curiosity, including a few young men who seemed to have been napping during the lecture.

"Can I ask what this is about?" the professor said, his eyes shining with annoyance.

"I'm Lieutenant Kane." He flashed his badge. "We have a few questions for Mr. Beaumont about...a personal matter."

Newman noticed a young man wearing a black t-shirt with a drawing of a surfboard and the caption *Surf's Up, Dude*. He sat in the back corner of the room and slunk into his chair as if to hide. Newman guessed him to be Benjamin.

"I see. All right, Mr. Beaumont, you're excused."

With a sigh, Benjamin dragged himself to his feet and gathered his books. As he left the room, the professor reminded him of what assignment he needed to complete for the next time they meet.

When they were out in the hall, Kane introduced himself and Newman.

"We're sorry to pull you out of your class," Kane began.

"Yeah, right. What do you want from me?" Benjamin muttered. He leaned against the wall, holding a stack of books in one arm and sticking his free thumb in the pocket of his jeans, "So...this is about Bree, I'm guessing?"

"Yes," Newman answered.

Benjamin frowned.

"We understand you were close to her," Kane began. "Must be hard dealing with classes and having to cope with losing someone you cared about."

"Yeah, Bree was a good friend. She was there for me when everyone else wanted me to go away." He hung his head with a sigh and closed his eyes.

"When was the last time you saw or spoke to her?" Kane asked.

"I think it was the other morning. She called to tell me she missed seeing me around, and to ask how I was doing."

"How did she seem?"

"How should I know? I'm not a mind reader," Benjamin said.

"She seemed, I don't know. Normal."

"Where were you Tuesday night between seven thirty to nine thirty?" Newman asked.

Benjamin paused before answering. "Atlanta."

"What was in Atlanta?"

"Nothing much. It's personal."

"Fair enough," Newman said. "We spoke to your father earlier, and he mentioned her husband threatened you to stay away from Bree. Any idea why he would he do that?"

Benjamin frowned. "He thought something was going on between us. Sullivan was always jealous of our relationship."

"What kind of relationship was that?" Kane asked.

Benjamin lifted his head to gape at him with obvious surprise. Several minutes crawled by before he shook his head and spoke.

"It wasn't like that, okay? I spent a lot of time with her, but she was helping me work through some stuff."

"Like?" Newman pressed.

"Personal stuff. I don't..." Benjamin let out a breathy chuckle, scratching his forearm. "I don't like to talk about it."

"Did you ever have issues with Bree?" Newman asked. "Did you have a disagreement with her within the last few weeks?"

He scoffed. "No. Why would you think that?"

Newman paused before saying anything more, well aware Benjamin had bunched his fists. He couldn't tell if Benjamin was telling the truth, but decided to let the subject go for the time being.

"What do you know about her marriage?" Kane asked.

Benjamin shrugged. "I can't say since I wasn't a part of it."

"Sylvia Richardson said she overheard the end of an argument with Bree and her husband," Kane informed him. "It was right before she died. Know anything about that?"

"Not really," Benjamin said. "I know Sylvia was worried about them because he and Bree have been arguing a lot. I'm not sure what about. Bree didn't talk to me about her marriage. Why would she? She obviously only thought of me as some lame kid."

Newman ran a hand through his hair, noting the annoyance lacing his attitude. Kane scribbled information in his notepad.

"Do you guys think it's someone she knows?" Benjamin asked.

Newman studied him before answering. "It seems that's the case. By the way she was killed. It seemed to be personal. Can you think of someone who would want to hurt her?"

Benjamin frowned. "No."

"Okay, thank you for your time." Kane extended his hand. "We're sorry for your loss."

Benjamin linked his arms over his chest, instead of accepting the lieutenant's hand. Kane cleared his throat and motioned to Newman that it was time to go. They proceeded to leave when Benjamin called out to them.

"How are Sullivan and Ally doing, anyway?"

Turning back, Newman said, "They lost someone they loved. How do you think?"

Newman allowed the question to linger as he turned back. Walking to the car, he called DeLong to give him an update.

Chapter 18

DELONG WATCHED AS SULLIVAN paced the living room. He already updated him about what he could based on the interviews he'd made.

It was obvious his brother was becoming more agitated. DeLong wanted to do or say something to ease Sullivan's pain, but he wasn't sure how.

"I was so sure it was Woo," Sullivan said, his voice hoarse. "I mean, he's the only one in history who has tried to hurt her."

"That you know of," DeLong pointed out. He leaned in his chair, his mind swirling with the shards of pieces he'd learned during his investigation. "You're sure she never mentioned someone texting her? Maybe she hinted she'd gotten involved with someone or something when she shouldn't have? Think, Sully."

"No," Sullivan said through his teeth. "I already told you. She never said anything to me. Don't you think I've been wracking my brain trying to come up with something? Anything?"

"I'm sure she thought it was nothing to worry about," DeLong offered.

Sullivan picked up a book from the end table, thumbed through it, then slammed it back down with a curse. "I don't get it. Any of it. I don't understand what happened to us. I just..."

"I know," DeLong said. "I'm sorry. I know it's tough for you right now."

Sullivan scoffed and glared at his brother.

"Really? You know it's tough?" He shook his head as though he didn't believe what he'd heard. "And how do you know, Jim? I mean, really. How do you know? You've got this perfect little family who forgives every stupid thing you do at the drop of a hat. You don't have to hide anything about your past. They'll love you no matter what you've done. Everything's so easy for you."

DeLong gripped the edge of his chair, pushing his emotions down. He knew Sullivan was referring to what happened in the juvenile detention center. *Ignore it, Jim*, he warned himself. *Just ignore it. Now's not the time.*

"Sully, just sit for a few minutes, okay?" DeLong insisted. "Take a breather."

"I'm sick and tired of being told to relax," Sullivan snarled, although he complied a few seconds later, but not before cursing and punching the wall. "Of all the men in the police department, why did you have to pick up the case? I mean, isn't it a conflict of interest or something?"

"Stop." DeLong held up a warning finger. He leaned forward, narrowing his eyes. "You can hate me all you want, Sullivan, but I'm the lead investigator because I'm good at what I do. Whether or not you want to believe it."

As he spoke, Ally walked into the living room, holding her bunny to her chest. She frowned at the two men.

"Why are you fighting?"

DeLong swallowed and softened his expression.

"We're not," he assured her, forcing a smile. "Come here."

Ally obliged and DeLong pulled her into his lap. He wrapped his arms around her. "Everything's going to be all right, okay?"

"You're going to find who killed Mommy, right?" Ally pivoted to stare into DeLong's eyes.

"Yes, I am," he said. "I promise."

She hesitated, giving him a fleeting smile before sliding off his knee and walking over to give her dad a hug. She whispered something into his ear, then left the room.

DeLong watched as his older brother bounced his knees. Sullivan grabbed a *Sports Illustrated*, flipped through, then tossed it on the table with a frustrated groan. He rose to resume his pacing.

"Why don't we go outside and talk?" DeLong suggested.

Sullivan looked at him as though he suggested they do something outlandish. "Why?"

"Well, you know, it's been a long time since we've seen each other, and it's a nice day. I'd like to have a conversation with my brother. Can't fault me for that."

"What makes you think I want to have a conversation with you?" Sullivan folded his arms across his chest. "Just because you are the lead investigator of my wife's murder, doesn't mean I want to talk to you. It certainly doesn't mean I want a relationship with you. The only relationship we have right now—the only one we'll ever have—is a professional one. That's it."

DeLong frowned at the finality of his brother's words but didn't dignify it with a response. Instead, he rose and made a beeline for the backyard, retrieving his phone. His brother wanted nothing to do with him—fine. But he wasn't about to allow him to wallow in his grief alone.

As he rang his mother, he lowered himself into a green lounge chair, immersing himself in the heat.

"Hi, Jimmy." His mother paused a beat. "How are the two of you doing?"

DeLong craned his neck to peer through the window and saw Sullivan reading his magazine. He considered what he wanted to tell her. He didn't want to say anything that would upset her. She didn't realize what they went through as young boys. DeLong didn't want her to know. If she did, she may not—

DeLong shook his head at the thought, knowing what he was thinking wouldn't be true. His mother loved them and only wanted her sons to find peace with themselves and each other. He couldn't help but wonder what her reaction would be if she learned every dark detail.

"It's a process." He cleared his throat, removing the packet of cigarettes from his shirt pocket. Once one was lit, he inhaled, held his breath and pushed it back out.

It amazed him how tobacco always seemed to ease his nerves.

"I hope the two of you will find your way to each other," she said, tears lacing her words. "You used to be so close."

DeLong didn't respond. He wasn't sure what to say. Instead, he remained quiet.

"What can I do to help? Just let me know, and I'll do it, son."

DeLong turned back to the window to see his brother still reading. "Well, Mom, I won't beat around the bush."

"I wouldn't expect you to."

"I think you should come here. Sully won't admit it, but he needs someone to be there for him. You know how he feels about me, so I can't be that person. And honestly, as the lead investigator, I need to step back as much as I can."

"I understand, son." His mother sighed. "Just tell me one thing."

"What's that?"

"Do you suspect him?"

DeLong considered the question. "It's too early in the investigation for me to decide that, Mom. We're still piecing together her timeline for Tuesday before she was...killed."

Another sigh.

"Are you feeling okay, son?"

Chills crawled up his back, and he wiped the sweat forming on his forehead. How did his mother always know how he felt from states away?

"I'm fine, Mom."

"You're not getting sick, are you?"

The call waiting beeped, and he re-informed his mother that he was all right, but needed to go. After he told her he'd see her when she arrived in town, he switched calls.

"This is Detective DeLong."

"Um, hi." The voice on the other line sounded familiar, however, he couldn't place it.

"Who is this?"

"J.J."

"J.J.," DeLong muttered. "You're one of the kids at PLC, right?"

"Yeah. I was just wondering if you know anything yet about Miss Bree?" J.J.'s voice sounded timid.

"Not yet," DeLong said. "Sometimes these cases take a little bit." He paused. "Is everything okay, J.J.?"

"You don't, um, suspect any of us, do you?"

"Should I?"

J.J. paused. "I was just wondering because you were asking us all of those questions before."

"It's my job to ask questions."

"Yeah. Right. Well, people ask too many questions."

"What do you mean, J.J.?"

Before J.J. could respond, DeLong heard someone in the background calling out for the boy.

"Has someone asked you too many questions?"

"J.J.! Get over here!" The second voice sounded as though it had moved in closer. "Who are you talking to?"

"I need to go," J.J. said.

The call ended before DeLong could reply.

Setting the phone on the table next to him, DeLong leaned in his chair, letting the warmth of the sun envelope him. He closed his eyes to reflect on the situation with his brother but the vibration of his cell phone interrupted his thoughts. He glanced at his caller ID to see it was Newman.

As he answered, he prepared to exchange information. After, DeLong ended the call and pocketed the cell.

He opened the glass door and stepped back inside. Sullivan was reaching into the refrigerator for a beer.

"I want you to tell me what was going on between you and Bree." DeLong put his cigarette between his lips for another hit of tobacco.

Sullivan turned and popped the can open. "Excuse me?"

"When someone like Bree dies," DeLong began, "It could very well be a robbery gone wrong. However, someone covered her face. You don't do that unless you have shame for what happened. So, in the case it's not robbery, it's likely someone she knows."

He studied his brother. Sullivan kept his face straight though his left eye twitched—a nervous tic. To cover, he tilted his head back for a long sip of beer.

DeLong continued, "When I interviewed Sylvia Richardson, she stated you and Bree were having an argument before she was killed."

Sullivan remained silent.

"Get where I'm going? *Right* before, Sully," DeLong said. "Benjamin Beaumont also told my team you and Bree were having marital problems. James Simmons *also* told them you were angry over an argument with Bree that day."

Sullivan narrowed his eyes. "Are you insinuating I murdered my wife? That I *killed* the mother of my child?"

"Did you?" DeLong said, unwilling to back down.

"Are you out of your mind?" Sullivan cursed him slamming his beer can on the counter. The liquid splashed over the mouth of the can. "I love my wife. Why would I kill her?"

DeLong tossed his cigarette on the ground with an angry curse. He stepped the rest of the way inside, pushing the door shut with force.

"If you love her so much, you wouldn't keep secrets about your marriage from the lead investigator!"

Sullivan's eyes went dark, his breathing grew heavy.

DeLong crossed his arms over his chest, waiting. Sullivan took another sip of his beer.

Then another.

DeLong realized his brother's hands were shaking.

"Fine," Sullivan muttered. He narrowed his eyes and stepped to where DeLong stood so they'd be nose-to-nose.

DeLong felt Sullivan's hot breath washing over his face.

"She was doing what she always did—begging me to call my drunken brother. All right? Happy now? She didn't care about what you are. She wouldn't shut up about blood being thicker than water or whatever. She definitely didn't care that I didn't care to have a brother."

They stood in angry silence, the second hand from the wall clock filling the air.

DeLong swallowed, trying to think of something to say.

"You've got to get past it, man," he pleaded, working hard at keeping his emotions at bay. "I'm only here to help."

"You know, I feel sorry for your family," Sullivan hissed. "I'm sorry they're stupid enough to give you chance after chance. They're too stupid to know you're nothing but a disappointment. Especially after everything your own wife told me about what happened the last time." Sullivan backed away, eyes blazing. "Oh, yeah. She told me that day I went over to your house."

Sullivan laughed, a harrowing sound.

DeLong felt heated anger rushing to his face.

"Can't say I blame Sam for the affair, but, wow! She chooses the one person in the world you trusted most. The *only* one who believed you didn't belong in juvie. Don't you see the irony in that?"

DeLong grabbed a fistful of shirt, shoving Sullivan against the counter.

"Enough. They have nothing to do with this. Whatever *this* is." He sliced his hand through the air for emphasis.

"It sickens me," Sullivan hissed, his eyes blazing. "It does. You've always had everything going for you. No matter what you've done. Now. Let. Me. Go."

Sullivan undercut DeLong in the stomach.

He keeled over, trying to catch his breath.

Retaliating, DeLong threw a right hook and connected his brother to his jaw.

Sullivan let out a groan as he fell back on to the table. He recovered and threw another punch, but DeLong blocked it and force Sullivan's arm behind his back.

"Enough! This has got to stop!"

Sullivan's breathing grew heavy, more from anger than exertion.

When he thought his brother had calmed, DeLong loosened his grip on his arm. "I told you not to go that night, Sully. Remember? I begged you. Something wasn't right. If you hadn't..." he trailed off.

"Don't you go there," Sullivan growled through his teeth.

"Why not?" DeLong challenged. "You do. Day after day. Year after year. You're still there, Sullivan. And you blame me for everything because you can't blame yourself."

Sullivan shook his head. "You're wrong, Jim. I died in there."

Sullivan stalked away, waving his hand in the air in resentment. DeLong gazed after him, wiping away the blood from his lip.

Chapter 19

DeLong found two medium-sized poster boards in his brother's home office. He used them to create links between potential suspects and Bree's murder.

He used the kitchen as an office space to sort his mind out. In the middle of the board, he taped a photo of Bree.

He wrote at the top: *Tuesday evening, Augusta Canal, struck multiple times by a large rock, died around ten o'clock.*

DeLong drew a line near the bottom of the board, stating she was last known to have been home around six o'clock. He added—*Witness: Austin Beaumont noted she'd come home, then left a moment later.*

DeLong wrote next: *Bree was overheard talking to someone, possibly Benjamin Beaumont, via telephone. She sounded upset.* Drawing the line, he added: *witness—Sullivan DeLong.*

Next, he considered what Austin Beaumont had said earlier: Sylvia was a likely suspect. On the board, he scrawled under her name, *could be jealous because of possible feelings toward Benjamin—she denies it.*

Underneath his brother's name, he added: *Beaumont overheard Sully threaten Benjamin.*

He also included that Camille Beaumont had said her husband told her he'd teach Sullivan a lesson if he threatened their son again. But DeLong wondered if Austin Beaumont would kill Bree to pay back Sullivan? DeLong wasn't sure. He decided it wouldn't be far-fetched.

To the side, he drew a question mark. Underneath, he wrote: *according to Zoe, Bree received text messages from an unidentified person. Claimed he loved her.*

With hesitation, he wrote his brother's name and underneath included: *argued with Bree that day.*

His head pounding its way out of his skull, DeLong frowned at his words. His heart told him there was no way his brother could have killed his wife. His thoughts and training told another story, reminding him it happened often.

Moving on, his glanced at the other poster board where he had taped photos or written the names of most everyone they'd spoken with and their connection to Bree. He made a note that Stephen Woo was no longer a person of interest because he had an airtight alibi.

DeLong stared at the two boards, attempting to discern what seemed the most likely. The trail appeared to lean toward either Benjamin or Sullivan.

There was no way Sullivan would have murdered his own wife.

Right?

DeLong swallowed and put his head in his hands, trying to ease the sick feeling churning in his stomach.

He heard someone enter the kitchen. Glancing up, he watched Newman pull out a chair to sit at the table. He was looking at the work the detective had done.

"We're getting nowhere," DeLong groaned, putting his elbow on the surface and propping his chin in his hand.

Newman studied his friend before speaking. "What happened to your lip?"

Without realizing, DeLong put a finger on the cut his brother gave him. "I ran into the door."

"I see." It was obvious Newman didn't believe him, but he let it slide. "I think maybe you need to go home, man. You're not well. Your eyes are glassy."

DeLong shook his head, despite his skin feeling as if it was on fire. "Out of the question. I need to figure it out. I *have* to figure it out."

Newman frowned but didn't respond.

They sat in silence while Newman continued to study the two poster boards.

DeLong's mind drifted to the figures he saw in the shadows the night before. Were they only a figment of his imagination? Was he having some a waking nightmare? Maybe it was his fever that was the source of his hallucination. Or was Bree doing what Manny Grimes had done in a previous case? Speaking to him from beyond? Trying to help him find her killer?

"Hey, Jeff." DeLong pushed to his feet and did a quick glance around the adjoining rooms to be sure no one was listening. He returned to his seat and leaned across the table. "Do you believe in ghosts?"

Newman snickered but soon realized DeLong wasn't kidding.

"I haven't thought of it. Why, do you?"

DeLong frowned. "I don't know. I didn't use to. I know people say they have feelings from the afterlife or something."

"I used to know a guy who swore the dead owner of his house was moving things around," Newman stated. "But the guy was senile, so I can't validate his claims."

"Well, I'm not senile," DeLong mumbled. "I don't think."

"Is there something going on with you?" Newman's eyes flashed with a mixture of curiosity and concern.

"Remember Manny Grimes?" DeLong asked. "Remember how I found the body?"

"Yeah," Newman said. "You told us the time frame between those kids finding the body and you arriving with the body *not* there, was only enough time to dump him nearby. So you decided the school basement was the best place."

DeLong nodded. "Well, there's actually more to it than that. I didn't just happen to find Grimes in the basement."

He hesitated to let Newman reflect on what he was saying.

"Manny Grimes led me to his body."

The investigator narrowed his eyes. "Okay, so what you're saying is that Manny Grimes told you to look in the basement."

"Ever since I first went to his house, I had started...noticing...things. That first time, a lamp in his attic window was blinking."

Newman shrugged. "Sometimes lights do that."

"But when I went up there, the lamp was broken. After I got back to my truck to leave, I could have sworn I heard someone say, 'help me.' And I've heard it several more times after that. I even saw Grimes standing in my doorway right before I found him. He was as clear as you are, Jeff. He told me to help him, to 'go to MC.' Then after that, something led me back to that school. And I saw him standing where he died. I followed him to the basement. To his body. Throughout the investigation, I felt him around me. Pushing me. Guiding me."

Newman listened with intent. After DeLong finished speaking, the kitchen went silent, except for the humming of the refrigerator.

"You think I'm crazy, don't you?" DeLong asked. "Honestly, I can't say I blame you."

"I don't think you're crazy at all, Jim." Newman smiled. "I think this is awesome."

"That makes one of us," DeLong muttered. "It's happening again."

Newman's eyes grew. "Grimes is back?"

DeLong shook his head with fervor. "I think this time, it's my sister-in-law."

He explained seeing the hooded image on the computer screen and the shadow figures struggling in his backyard.

"You think Bree's telling you what she saw when she was killed?"

DeLong shrugged. "I don't have a clue. I know it's creeping me out. I don't want to be going crazy, Jeff. I mean seeing these things? That's crazy, right?"

"Yes," Newman agreed, nodding, eyes wide. "It is loads of crazy."

Newman leaned back in his chair, his face changing from amused to serious.

"But this is *you* we're talking about," he continued. "You're a lot of things, Jim, but crazy, you are not."

"Right. So what should I do about it?"

Newman paused as he considered the question.

"Well," he began. He leaned forward and rapped his knuckles on the surface of the table. "Most people say spirits or ghosts come to the living because of unfinished business. I'd say a murder investigation is pretty much unfinished. Maybe if you open yourself up to what they need from you, you'll find answers you need."

"You say this as though I'll see more from future victims."

Newman beamed. "Well, you've already come across two. Who's to say you won't?"

"For goodness' sake," DeLong grumbled. "I sure hope not."

"Just keep an open mind if it happens again," Newman suggested. "If this is Bree trying to contact you, she may make our job a tad easier—well, yours, anyway. I still have to process everything in the lab. I'm not so sure ghosts would qualify as valid witnesses."

DeLong cleared his throat. "Just promise you won't go running your mouth about this."

Newman held two of his fingers in front of him. "Scout's honor." He leaned across the table as the front door opened. "This is cool, you know. You're like the Murder Whisperer."

"I'd rather be known as Detective Jim DeLong of the Piedmont County Sheriff's Office." He rolled his eyes.

He rose to open the fridge and retrieve a bottled water as Officer Buckwheat entered the kitchen. Newman peered at the two poster boards, mumbling to himself.

DeLong slipped out the back and give his wife a call.

Chapter 20

W HEN NEWMAN LEFT TO check on his wife at home, DeLong called the computer technician. He had hoped there was something to be found on Bree's laptop and personal computer.

Anything would be good at this point, DeLong decided.

When Amanda Shilling answered, he heard the smack of her gum. He knew she was in deep concentration whenever she chewed gum.

The government once offered Amanda a job as a hacker which she almost accepted. Then she decided the government was corrupt and didn't want to help them in any way. She was a free-spirited twenty-year-old who had a passion for painting, computers, and God.

DeLong enjoyed his dealings with her and even preferred when Amanda was involved with his cases.

"Hey, Amanda," DeLong said. He slipped outside and lit a cigarette, telling himself it'd be the last time.

"Hey, LT," she chirped. "Glad you called. Got something for ya."

"I was hoping," DeLong responded. He settled himself into a lounge chair. "So what d'ya find?"

She gave him a quiet laugh and said, "Well, it's gonna cost ya, dude."

DeLong's lips curved into a faint smile, knowing what was coming. "What's the price this time?"

"Well, let's see." She popped her gum. "I'd like takeout in the next few days. I think this Monday would work. And I also want you to say it."

"Hmm." DeLong pretended to think. "You must either be greedy, or you've found something I'll like."

"Well, you'll have to pay up before I offer up," she said in a sing-song voice.

"Lunch, I can do, no problem. But the other thing, do I have to?"

"The other thing is the most important."

"Okay, then." DeLong let out a heavy sigh as though he felt defeated. "I think Amanda Shilling is the best computer hacker I've ever known, and I don't know what I'd do without her."

"How sweet of you, LT," Amanda squealed, pretending to be choked up.

DeLong rolled his eyes though he couldn't help but smile. "All right, so, I paid up. What do you have for me?"

"Sit back, and prepare to be dazzled," Amanda muttered. He heard the sounds of her fingers clacking against the keyboards. "Okay, so I ran a hard-delete check on her emails and found a few letters from an address: skullz4@yahoo.com. It dates back from a few years ago. Whoever sent her the emails has definite anger issues for sure. In colorful language, he threatened to...hurt her for ruining his life."

"Maybe that's the same person who texted her when Zoe looked at Bree's phone," DeLong stated more to himself. "Did she ever respond?"

"Yes." Amanda continued clicking on the keyboard. "She tried to assure him she wanted to help, but it was up to him."

"I don't suppose you know this guy's name?" DeLong questioned.

"Nope. He never signed it, not even with initials."

"Curious," DeLong said, deep in thought.

Amanda paused before continuing. "The emails were consistent until.
.."

"Until what?" DeLong asked. "What happened next?"

Amanda let out an audible swallow, then said, "She emailed him on March 15. 'I saw you yesterday at my daughter's school, then today at the store. Why are you following me?'"

DeLong was putting his cigarette in his mouth for another drag when he froze, his hand in mid-air.

She was being followed?

"That was two months ago. Did he respond?" DeLong asked. He pulled in a deep breath, allowing the tobacco to feel his throat. Once he pushed the smoke back out, he rose and paced the pavement of the patio.

"Yes." Amanda cleared her throat. "He said only two words, capitalizing them: 'I'm watching.' I tried to find out the name of this guy, but nothing came up. Not yet, anyway. But I will find something. I just need to dig deeper."

"What about the IP address?" DeLong asked though he knew it would only be an insult to the young hacker's intellectual level. "Can you follow that?"

"I already did," Amanda said. "He used the computers at the Piedmont County Library."

"Is that all you found?" DeLong asked.

"Yeah," Amanda said. He heard the tapping of a keyboard.

"Can you compile Bree's exchanges with this guy and send them to me?" DeLong asked, blowing out more of the tobacco smoke.

"Already working on it," Amanda said.

"Thanks," DeLong said.

So Bree was being threatened? By whom? Who else knew what was going through Bree's mind during that time?

Did Sylvia? Or his brother?

So far, no one had come forward.

"Thank you," he said again into the receiver. His mind was going into overdrive, trying to make sense of what Amanda had said. "You really are the best."

Amanda hesitated before she replied. "How are you doing anyway, LT?"

The tone of her voice moved from lighthearted to disquiet. It wasn't a secret anymore that DeLong was investigating the murder of his estranged brother's wife.

"I'm good," DeLong assured her. He wasn't sure if it was the truth or a lie.

He thanked her again and ended the conversation.

Chapter 21

Sullivan lay on his bed, his cell phone to his ear. James Simmons had called to find out if there had been any development. Sullivan informed him everything he already didn't know about Bree's death. He heard the distress in Simmons' voice, and it got to the point where he was tired of hearing everyone's concerns.

Being concerned wasn't going to find his wife's killer.

"Is there anything I can do to help?" Simmons said.

"Unless you can bring me the head of this guy, then no."

"I'm so sorry," Simmons said again for the hundredth time. "I can't even begin to imagine what you're going through. How is your daughter dealing with all this?"

"She's..." Sullivan rolled to a sitting position. "She's taking it pretty well—so far. It's a long process, but I think she'll be okay. She's in her room playing right now. I'm going to keep her out of school for a few days."

"I'm sure the police are doing all they can."

Sullivan scoffed. "The police. Yeah, right. My brother's actually the lead investigator. Did I tell you that? I don't trust him, you know."

"Why's that?"

Sullivan heard the crinkling of papers, then the sounds of a shredder came alive.

"How many times have you heard me mention my brother?" Sullivan said into the phone.

"You've never mentioned him," Simmons answered, "come to think of it."

"Exactly. Jim DeLong and I may be blood-related, but..." Sullivan trailed off. He asked how things in life could get so messed up.

One mistake and you pay for it until you die.

He couldn't think about his brother without falling back into unwanted memories. "I just can't deal with him. Especially since he's the one who ended up with the drinking problem and caused my family more headaches than ever before."

"I don't know what happened in your childhood," Simmons began. "And you know I'll never ask because I know you don't want to talk about it. But, Sullivan, you can't keep blaming your brother. That's not going to get you anywhere. Family's important. No matter who they are or what they've done."

Sullivan scoffed. "You're sounding like Bree."

"Well, Bree was right," Simmons said. "And you know people change. They make mistakes and they can overcome it. Give him a chance. He may surprise you."

Sullivan didn't respond.

"But," Simmons released a sigh, "if you don't want your brother to investigate, why aren't you protesting to the sheriff's office?"

"Maybe I should," Sullivan said with a sigh.

"Or maybe you trust him more than you think."

Instead of replying to his friend's statement, Sullivan informed him that he needed to go.

After they ended the call, he remained on his bed for several minutes. Sullivan pressed his fingers to his eyelids, well aware his hands were shaking.

He rolled off the bed and opened the dresser drawer to bring out a small, rectangular box. He stared at the container for a few minutes before lifting the lid.

He set the top aside and stared at the contents he kept.

Inside was a single folded news article.

With care, he picked it up and unfolded the old article. He read the printed words highlighting the career accomplishments of Detective Jim DeLong. The only recent photo he had of his brother came from the article, looking over a crime scene from a few years ago.

Sullivan picked up a glossy photo taken when they were kids.

Before they met Drake.

Before they were sent to juvie and their lives changed.

In the picture, they were friends, and Sullivan found he missed the friendship. He missed the way things used to be.

But it was long gone now.

So much had happened. He'd endured so much pain. Looking at his brother was nothing but a painful reminder.

And he didn't want to remember.

With a sigh, Sullivan returned the news article and photo to the box and replaced the lid. He set his memories back in the drawer.

He slid the drawer shut and went to sit on the bed, staring into the oval mirror on top of the dresser. He wasn't really looking—his mind drifted to seeing Bree's lifeless body at the morgue.

It still felt unreal to him. They'd fought before, and she had even left him a few times, only to teach him a lesson. But no matter what, his wife always returned home to him.

He kept expecting she'd return. That she'd come home. But Sullivan knew it wouldn't happen. Bree was gone for good.

Someone would pay for what happened to her.

He would see to that.

Chapter 22

AFTER DELONG FINISHED HIS conversation with Amanda, he called Newman and informed him of what he had learned. They ended the conversation with Newman telling him he was at his office to get a little bit of work done. He would join him at Sullivan's house.

When Amanda emailed DeLong the zip file, DeLong read through the exchanges Bree made with the unidentified person before going inside.

He felt a chill crawl up his spine as he read pieces of the messages.

You've ruined my life.

I only tried to help, Bree had responded, *You're in charge of your own life.*

You better get yourself a bodyguard, little lady.

Don't threaten me, Bree had written.

Threaten? I don't threaten. I'll do things to you your husband has never even heard of. Then I'll kill you. And I'll do it again. And again.

DeLong closed the zip file and pocketed his phone. Whoever threatened Bree seemed intent on sexually assaulting her before and after he killed her. But there was no sign of sexual assault.

What did that mean?

DeLong tossed his cigarette to the ground with a sigh and snuffed it with the toe of his shoe. A breeze of cool air passed through him. Chills crept up his back as the all too familiar words whispered to him.

Help me.

DeLong froze, holding his breath. He closed his eyes to listen to the silence.

Reopening his eyes, he looked around the yard as though he might see someone walking his way. Remembering Newman's suggestion about paying close attention, he stepped further into the yard.

"Bree?" He kept his voice low in case his brother or someone was nearby. The last thing he needed was for someone to hear him communing with the dead. "Bree, are you there?"

DeLong felt inane, but he persisted.

"If you're really there," he continued, "and you can hear me, give me a sign."

He wasn't given a sign.

He cursed underneath his breath, pressing his fingertips to his eyelids. He still felt the fever invading his body though it had eased since earlier that morning. But maybe it was his sickness making him hear things. Maybe he needed to go home, put his investigation aside and rest until the next day.

DeLong turned on his heels to head back into the house.

As he walked past the bistro table, he heard another soft murmur in the breeze.

Trust.

Again, he froze.

Trust? What was that supposed to mean?

What was Bree trying to tell him? That he needed to trust someone? Did he need to earn his brother's trust? DeLong frowned. Why couldn't these so-called voices tell him straight what he needed to know? He listened for some other clue, but nothing ever came.

With another curse, DeLong stepped into the house and made a beeline for Sullivan's bedroom. He thought of their recent fight, and the years the brothers had wasted by their silence. Then he considered the shame he'd brought on himself and his entire family by his drinking. He thought about what Newman said the afternoon before, about him not forgiving himself for everything he had done over the years.

It was true he hadn't.

He had fallen back into his drinking habits almost two years ago and even today felt guilty for all he'd done. At his brother's door, DeLong placed a palm on the surface and focused on his breathing.

He began to hyperventilate.

His brother hated him.

Memories of being in juvie were now at the forefront of his mind and he couldn't push them away. They were tangled with the present day issues.

His sister-in-law was murdered.

Everybody's laughing. He's being pushed to the ground. The noise all around him grew louder, louder.

Someone was threatening to assault her.

Get off him! *The screams were somewhere close by.*

Bree's lifeless body was found in the canal.

The sound of tearing flesh, the taste of salty tears. A boy cries...

DeLong jerked his head as though the thoughts crowding his mind would be shaken loose. He pushed out his breath and rapped his knuckles on Sullivan's door. When the elder brother opened it, he cleared his throat, wanting to speak before his brother turned him away.

But, he couldn't concentrate. The memories that'd been long-buried continued to push its way to the surface.

"Um, I was just...talking to my computer tech." He paused, trying to get his bearings. A lump lodged itself in his throat and his heart skipped several beats.

Sullivan narrowed his eyes. "What's wrong with you?"

"Huh?" DeLong blinked, finding himself jarred back to the present. The sounds in his head died away. "Um, nothing, sorry. I...never mind. Listen, has Bree ever mentioned she was being threatened? Even if she passed it off as harmless or a prank?"

"No, she didn't. Listen, Jim, do me a favor and quit dancing around the issue, all right? I'm tired and I'm beat. Don't treat me like I'm just another case. Please."

With a nod, DeLong went into detail about the emails, then passed his phone over once he pulled up the zip file.

As Sullivan read through the messages, his face whitened. He shook his head as he scrolled through the emails. Seeming to be in a daze, he handed the phone back and made his way to the bed, falling short of the edge.

"Obviously someone she failed to help hated her," DeLong said. "Maybe he was looking for someone to blame after being sent to prison. Or maybe she betrayed this person. Can you think of anyone Bree was invested in who may have had this reaction?"

Sullivan considered the question as he covered his face with his hands. "I'm sure there were a lot of kids, even adults. Bree was good at what she did, but even she couldn't save everyone. There is something that comes to mind though. One of the teenagers from two, maybe three years ago was high on some kind of drug. Not sure how he got it, or what it was, but he started screaming at her when she confronted him. I remember he grabbed her arms and pushed her. She hit her head pretty hard."

"What happened to him?"

"I'm not sure. One of Bree's volunteers called the police, and he was arrested for assault. His name was Gary or something like that."

"Okay, I'll check into it," DeLong said, writing the name in his notepad.

"I don't understand this," Sullivan whispered. "If Bree felt threatened, if she was followed, why wouldn't she have come to me with it? Why would she keep this to herself? I don't get it."

"She probably didn't want to upset you," DeLong answered. "She cared about people. Bree probably wanted to see the situation play out, hoping it would have a good outcome."

"But I could have protected her from him. I could have..." Sullivan's voice went softer as he spoke. He rested his head on the edge of the bed and closed his eyes.

"When's the last time you slept?" DeLong asked. "And I don't mean getting drunk and having to sleep it off."

"I'm not sure," Sullivan admitted.

"Don't go down that road, Sully," DeLong warned. "It's not a place you want to be."

Sullivan scoffed. "I'm nothing like—" He stopped himself short to bite into his lower lip. Rubbing his hair, he blew out a sigh. "I'm sorry. I didn't mean—"

"I know," DeLong interjected. "It's fine."

"No," Sullivan stated with a firm shake of his head. "It's not fine. You're trying to do a job and I haven't been making it any easier for you. I know that."

DeLong swallowed, unsure of how to respond.

"I'm just..." he trailed off again. Fresh tears forming at the corner of his eye.

"You don't need to say anything," DeLong insisted. "I won't rest until I get to the bottom of all this. That's a promise I intend on keeping."

Sullivan met his brother's gaze and held it.

"I know," he said after a few seconds of silence. Sullivan paused as his eyes scanned his brother's face. "Maybe you should go home. You still look like the walking dead."

DeLong smirked and leaned against the dresser. "When Newman gets here, we're going to pay another visit to Sylvia Richardson and ask her if she knew anything about the emails. Then I'll go home."

Sullivan only nodded.

"You're telling me everything you know, right?"

Sullivan pushed to his feet with a frown. "Why don't you say it? I'm still on that list of yours, aren't I?"

"What list?"

Sullivan stepped closer to DeLong, so they stood eye-to-eye. "Don't beat around the bush, brother. You know what list. Bree and I were having problems. Even had a terrible argument the day she died. On top of it all, I tried to kill someone once before. Put all those factors together, that makes me the most viable suspect." Sullivan's words were full of tears rather than ice. He crossed his arms and then stuffed them into his pocket.

"No," DeLong said, shaking his head. "I don't think for a second you killed Bree. Never did. But let me make something clear to you." He took a step closer until his nose was only an inch from his brother's. He straightened until he loomed even taller than was normal. "If I do find out you're lying about anything...anything at all...*that* makes you the most viable suspect. That aside, I will not get into the past with you. After this is through, if you want to hash it out, then be my guest. But until my job here is done, I'm conducting a murder investigation, and I want you to treat me with respect. If you don't, I'll arrest you just because I can. Understood?"

As if on cue, DeLong heard Newman shout his name from the front of the house. Without another word, he turned to meet with the investigator.

Chapter 23

DeLong and Newman pulled up to the curb by Sylvia Richardson's house. They saw her kneeling by a rose bush, pulling weeds. At the sound of a vehicle, she twisted her body, shielding her eyes from the bright afternoon sun. Sylvia tossed the weeds in a nearby trash bag and pushed to her feet.

DeLong climbed out the driver's side to greet her.

"Miss Richardson, how are you doing?"

"Um, okay, I guess," she said. "What can I do for you? Have you come up with any development?"

"It depends," DeLong said. He introduced her to Newman. "We have a few more questions for you if you can spare the time. We won't take too much."

"Okay," Sylvia said. She removed her gloves and stuffed them into the back of her jeans. "Come on inside. If you don't mind, I'd like to get cleaned up first."

They followed her into the house and settled in the living room. Sylvia excused herself and disappeared into another room. She reappeared a few minutes later, hair brushed and pulled into a ponytail, face free of the sweat. She'd also slipped on a cleaner t-shirt, but kept the same jeans.

"Thanks for waiting." She sat in a leather chair and crossed her legs. "What can I help you with?"

"We came across some messages on Bree's laptop," DeLong began. "It seems an unknown person had been emailing threats to her—the address is skullz4@yahoo.com. Do you know anything about that?"

She remained quiet for a few minutes before she scratched her right cheek. "Not that I remember. You said he was threatening her?"

DeLong handed her photocopies of the emails he'd printed at his office before arriving at Sylvia's. He watched her expression as she read through the messages.

Sylvia returned the evidence, breathing out a curse. "I had no idea. Bree rarely complained. I mean about anything. She didn't like letting anyone know she was upset." Sylvia closed her eyes and pushed out another breath. "She was never without a smile on her face, you know?"

"My brother mentioned a scuffle with someone from a few years ago," DeLong said. "He thinks his name was Gary. Do you remember anyone like that?"

Sylvia bit her lower lip. "Yeah, Gary Parrish. But I haven't seen or heard from him in the last couple years. Last I heard, he was in prison."

"What happened between Bree and Gary Parrish?" Newman asked. "Do you remember?"

"How can I forget?" Sylvia muttered. "Gary was arrested for drug possession and assault. He'd gotten high at some rave party. When he got home, he found his little sister in his room and lost it. He beat her. His parents called the police on him."

Sylvia hesitated before continuing.

"Gary was sentenced to juvenile detention for a year. When he got out, he needed to complete community service at PLC. But he was so angry, no matter what Bree or anyone did, he got worse. He got his hands on drugs and tried to put it on one of the other kids. That last day, it all happened so fast. He'd pushed Bree to the ground. She hit the side of her head on the coffee table. He called her every name he could think of. I saw his eyes, wild and scary. Gary ran off but was eventually picked up by the cops. As far as I know, he's been in prison ever since."

Sylvia lowered her head to her hands. Her shoulders shook as she let silent tears flow. DeLong moved from his chair to the couch and laid a hand on her back.

"It's okay," he assured her. "I know it's hard, but Bree would want you and her family to be okay. To work through this."

"But Bree's dead," Sylvia said. "She's dead, and if I'd tried to get her to talk to me, then maybe I could have saved her. I could have at least tried."

"There wasn't anything you could have done," DeLong said.

Sylvia sniffed. "When I got involved with Protecting the Lord's Children, she and I grew a stronger bond. Nothing could break it. I wish she would have come to me if her life was in danger."

"I'm sure she was thankful for your friendship," DeLong said.

"She helped me more than I can say. I'm the one that should be thankful." Sylvia's lips curved into a small smile. "How's Ally doing?"

"She misses her mother," DeLong said. "But I think she'll be okay. She has Bree's strength."

Sylvia nodded and swallowed. "I should go see her."

"I'm sure she'd love that," DeLong said.

Sylvia fiddled with the cross necklace hanging from her neck.

"We'll get out of your way, Miss Richardson," DeLong said. "Thank you for taking the time to talk to us again."

Sylvia rose and walked her visitors to the door.

"Thank you, Detective DeLong," she said as they left.

Newman waited until they were in the car before he spoke. "How are you holding up? I know it's tough investigating the murder of your sister-in-law while your brother is giving you a hard time."

"Don't forget about me seeing and hearing things," DeLong added as he turned the ignition.

"Oh, right." Newman snapped his fingers. "Let's definitely not forget that. So, how are you dealing with it?"

DeLong steered the truck from the curb and headed out of Sylvia's neighborhood.

"I'm fine," he answered. "So many things are happening at once, it's hard for me to keep them straight."

"I can understand that." He punched DeLong's shoulder. "What we need to do is plan a guy's night. What do you say?"

"Sounds good," DeLong said. "Can't tonight or tomorrow. Maybe Saturday, or sometime next week?"

Newman nodded in thought. "We'll play it by ear."

As DeLong drove, Newman retrieved his phone to check his messages, then called his wife.

When he pulled to a stop at a red light, DeLong texted Lieutenant Kane and asked him to run a background check on Gary Parrish and locate him.

After the light turned green, he pressed his foot on the pedal and continued driving, deep in thought

Chapter 24

DELONG SAT AT HIS desk in his office reviewing Gary Parrish's list of offenses and jail time with Newman hovering over his shoulder. Parrish was on parole as of four and a half months ago and placed on probation. So far, he seemed to behave himself. Of course, that didn't mean much of anything.

DeLong leaned back in his chair with a sigh. Newman rounded the desk, pacing with his arm behind his back.

DeLong removed his cap and scratched his head with a sigh. "We'll pay Gary Parrish a visit tomorrow."

"Okay," Newman agreed.

DeLong knew he should go home, but he didn't want to. He'd already answered a text from Samantha asking if he felt better and when would she expect him. He told her yes, he felt better, and he'd be home soon. But despite that he still felt under the weather, he wasn't willing to call it a day.

DeLong retrieved his notepad from his pocket and flipped it open.

"Why don't you go on home and I'll see you in the morning, Jeff?" DeLong suggested.

"Are you going home?" was the investigator's response.

Newman had moved to the window and was gazing through the open blinds. The evening was overcast and threatening more rain.

"In a little bit," DeLong said. "But I want to look over my notes. I know if I go home now, my wife will dope me up with medication and I'll be too drowsy to think."

Newman lifted the corner of his lips to a smile.

"I'll only leave when you do."

DeLong pushed out a breath. "Fine, have it your way. Let's review our suspects. So far, we've got Austin Beaumont who wasn't too happy to find out Sullivan threatened his son," DeLong began. He shook his head. "He is the weakest case of them all, I believe. I don't think he did it."

"There's Benjamin Beaumont," Newman added. "Rumor has it he was interested in more than friendship with Bree. And he has apparent anger issues. And there are those text messages and emails Bree received from an unknown suspect."

"Right," DeLong agreed, "And there's Sylvia Richardson, too. Austin claimed, she's in love with Benjamin. He thinks she may have wanted to take out the competition. But Benjamin denies any romantic feelings, so does Sylvia."

"Because suspects don't lie," Newman said as he rounded the desk to sit in the chair across from DeLong.

They remained in silence for a few minutes. The sound of rainfall descended onto the roof of the building.

"And then there's your brother," Newman stated, echoing DeLong's thoughts.

DeLong looked across his desk at his friend.

"And there's my brother," DeLong admitted. "He and Bree were having marital problems. He admitted to fighting with her that day."

As of now, all he had was theories and conjectures. Not a shred of proof. Any one of his suspects could have murdered his sister-in-law.

But the question was which one? Or was it someone they hadn't come across yet?

The only thing he had was the weapon—a large gray rock with a partial fingerprint—but it didn't match anyone in CODIS. There was also the red handkerchief with gold flowers designed with the words *love always*.

Was Bree's death only an accident? If it was Benjamin, did he go on a blind rampage, killing her because she wouldn't return his love? If it was Sullivan, did he kill her because of an argument?

He thought about the voice he heard earlier.

Trust.

A year and a half ago, when Manny Grimes appeared to him, he had helped lead DeLong to his body and find the killer.

Was it possible for Bree to be doing the same thing?

Could she be telling him it was someone she trusted?

Like her husband?

"What are you thinking?"

Newman shattered his thoughts and DeLong blinked, trying to make sense of what he knew and what he didn't. He realized Newman was watching him with concern.

"I'm not sure what I'm thinking," DeLong said. He skimmed through his pad, then tossed it with frustration on the desk. "All I know is we're missing something. There's a piece of the puzzle we're not seeing."

DeLong rose, glanced outside at the rain. It wasn't falling hard, and he assumed it wouldn't last too long, or get worse. "Come on. I want to go back to the scene."

"But we already went through it," Newman protested, pushing to his feet.

"I know," DeLong said. "But maybe there'll be something we missed. We still haven't found her handbag. Bree wouldn't have gone anywhere without her handbag. Assuming the killer didn't take it from her, she may have dropped it somewhere."

Newman nodded in agreement, then sighed. "Okay. If you want to go back, then I'm with you."

Chapter 25

"How are you doing?" Sullivan asked Ally when he entered her bedroom.

His daughter sat on the floor, her legs in a lotus position. Her blue bunny rested in her lap and she held Barbie and Ken in her hands. Ally whispered underneath her breath, but stopped in mid-sentence and looked up at her dad.

Sullivan stepped farther into her room and lowered himself onto the bed.

"Okay," Ally answered, her voice small. She set her Barbies on the floor and gripped her bunny.

"Do you want to talk?"

Ally twisted so she could gaze up at him. "About what?"

"Anything. Your mom, how you're feeling...I want you to know you can talk to me."

"I'm okay, Daddy," she said, though her frown said otherwise. She peered up at him.

"I miss her, too," Sullivan said. He pulled her into his lap and held her tight. "But we'll be okay. I promise."

The doorbell rang, so Sullivan kissed his daughter's cheek and left the room to answer it.

When he pulled the door open, he saw Sylvia standing on the other side.

"Hi," she said, offering a half-smile. "Hope you don't mind me dropping by like this. I wanted to check on you and Ally."

"Of course not." Sullivan ushered her inside. "How are you doing?"

Sylvia sniffed and put a hand on his arm. "I'm doing okay, considering. How are you holding up? Do you need anything?"

"I don't think so, but thanks. Come on in. Do you want a drink?"

"Sure," Sylvia said. As she took a seat on the leather chair in the living room, Sullivan went to the fridge to grab two beers.

He returned, handing her a can.

She popped her can open, but didn't drink.

"I'm still trying to make sense of this," she whispered. "It's like a dream where you can't wake up."

"I know," Sullivan agreed. "I've been trying to figure out exactly what happened, or if I could have done something to save her. But I'm at a loss. I just don't know."

"What do you think about Detective DeLong?" she asked, taking a sip. "I know he's your brother, but I also know you guys aren't exactly friends. Bree told me a about the two of you. Isn't it weird he's the one investigating the case?"

Sullivan hesitated before responding. He took a long sip of his beer and sighed. "At first, it was weird," he admitted. "But, you know, I have to say I'm glad he's on this." He snickered. "But I'll never admit it to him. I wouldn't be able live that down."

Sylvia lifted the corner of her lips into a smile. "I'm sure he's probably figured that out by now."

Shaking his head, Sullivan leaned back on the couch and crossed his legs. "I don't think so. I haven't exactly been easy to get along with."

"Why not?" Sylvia asked.

"Let's just say he brings out the worst in me. It's nothing he does. It's me. I can't seem to let go of the past. I spent so much time and effort over the years hating him. But the truth is it wasn't him I hated. It was me."

Sylvia opened her mouth to respond until she noticed Ally peeking around the corner.

"Hey, gorgeous." Sylvia set her beer on the coaster and outstretched her arms. "Want to come and give me a hug?"

Still clutching her blue bunny, Ally moved into Sylvia's arms.

When they parted, Sylvia talked to Ally, who nodded a few times.

Sullivan rose and made his way into the kitchen, glad his daughter interrupted the conversation. He hadn't intended on speaking his mind to Sylvia. It slipped out before he realized what it was he was saying. He looked out the back door window into the evening. The rain fell to the ground, mesmerizing. He let his mind drift as he stared into space.

Some minutes later, he felt something touch his shoulder. Startled, Sullivan spun until he was face-to-face with Sylvia.

"Sorry, I didn't mean to frighten you," she said with a smile. "You must have been a million miles away. I said your name several times."

Sullivan offered her a smile. "Yeah, I was thinking."

"I'm going to head out. I wanted to see how you guys were doing," Sylvia said. "Is it okay with you if I come by again and visit Ally?"

"Of course. Ally would like that. It might help take her mind off things. If nothing else, she'll probably be open to talking with you. I think she may be worried about upsetting me if she talks about her mom."

"Okay, then I will," Sylvia said with a nod. "Are you sure there isn't anything you guys need?"

"I'm sure," Sullivan answered. "But thanks."

"Well, I'm a phone call away if you think of something."

Sullivan pulled her into a hug. "I appreciate that. Thanks for stopping by."

He walked her to the door and watched as she climbed into the car. Before pulling away, she waved. He reciprocated and then watched as Sylvia drove out of eyeshot.

Several cars were in the parking lot of the pavilion, and DeLong noted people walking the trail in the rain.

The police tape still blocked off the crime scene, so people avoided the area. As he and Newman extended their search outside the perimeter, they tried imagining the murder.

"Austin Beaumont says Bree left her house shortly after six o'clock," DeLong began. "So, considering she came straight here, she would have arrived...about twenty or thirty minutes later, depending on the traffic that day."

"The wedding began around six thirty," Newman added, "but no one noticed anything out of the ordinary before or after. So she could have been at the pavilion for three hours, give or take. Do you think Bree may have planned on meeting her killer here?"

"Either that or they knew her well enough to know she'd be here."

"Or she was being followed," Newman said. "If her killer is the same guy who wrote the emails, then it's possible."

DeLong didn't respond. He still wasn't happy with the idea someone was stalking her. He hated she never came to him with the emails. Was she worried he'd go to his brother about it? Did she not trust him enough?

"Okay, so are we going to assume she wasn't meeting anyone here?" Newman asked.

"Until we find otherwise, I think that's a pretty good assumption," De-Long said. He walked along the trail, away from the crime scene, keeping his eyes on the ground. "It'd make sense Bree would try to defend herself. But she didn't have any fibers or DNA on her..." He drifted off into silence as they moved down the trail.

He stopped when he came to a bed of yellow flowers. DeLong kneeled to get a closer look at what caught his eye.

"Well, will you look at that," Newman muttered. He snapped a photo with his camera.

"Got some gloves on you?" DeLong asked.

Newman handed DeLong a pair of latex gloves. Slipping them on, he reached into the bed of flowers to retrieve the small, yellow handbag. It blended well enough to be overlooked. DeLong turned it over for inspection, then unzipped the purse.

Inside, he found lipstick, eyeliner, an iPhone, and a red wallet. DeLong removed the wallet and looked inside. He found two credit cards, a debit card, and Bree's driver's license, along with a family photo and a twenty dollar bill.

DeLong exchanged glances with Newman, then tried to power on the phone, only to find it was dead.

"Well," DeLong said as he pushed to his feet. "Once we get her phone charged up, maybe we can pull something off it."

Without waiting for an answer, DeLong continued down the trail, keeping his eyes peeled for more evidence.

"Over here," Newman said.

DeLong went to where the investigator had stopped next to the bridge's railing. A piece of it had broken. What interested them, though, was a dark red substance lingering on the splinters.

Newman set his kit on the ground, searched for his Luminol and sprayed the substance. A second later, it indicated blood. Newman snapped a picture of the railing and collected the evidence.

"It could be anybody's blood," Newman pointed out with a sigh. "But it'd be nice if it turns out to be our killer."

DeLong scanned the area where a handful of people were walking or jogging toward them. The air had thickened with humidity and DeLong wondered how they could stand running in the sweatpants a few of them wore. He always wore shorts and a t-shirt, and even then, he found it difficult to jog in the heat of the day. He preferred to do his daily runs during the cooler hours of the early mornings or late evenings.

"Let's get back to the truck," he suggested when he decided there was nothing more to be seen. "I want to put a little juice into the phone."

Chapter 26

NEWMAN DROPPED OFF THE blood sample for processing and went home for the evening to check on his wife and baby.

Meanwhile, DeLong decided to pay his brother one final visit before calling it a night and give him an update on what he could. By the time he parked in the driveway, Bree's cell phone reached its full charge.

He turned it on to find it locked with a four number passcode.

With the phone in hand, DeLong climbed out of the truck and padded to the door. He knocked and tried the doorknob. Finding it unlocked, he stepped inside and announced his presence.

"In the kitchen," Sullivan called out.

"Hey," DeLong said when he found his brother. "You should keep your door locked."

"Yeah, I know," Sullivan said with a soft snicker. "One of Bree's many pet peeves."

"Some things never change," DeLong muttered.

Sullivan looked up from the sandwich he was making, narrowing his eyes. "Hey. I thought you were going to go home and rest."

Instead of answering, DeLong held the phone out in front of him. "Found this at the crime scene, along with her handbag."

"That's Bree's phone!" Sullivan said, mouth agape. The knife he held fell from his hand and clattered to the floor.

He reached for the phone, but DeLong pulled away. "I can't let you have it right now. It's evidence. But do you know her passcode?"

Sullivan frowned. "No."

"Okay. I'm going to let my computer tech hack into it. I'm hoping we'll be able to get something from it. We also found a section of the bridge where the railing was broken off. It had blood on it. Jeff is having one of his guys process it."

"How will that help?" Sullivan asked.

"Well, if it's Bree's blood, then we'll have a better idea where she started that day. We can question some of the witnesses again and see if they remember a young blonde arguing with a male—or anyone for that matter—by the bridge. If it belonged to one of our suspects, then we'll know how to proceed in arresting someone."

"So it means you're getting close to ending this, right?"

DeLong studied his brother before speaking. "We have a few suspects with the means and opportunity. But we haven't been able to count many of them out yet." He reached over and put his hand on his brother's shoulder. "But I'm optimistic. I have a good team working with me."

Sullivan didn't respond. They stood in the kitchen in awkward silence.

DeLong craned his neck into the living room and saw Ally sitting on the floor, eyes glued to the television.

"How is she?" he asked, turning back to his brother.

Sullivan took a sip of water. "She's...going to be fine, I think. Allyson has her mother's strength."

"And you? How are you doing?"

Sullivan paused as he grabbed a clean knife and spread more grape jelly on the already gooey sandwich. He set the knife down with a sigh. "I'm not sure," he said. "I can't decide how to act or what to do. I'm trying to be normal for Ally's sake. But, I'm not sure what normal is anymore."

"I keep thinking about how I'd feel if I were in your shoes," DeLong admitted as he searched for a glass. When he found one, he filled it with iced water. "I'm not sure I could handle it well. I almost lost my family once at my own fault. To think I would lose them at the hands of a killer, it's..." DeLong paused, swishing his water in the glass, careful not to spill the liquid. "...unfathomable."

They stood in silence, listening to the soft drone of the television in the other room. DeLong heard Ally giggle.

"Jim?"

"Yeah?"

A pause.

"What reason could anyone have to kill my wife? That's what I'm trying to figure out. I just can't—" Sullivan trailed off, taking a sip of his drink to hide the fresh tears threatening to fall.

DeLong looked at his brother, studied him. "I don't know, Sully. Bree's heart was always in the right place. Maybe she was trying to help the wrong person. Or maybe she saw something she wasn't supposed to see."

"If that's true, she would have told the police. Right? She would have at least said something to you."

"When people are afraid, they don't always do ordinary things. They tend to not think straight."

They fell into another heavy silence. Sullivan removed his eyeglasses, rubbed his eyes, and then cleaned the lens with his shirttail. He replaced the glasses on the bridge of his nose.

"When all this is over..." he began after a few minutes ticked by.

He paused and DeLong waited for his brother to finish what he wanted to say. Sullivan looked into his eyes, but DeLong couldn't read what he was thinking or feeling.

"When this is all over, I think it would be good for us to get to know you and your family more."

DeLong remained silent, unsure if he heard what he thought he heard. He cleared his throat, letting out a tense laugh. Running a hand through his hair, he met Sullivan's gaze.

"Yeah?" he said.

Sullivan nodded with sincerity. "Yeah."

"I would like that," DeLong said. "I would like that a lot."

Chapter 27

Aᶠᵗᵉʳ ʜᴇ ʟᴇꜰᴛ Sᴜʟʟɪᴠᴀɴ's, DeLong met Amanda Schilling at her lab to give her the cell phone. Newman already retrieved fingerprints, but they agreed the only prints would likely be those of its owner.

He found Amanda in the break room, devouring a plate of fried chicken, mashed potatoes, and green beans.

Amanda was a slim, blonde girl who wore a Bon Jovi shirt almost every day. She painted her lips wild colors each day of the week, claiming she missed the rebellious years of her youth.

"It's better late than never," she'd say.

Amanda bounced her head from side-to-side as she listened to her headphone—Bon Jovi most likely since she claimed they were the *only* good thing about music.

Her back was to him, so DeLong dangled a Snickers bar in front of her.

She reached for the candy but missed when he snatched his hand back. Amanda removed her headphones to turn and glare at him.

"Not nice, Detective," she said, her blue lips turning into a mock frown.

"Don't worry," DeLong said. "You'll be rewarded after you do me a little favor."

She put her hand on her hip.

"I'm thinking I do way too much for you, LT. I'm beginning to feel as if I'm being taken advantage of. Do you even deserve it?"

"No, I don't," DeLong said. He dangled the candy bar in front of her eyes. "But I once again require the help of a brilliant hacker."

"Well," she said, her lips curving into a smile. "Since you put it that way. As long as the lunch you owe me on Monday is Chinese."

"Consider it done."

"Very well. What do you have for me?"

DeLong handed her the cell phone. "We found Bree's phone. My brother doesn't know her passcode, so I told him I'd give it to the brilliant hacker."

Amanda accepted the phone and led the way to her computer, licking her fingers of the remaining chicken crumbs. "I thought you had something that's more of a challenge." She lowered herself into her chair. DeLong looked over her shoulder as she hooked the cell to the computer and clacked against the keys. "I'm actually a little insulted."

"Next time, I'll try to bring you something that's a headache."

"I'd appreciate that."

Seconds later, she had the phone unlocked. Before returning it to DeLong, she turned to him and smiled, her palm facing upward.

"I'd like my Snickers, please."

When they swapped items, DeLong looked through Bree's phone. Amanda waited as she opened her treat.

"Anything?"

"Nothing out of the ordinary, yet. She called that ministry she ran, Sullivan, my wife, and Sylvia, her partner. Some out of the area, a couple unknown numbers from around here. She has a few voicemails."

DeLong played the messages on speaker. Three were from her husband, one of which was on the day she was found. The time stamp was after DeLong called him. The final message, however, raised curiosity.

"Mrs. DeLong, this is Dr. Maxine Kendricks returning your call. If you will, please call me back." The voice hesitated, and then ended with, "I'm not sure how I can help, but I will do everything I can."

DeLong exchanged glances with Amanda.

"What kind of doctor is Maxine Kendricks?" DeLong asked.

"Not sure," Amanda said sliding into her seat. "Let's find out."

She worked her magic until she tapped the screen. "Dr. Maxine Kendricks is a psychiatrist at Psychiatry and Behavioral Health Center."

"Why was she seeing a shrink?" DeLong mused out loud. "Sully never said anything about that."

"Maybe he didn't know."

"What are Dr. Kendricks' office hours?" DeLong asked, glancing at his watch. It was nearing six o'clock.

"Let's see," Amanda muttered, looking at her computer screen. "Monday through Friday from eight in the morning to four in the evening."

He thanked Amanda and told her he'd come in on Monday with her Chinese.

Leaving her office, he attempted to wrap his head around the new development in the case. While he knew he wasn't getting any closer to finding his sister-in-law's killer, he felt he was finally catching a break.

So Bree was talking to a shrink. He wondered if Bree mentioned it to Samantha. He decided to ask Sullivan and Samantha, then on Monday, he'd pay Dr. Maxine Kendricks a visit.

From the doorway, Sullivan watched Ally flip through the channels, unable to find something to keep her interest. She sighed and kept the channel on *Power Rangers*, tossing the remote to her side. Ally pulled her knees to her chest and wrapped her arms around them, her mouth turning into a frown.

He made a beeline to the couch and sat.

"There's something I need to do," he said.

Ally turned to gaze up at him.

"How would you like to go over to Aunt Sam's and play with Bella while I run a few errands?"

Her eyes brightened. "Okay."

"All right, then. Turn off the TV and let's get on out of here."

Once they locked the house and settled in the car, Sullivan turned the rearview mirror so he could look at Ally. She sat in the back seat, elbow on the door, head against the window.

He turned the ignition and switched on the radio to fill the silence. He wanted to give his daughter peace of mind, so he decided a visit with her cousin would help. It would also help him spend a couple hours to himself without having to worry about her.

As Sullivan drove to his brother's house, he tried to think about the funeral arrangements. Bree always wanted to be cremated and have her ashes spread across the Blue Ridge Mountains where she'd spent most of her childhood.

Sullivan wasn't sure he wanted her body to be burnt to a crisp. He wanted to visit her, to talk to her. How could he do that when her ashes were swimming in the air three hours away?

He knew he wanted to order daisies—they were her favorite flowers. He needed to phone their pastor about officiating.

There were so many things to be done, and Sullivan wasn't sure he'd be able to do them himself.

When he pulled into the driveway, he turned off the car and climbed out. He opened the back door to let Ally exit.

They walked hand-in-hand toward the door.

"I want to ring the bell." Ally said, reached her hand to the button. She had to hop to press it.

"Excited to see Bella again?" Sullivan asked.

Ally nodded as the door opened.

"Sully," Samantha said, a smile lighting her face. She leaned toward Ally so she could be eye level. "Hey, pretty girl. Are you going to give your Aunt Sam a hug?"

Ally moved into Samantha's arms and then pulled back. "Where's Bella?"

"In her room. Why don't you go up and see her?"

Ally pushed her way into the house. Sullivan heard her footsteps storm up the stairs as Samantha pulled him by the arm to usher him into the house.

"I'm so glad you're here, Sully." She guided him into the living room. "Would you like something to drink?"

"No, I'm good, thanks," Sullivan said. He lowered himself to the couch.

"Okay." Samantha sat next to him. She crossed her legs and folded her hands over her knees. Her eyes scanned him. "Jim's not home yet, but I hope he'll be finished with work soon. He needs rest."

"Yeah, he looked sick when I saw him." When Samantha frowned, he added, "But I saw him about an hour ago and he seemed much better."

She smiled at his sentiment. "Good."

"He's determined," Sullivan noted.

"Yes, he is," Samantha agreed. "He loves his job, but sometimes he works too hard."

Sullivan nodded. "I can tell. I know it's his job, but I should tell him how much I appreciate—"

Samantha leaned over to put a hand on Sullivan's elbow. Her eyes shined with care. "This may be his job, but you're still his family, Sullivan. I don't know what went on between the two of you. I never asked him because whatever it was, I want him to *want* me to know. I don't need to pressure him to tell me every part of his life. But, Sullivan, he's still your brother. He may not show it, but he loves you deeply. And he loved Bree."

"I know," Sullivan said, his voice hoarse. He put a hand over Samantha's. "And I also know I haven't been the best brother in the world. But I want to change it."

"I'm glad," Samantha said.

Sullivan swallowed, wanting to change the subject.

"Do you need help with the funeral arrangements or anything?" Samantha asked, breaking through his thoughts. "Because I'll do whatever I can to help you. I want you to remember that."

Sullivan offered a smile. "I know. And, yes, I'd appreciate your help. I don't—I don't think I'd be able to do this alone."

"You don't have to, Sully. Jim and I are both here for you."

"Thanks, Sam," Sullivan said. "Listen, I have a few errands I need to do. Can you keep Ally for a little while?"

"Of course. She can stay as long as you need."

Sullivan rose, Samantha following suit.

"Thanks. I won't be too long."

Leaving Samantha in the living room, he walked up the stairs, eyeing the family photos lining the wall. He followed chatter and giggles until he found the girls playing in Bella's room. They had changed into Disney princess costumes.

"Hey, girls." Sullivan leaned against the doorframe, his thumb hooked in his belt hoop. "Bella, do you remember me? I know I haven't been around much these years."

Bella tilted her head in laughter. "Uncle Sully!" She ran to him for a hug.

"What are you girls doing?"

"Getting ready for a ball," Ally said.

"That sounds like fun."

"Do you want to come with us?" Bella asked.

"No, I've got errands to run," he explained. "Maybe another time?"

"Maybe," Bella agreed as she clipped on earrings. "But a ball is a rare occasion. There might not be another chance."

"Okay, well, I'll just have to hope there will be. Ally, come on over here and give Daddy a hug."

When Ally did, he told her he loved her, then kissed her forehead.

"I'll be back soon. Be good and have fun with your cousin."

The girls resumed their playing, and he met Samantha at the bottom of the steps. He gave her a hug, thanked her, and then left the house.

He wasn't sure where he wanted to go. All he knew was that he wanted to be alone for a while.

It didn't take long for him to realize he was en route to where his wife now rested on a pullout table in the freezer.

He didn't want to go in, but he did anyway.

He needed to see her.

Just one more time.

Sullivan knocked on the closed door and waited for Dr. Harmon to appear in the frame. The doctor gazed at him, tilting his glasses with one hand and holding a clipboard with the other.

"Mr. DeLong," the doctor remembered.

Sullivan cleared his throat.

"Can I see her?"

Dr. Harmon hesitated before nodding and ushering Sullivan inside. They ambled over to the storage cabinets. The doctor opened the square gray door and rolled a table out of the freezer.

He looked at Sullivan. "Are you certain you want to do this again?"

With a swallow, Sullivan nodded. At the confirmation, the doctor folded the sheet to reveal the broken face.

Bree lay still.

Peaceful.

Dr. Harmon stepped back to allow Sullivan a few minutes of solitude.

Bree was cleaned up as best as she could be, but her face was still covered with deep gashes and bruises.

With shaky fingers, Sullivan touched her cheeks. Ice cold.

Tears streamed down his face. Even though he hadn't seen her alive in three days, he still couldn't believe his wife was on the table in the morgue.

He leaned toward her and kissed her lips, whispering a promise to find her justice. No matter what happened.

No matter what it took.

He told her he loved her and that Ally did as well.

"Thank you," Sullivan said, his voice hoarse.

He forced himself to walk away, keeping his tear-stained face hidden from Dr. Harmon.

He left the morgue and opted to go home. He'd allow Ally a little longer with her cousin.

When Sullivan arrived at his house, he let the car idle, looking over the quiet dwelling. Fresh tears fell from the corners of his eyes.

He wiped them away and turned off the car. With unsteady knees, he exited the vehicle and made his way to the front door. He hesitated before unlocking it and stepping over the threshold.

He hadn't spent a lot of time out of the house in the last few days, but now, the home he'd bought five years ago felt unfamiliar. Sullivan made his way to his room and opened his closet. Once inside, he pulled out one of Bree's t-shirts and sniffed it.

It still had her scent.

Sullivan took the shirt with him to his bed and sat, smelling his wife. For as long as he held the shirt, Bree was with him.

Nothing else mattered.

Chapter 28

RHONDA McIntosh grabbed her scrunchy from the locker and pulled her hair in a careless ponytail. She yawned, exhausted from the past few days. Her best friend recently married, and she and her friends had been up late most nights celebrating. Now the excitement had ended, and her friend and new husband were off honeymooning in Africa. They were no doubt having the time of their lives, but it was time for Rhonda to return to reality.

She loved her waitressing job but felt like taking a few more days off for some much-needed sleep.

But the bills wouldn't pay for themselves.

So now she fought sleep as she clocked in, a yawn following each punch of the number on the keypad.

"How was the wedding?"

Rhonda released another yawn and looked to see Charlene rummaging through her handbag. Charlene muttered a soft curse when she couldn't find what she was searching for.

"Wonderful," Rhonda said with a broad smile.

"Must be nice to have found love," Charlene said. "I wish I could."

"Eh, you will," Rhonda muttered.

Charlene often complained about not finding love. Rhonda, on the other hand, was a big believer that it would happen when it happened. She was in no hurry. Whenever she found love, she wanted it to be deep and last for the rest of her life.

Just like it would with her friend and her new husband.

"Hey, the wedding was at the Savannah Rapids, right?"

"Yeah. It was amazing. I love that area. You know, I've never even been there before. On our break, I'll have to show you some pictures I took."

Charlene found what she was looking for and squeezed the bottle of lotion. She spread it on her baby-soft chocolate skin.

"I guess you didn't hear about what happened, then?"

Rhonda wavered her head in response.

"Someone got killed. I think it was while the wedding took place. Around eight or nine, something or other. I can't believe you haven't heard about it."

Rhonda's mouth flew open as she released a gasp. "No! I didn't hear anything. Who was it?"

"I'm not sure. But it's all over the news. She was found in the canal the morning after the wedding."

"That's awful! I can't—"

Rhonda froze. Her eyes widened as she remembered seeing a man and a woman at the pavilion.

"Oh my goodness," she whispered. Rhonda fell against the lockers, ignoring Charlene, who asked her what was wrong. Rhonda's wide eyes found their way to Charlene's confused face. "I think I saw her."

"You saw her get killed?" Charlene asked, a tone of more excitement than concern.

"No, but I saw her fighting with someone. She was arguing with some guy on the bridge. There was so much going on that day, I didn't think anything about it. You said it's been in the news?"

"Yeah, nonstop."

Rhonda pushed herself off the locker and went to the television at the bar. She changed the channel to a news station, despite an angry patron cursing her for interrupting his baseball game. On the screen was a recent photo of a woman. The headline read: Wife and mother found dead in the Augusta Canal.

She'd seen the woman before.

During the time of her friend's wedding reception.

Her heart seemed to lodge itself in her throat as the thought circled in her mind.

In the photo, the woman stood next to her husband and daughter.

"Is it her?" Charlene inquired with a hopeful edge in her voice.

"Yeah," Rhonda said. "I think so. I mean, she wasn't near where we were, but I think it's the same woman. She was on the bridge."

"Wow," Charlene breathed. "You witnessed a murder and didn't even realize it. This is the kind of stuff that happens in movies!"

Without responding, Rhonda grabbed the phone next to her and dialed the number from the bottom of the screen.

"Piedmont County Sheriff's Office, how might I direct yer call?"

"Um, my name's Rhonda McIntosh. I think I need to speak with someone that's involved in that woman's murder. The one that was found at the pavilion."

"Detective DeLong's not in at the moment, but I'll send ya to Captain Lowell. Hold, please."

Rhonda waited until a man picked up the receiver.

"Captain Lowell."

Introducing herself again, she informed him that she was at a wedding and saw the woman arguing with a man.

"What time was this?" the captain asked.

Rhonda bit her lower lip as she tried to think about the day of the wedding. "It was around seven thirty, I think. It was raining, and I was helping move some of the things inside. I looked in their direction for just a second, but didn't think anything of it."

"Would you be able to come in and make an official statement? We'll also have you describe this person you saw to our sketch artist."

"Um, well, I'm at work right now," Rhonda said. "I don't get off until later. But do I want to get involved? I mean, I don't want my life to be in danger or anything. What if this guy finds me?"

"I assure you, you'll be perfectly safe," Captain Lowell said. "Why don't you stop by after you get off work?"

Rhonda considered it and agreed. She replaced the phone on its cradle and glanced over at Charlene.

"He wants me to come in and give them a statement after work."

"That is so cool!" Then Charlene realized what she said, and added, "That you'll be helping the police. I mean, the situation isn't cool. But that you'll be helping them is."

Rhonda frowned and looked up at the television screen. The news droned on about the woman who had been murdered while she attended her best friend's wedding.

Chapter 29

DELONG FOUND SULLIVAN IN his room, holding a woman's shirt. His eyes were closed, his breathing relaxed. He was reluctant to wake him. He seemed to have found a sense of peace, and DeLong didn't want to disturb that peace.

He had already checked the rest of the house for Ally but she was nowhere to be found. Concern rose within him.

"Sully," DeLong said.

When his brother didn't budge, he shook Sullivan's shoulder.

"Come on, time to wake up."

Sullivan's eyes were slow to open, and when he focused on DeLong, he rolled his legs off the edge of the bed, rubbing his eyes. "I didn't realize I'd fallen asleep."

"Where's Ally?" DeLong asked.

Sullivan glanced at the clock on the bedside table.

"Your house. I wanted her to have a little normalcy for a change. I asked Sam to watch her while I ran errands."

"Okay. I think that's a good thing," DeLong said. Relief flooded through him, but he tried not to show it. "Children, especially her age, are delicate."

"What are you doing here?"

"I want to ask you something," DeLong said as he lowered himself next to his brother. "Was Bree seeing a psychiatrist?"

Sullivan sighed, looking over at DeLong. "No. At least not that I knew of. Why?"

"Have you ever heard the name, Maxine Kendricks? Maybe Bree mentioned the name in passing or something."

"I've never heard that name before." Sullivan rose and paced. He stopped at his dresser and leaned against it, linking his arms. The brothers stared at one another through the mirror. "What are you saying?"

"Well, Bree had a voicemail from a Dr. Maxine Kendricks," DeLong began. "There wasn't much to say, but she requested for Bree to return her call. Dr. Kendricks said she'd do whatever she could to help her."

"Did you call this doctor and ask her?"

"Not yet. Her office is closed," DeLong said. "Newman and I will pay her a visit first thing Monday."

Sullivan closed his eyes. "So it seems my wife was hiding things from me."

"Sully, I'm sure it's..." he trailed off. He was about to tell his brother it was nothing. But how could he when he didn't know himself? The fact was someone killed Bree, so he knew it had to be something. Whoever killed her did so for reasons unknown. Now it appears she was seeing a psychiatrist behind her husband's back. What was the reason?

What else was his sister-in-law hiding from her family?

"Why didn't I see it coming?" Sullivan's tired voice seemed to echo against the walls. "I should have seen it coming. We didn't use to keep secrets from one another. Well..." he allowed a feeble chuckle, "...not a whole lot of secrets, anyway."

DeLong frowned, knowing what secret his brother was referring. He broke the gaze and looked around the bedroom, trying to find something else to focus on.

Sullivan sat again on the bed. He put his elbows on his knees, propping his hands on his forehead.

"I feel so helpless."

The brothers remained silent for a few more minutes until Sullivan rose to pace the room. He grabbed a fistful of his hair and let out an agitated groan. "Jimmy, I'm going out of my mind here. I've got to do something. I can't—I can't just sit here and do nothing while my wife's killer is running loose." He frowned. "As far as we know, he already left town."

"I'm not so sure about that," DeLong said. "Call it instinct, but whoever murdered her is still here. If I'm right and Bree knew this person...if she trusted this person...then they won't be drawing attention to themselves by leaving town. That'd be too obvious."

Sullivan nodded in agreement. "Yeah, I guess you're right."

They fell into another brief silence. Sullivan focused his attention on the floor and DeLong stared into a small photo of Bree and Ally.

"Do you ever think about it?"

DeLong turned back to see his brother watching him before he hung his head with a sigh. "All the time. I sometimes can't sleep I think about it so much. I have these dreams that keeps me up. It's like I'm still in that place."

Sullivan paused before speaking. "I'm glad Calhoun got you out, Jimmy. You didn't deserve to be there."

DeLong pushed out a heavy breath. "When I got out, I begged Russ to help you. And he did try. He really did. But there was no way to prove what they were doing. Those guards were so careful."

"Have you told anyone what happened in there?"

"I promised you I wouldn't. Calhoun was the only one who ever knew. I never even told Sam. I..." DeLong cleared his throat. "I couldn't face it. I was too ashamed. Too guilty."

"You have nothing to feel guilty about," Sullivan said in a low voice. "Neither do I, for that matter. I spent a long time over the years trying to figure out if there was a way for me to stop Corey Black from doing what he was doing. He...he was going to hurt you. You're my little brother. I didn't know what else to do. I couldn't think about anything." Sullivan rose and moved to the dresser. He put his hands on the edge and leaned against it. "I saw red, you know. I wasn't trying to kill him."

"You didn't," DeLong reminded him.

"But I'd come close, Jimmy. I came real close. And I wanted to."

"We can't change the past," DeLong reminded him. "We survived it. That's all that matters."

"But did we really? I'm not so sure."

Through the mirror, DeLong saw Sullivan blinking back tears.

"Yeah," DeLong whispered, his voice raw. "This secret is destroying us. I'm not sure how much longer I can live with it. I...I think I need to tell Sam. I need to tell someone."

Sullivan didn't respond.

They remained silent for a few minutes, reflecting on the dark secret they carried. A secret that would forever define their lives.

"I should go pick up Ally," Sullivan said.

"You're both welcome to stay with us for a while if you'd like."

"Thanks, but I'd rather for us to be alone. For now anyway."

"Well, I've put this off long enough, but I should warn you about something." DeLong hesitated as he led the way out of the room. "Mom is getting a flight here."

"You've got to be kidding me," Sullivan said with a curse. "I told her not to come."

"When was the last time you remember her doing anything other than what she wanted?" DeLong asked. He opened the front door and stepped outside. "Besides, it may be good for you and Ally. She can help with...you know...the funeral arrangements."

Sullivan sighed as he locked the door. "Guess you're right. But...forgive me if I sound like an awful son...I just can't handle her right now."

"I understand. I'll have her stay with us," DeLong offered. "At least for a few days. But you can't avoid her forever."

Sullivan turned to face his brother. "Thanks. And I promise to stop by and see her when she gets here."

"Good." DeLong gave Sullivan's shoulder a pat and turned to head for his car. He spotted Benjamin Beaumont climbing out of his jeep, his cell phone attached to his ear.

The young man must have noticed he was being watched because he stopped moving and turned his attention toward the DeLongs.

"Have you spoken to the Beaumonts lately?" DeLong asked.

Sullivan followed his gaze. "No. I haven't been conversational with anyone. The only person to even stop by to see us was Sylvia Richardson."

DeLong turned to look at his brother. "You didn't mention that. What did she say?"

"Well, I didn't think it was relevant. I mean, she was Bree's friend, after all. She only wanted to stop by and see if there was anything she could do. And to see Ally. Why? She's not a suspect, is she?"

"Sylvia's...a person of interest," DeLong said. "So are the Beaumonts. We have yet to rule anybody out."

"Including me." Sullivan kept his gaze on his brother.

DeLong didn't reply. He only turned back to Benjamin, who retreated into his house.

"Let's go," DeLong suggested. He followed Sullivan to his car. "Listen, if anybody else who hasn't been cleared of Bree's murder talks to you, I want you to tell me. Let me know what they said or what they did."

"Why? You think they're just going to tell me they murdered my wife?" Sullivan scoffed.

"Call it curiosity," DeLong said. "Just do this for me, okay?"

"Whatever you say, Detective," Sullivan said. "I'll see you at your place."

Sullivan climbed into his car and shut the door as DeLong used his keyless entry to unlock his truck.

Chapter 30

R HONDA MCINTOSH STEPPED THROUGH the double doors of the
sheriff's office and walked to the window. A round woman sat
munching on some celery, making a face with each bite.

"May I hep ya?" the woman said between crunches.

"My name's Rhonda McIntosh. I'm here to speak with, um, I think it
was Captain Lowell?"

The desk sergeant stared at her through her glasses.

"You're the one who called about the murder at the pavilion?"

"Yes ma'am," she stammered.

"Just a second, I'll let the cap'n know you're here."

Rhonda waited as the desk sergeant picked up her phone and called
Captain Lowell. The woman said a few words and then nodded, following
with a "yes sir" at the end. Replacing the phone on its holder, she exited
her small booth and stepped toward Rhonda.

"If yeh'll follow me, I'll take ya to 'im."

Rhonda followed, and they ended up at the door marked "Captain."

The desk sergeant knocked and opened the door when a voice told her
to enter. She peeked her head in to announce Rhonda's arrival and then
turned to inform her she could go in.

Rhonda swallowed and walked into the office, a nervous smile playing
on her lips.

The bald-headed captain was skinny and sported a black mustache. He
hunched over his desk, scribbling something on a sheet of paper.

"Have a seat, Miss McIntosh," he requested without looking up.

She obeyed, crossing and uncrossing her legs. It seemed hours passed
before Captain Lowell looked up for the first time.

"Okay," he said with a sigh, straightening the stack of papers. He set them aside and folded his hands on the desk. "Thank you for coming in, Miss McIntosh. Or is it Missus?"

"Oh, um, miss is fine, sir," Rhonda said. She smoothed out the wrinkles on her pants with her sweaty palms.

"Great. Anyway, if I remember correctly, Miss McIntosh, you told me you may have seen the murder of Bree DeLong? Can you tell me what happened?"

"Oh, no, I didn't see her get killed," Rhonda corrected. "But I saw her talking to someone. Well, more like arguing. It seemed pretty heated."

"Can you describe this person? Male or female?"

Rhonda described who she saw as best as she could although her memory was vague. She admitted she didn't pay too much attention that day. Captain Lowell asked if she would be willing to look in a book of possible suspects. She agreed, so he led her to a desk outside his office and placed a large book in front of her.

"Can I get you anything? Coffee? Water?"

"I guess water is okay." She stared at the thick book, then opened it and flipped through the pages to see if she recognized the man she saw arguing with the woman.

There must be a hundred faces in here, she complained to herself, taking a sip of the water that was brought to her. Rhonda wondered if she should have left well enough alone, but she couldn't stop thinking about the woman on the news. The woman she'd seen at the wedding.

She wasn't sure how much help she'd be, but Rhonda decided if she could help find the woman and her family some justice, then it was worth it.

So with a series of yawns, she continued flipping through the pages of the suspect book.

Samantha was in the kitchen washing dishes when the DeLong brothers entered.

"I fed the girls already." She kissed her husband. She looked over at Sullivan. "Are you hungry? I'd be happy to fix you a plate."

"No, thanks. It's getting late, and I want to get Ally home."

"I understand," Samantha said. "The girls are upstairs."

Sullivan thanked her and headed out of the kitchen.

"How is it going with the two of you?" Samantha wrapped her arms around DeLong's waist.

He shrugged. "I think it'll be fine. We've put our differences aside for the time being."

"I'm glad," she said with a smile as footsteps descended the stairs.

A second later, Sullivan appeared in the kitchen with Ally in his arms.

"Thanks again for watching her," he said to Samantha.

"It was a pleasure."

"We should be going."

"I'll walk you out," DeLong said.

He followed his brother to the car and watched as he helped Ally climb in the backseat. He told her goodbye, then focused his attention on his brother.

Sullivan gave him a quick nod. He held his hand out for his brother to shake. DeLong accepted the gesture.

He watched his brother climb in the driver's side and pull away.

For the first time in years, he felt as though everything would be all right, since he and his brother were on speaking terms. It was something he'd yearned for but never believed would happen.

As DeLong stepped back into the house, he reminded himself to be careful. Just because he and Sullivan were now on good terms, didn't mean everything would work out.

He still had to find out who murdered Bree, and Sullivan was still on the list of suspects. Without an alibi or proof that it was someone other than him, he'd have to remain a person of interest.

"How was your day?" Samantha said when he returned to the kitchen. She dished food onto a plate as she spoke. "Do you know anything yet?"

DeLong's eyes felt heavy, and he realized how hungry he was. At the same time, he felt sickened. It was times like these when he wished he could have a glass of whiskey. He yearned for release, something to take his mind off this case.

When the thought entered his mind, he forced it out, reminding himself that if it wasn't this investigation, then it'd be the next or the one after that.

Over time, he'd learned it only took one thought to slip up. And it wasn't something he desired to risk. Not again.

He'd been a police officer for years and loved his job. But sometimes his cases took a toll on him, and he felt like hanging up the gloves. He'd often picture what his life would be like if he retired. However, the thought of leaving the force left him feeling empty. It was who he was.

Who he wanted to be.

There was no such thing as an easy case. One might take a few days to solve, one might take months or even years to solve. Some were left cold. Either way, the circumstances of the crimes he saw were never easy.

Not when it came to strangers, and certainly not when it came to family.

"Not yet," DeLong said. "We've got more evidence, but they're only leading to more questions."

Samantha studied him, then placed the back of her hand on his cheek. "You're still warm, but not like before," she muttered. "I want you to take something so you can rest tonight."

"Did she ever say anything to you?" DeLong asked as he lowered himself to a chair. "You were pretty close with Bree. Maybe she confided in you about something."

Samantha shook her head. She stared off into space as she answered. "I would have told you from the beginning if I thought for a second she was in trouble."

"Even if she asked you to keep it a secret?"

Samantha hesitated. When the microwave beeped, she removed his supper and set it on the table in front of him. She sat in the chair across from him. "I can't answer that. It'd depend on the secret. But I will say if it was something I thought would be dangerous to her, then yes, I would have come to you, no questions asked."

DeLong stabbed a forkful of his meatloaf as he mulled over his investigation.

"Did she ever say anything about seeing a psychiatrist? A Dr. Maxine Kendricks?"

Narrowing her eyes, Samantha shook her head.

"We found her purse and phone at the pavilion. She had a voicemail from Dr. Kendricks. But it didn't offer any information."

"You think she was seeing a shrink in secret?"

"I'm not sure," DeLong answered. "Something doesn't add up. I haven't been able to put a finger on it yet."

"Yeah," Samantha sighed.

"And you didn't notice Bree was acting differently? You only saw her a few days before," he pressed.

Samantha turned her lips to a frown. "Jim, I'm not one of your witnesses."

"I know," he said. He set the fork on his plate and reached for her hand. He brought it to his lips and kissed it. "We just don't have anything much to go on."

"I wish I could tell you something that'd help."

"Me too," he whispered.

DeLong ate the rest of his meal in silence, mentally listing all the things he needed to do over the weekend and on Monday.

Rhonda didn't recognize anyone in the suspect book, so the captain wanted her to return the following Monday to speak with a sketch artist.

She agreed and admitted it would be best for her, anyway. She had a full work weekend and was off on Monday.

Sleep was drawing her in, and she'd had a long, rough day. Looking through the book at a countless number of faces made her even more tired.

Her mind went fuzzy.

Charlene wanted to know all the details when she left the sheriff's office, so she called her on the way home.

Chapter 31

S ULLIVAN WATCHED AS ALLY slept. It seemed she slept, and he was grateful for that. He tried to keep from showing his anger at Bree's murder for Ally's sake. But as the long days crawled by, he found it hard to contain the feelings.

He felt the need to scream and hit something until his knuckles became bloodied and broken.

Why did Bree have to die? Why couldn't she have been at home when he got there Tuesday night? Why did she have to be at the pavilion?

He closed his eyes and shook his head, trying to erase the thoughts of Bree's death.

Sullivan's mind drifted to his last conversation with his brother. The part where they had reminisced about their time in juvenile detention.

He couldn't seem to get away from the memories.

It was like a disease, eating him inside out. His brother was right: the secret was destroying them.

As the hours went on during his time being locked up in that place, Sullivan trained himself to forget about everything that had happened. It was easier to forget instead of facing the humiliation.

Sullivan shook his head, trying to clear his mind, but the more he tried to forget, the more he remembered.

He forced himself to think about tomorrow. About the things he needed to do.

In the morning, he'd have to make the funeral arrangements. It wasn't something he looked forward to, but his mother and Samantha would help.

He didn't want to say his final goodbyes. He wanted to walk into his bedroom and watch his wife sleep. He wanted to lie next to her and wrap his arms around her.

But, of course, that wouldn't happen.

Sullivan stepped into Ally's room and kneeled by her bed. He watched her eyes flutter against her lids as she dreamed. He put a hand on her head and stroked her hair before leaning in and kissing her cheek.

After he whispered in her ear that Daddy loved her, Sullivan left the room and made his way downstairs. He grabbed a bottle of water and went into the garage where he had created a gym some years before.

Sullivan closed the door, set his water bottle on the table and switched on the stereo.

U2 blared through the speakers.

He stood in front of the punching bag. Sullivan glared at it before he threw an angry jab.

The bag swung back, then returned to its original position.

He placed his feet in a fighting stance, set his fists in front of his face. Bouncing on his toes, Sullivan went for another jab, then an undercut.

Jab.

Jab.

Undercut.

He swung his arm in a left hook, connecting with the bag. Pain lingered in his knuckles as he threw a cross-punch.

With the pulsing music of U2 guiding him, Sullivan tossed a series of punches and hooks at the bag. He screamed in angst as he did so until he fell to his knees.

Sullivan lowered his head as he sobbed, grabbing his hair and pulling.

He felt a hand touch his shoulder so lightly, he thought he'd imagined it.

He looked up to see Ally standing next to him, her bunny in her arms. Her face was a mixture of fear and sleepiness. But she leaned into him, wrapping her arms around his neck.

As he sat on the ground, he held onto her, letting the tears come. Ally's body shook.

"Ally, I'm so sorry, honey," Sullivan whispered into her ear.

He pulled back to see the tears fall from her eyes. Ally's lips quivered as she attempted to control herself.

Sullivan kissed the top of her head and picked her up. He switched the stereo off and the deafening silence of the night greeted him.

"It's going to be okay, baby," Sullivan said.

"I miss her so much," Ally cried.

He set her on the counter and wiped her tears with his thumb. "I know baby. Me too. We'll get through this together, okay? I promise."

She only nodded and rubbed her eyes.

"Let's get you back to bed."

Sullivan carried her to the room and laid her on the bed. He pulled the comforter to her chin and kissed her forehead.

"Try to get some sleep," he whispered.

"Will you stay with me?" she asked, her voice thick with sleep.

"Yeah." Sullivan laid himself next to his daughter, and she snuggled close to him.

He felt comfort being near her. It was almost as though Bree was in the room with them. Sullivan prayed the Lord would keep Ally safe from harm. He prayed she would sleep, and for her pain to heal. Then he prayed for strength for himself. Strength that would help him get through the rest of his days.

Whatever may come his way.

Chapter 32

D eLong's mother arrived at the airport early Saturday morning, and although she wasn't pleased her elder son didn't want her to stay with him and Ally, DeLong convinced her it was for the best. After he picked her up from the Augusta airport, he drove her to his house.

He parked his truck in the garage, helped his mother retrieve her suitcases from the trunk and led her inside.

Samantha stood at the stove, fixing bacon and eggs. She turned at the sound of the door opening and smiled at her mother-in-law.

"It's so good to see you," Samantha said. She transferred the cooked bacon to a paper plate and made her way for a hug.

"And you too, my dear. You look as ravishing as ever."

"Thank you," Samantha said. "I made up the guest room for you, Felicity. If you need anything, don't hesitate to ask."

"Thank you, dear," Felicity said with a smile. She scanned the kitchen. "So where's my beautiful grandchild?"

"I'm playing hide-and-seek! Come and find me!" Ally's voice carried from somewhere in the house.

"Oh, well, let's see if my grandmotherly instinct is still intact," Felicity said as she searched the rooms.

As she searched the living room, then ascended the stairs, DeLong heard his mother say, "Well, she's not here..."

"Did you call Sully yet?" Samantha returned to her cooking.

"I'll call him soon," he said. "It's too early to wake him."

"What are your plans for the day?"

"Newman and I will take a short trip to North Augusta," DeLong answered. He attempted to snatch a piece of bacon, but Samantha slapped his hand away. "After that, I don't have any other plans. I'll probably force myself to take the rest of the day off."

"Good," Samantha said. "You need it."

"Well, Jeff needs it more than I do. And he won't unless I do. I can guarantee you that."

"Jeff's a good man," Samantha said. "You know, we should take him and his wife some dinner one day next week."

"I'm sure they'll like that."

"I found her," Felicity announced as she came around the corner, with Bella in her arms.

"I had to come out," Bella said with a pout. "She took *forever.*"

"Well, that shows what a great hider you are." DeLong leaned against the counter. "But I'd like to know what a great hugger you are."

With that, Bella climbed out of Felicity's arms and ran toward her father. He lowered himself to eye level so his daughter could wrap her arms around his neck.

"Are you close to finding out who killed Ally's mommy?" Bella asked. She pulled back and looked deep into her father's eyes.

"Daddy's doing everything he can to find out. Don't worry about them, okay? Everything will be fine."

"I'm not worried, Daddy. I know you'll find who killed Aunt Bree," Bella said.

"You do? How do you know?" DeLong asked.

"Because I had a little talk with Jesus, and I asked Him to help you," Bella stated.

"Oh, well, thank you for that, sweetheart."

"Breakfast is ready," Samantha informed her family as she carted dishes to the table. "Everyone hungry?"

"Famished," DeLong said.

"Good. Then let's eat."

Chapter 33

G ARY PARRISH LIVED IN a trailer park in North Augusta. When Newman and DeLong found which trailer belonged to him, they parked and stepped out of the car.

A young woman with stringy brown hair seemed to be trying to teach her son how to walk. The child took a step, then fell to his bottom. Her face brightened with amused laughter.

"Excuse me, ma'am," DeLong said as they approached. "We're looking for Gary Parrish."

The woman grabbed her son off the ground and turned to face her uninvited guests. "Who are ya'll?"

DeLong introduced himself, then Newman.

"Does Mr. Parrish live here?"

"Yeah," she said. "Ain't home now, though."

"When will he arrive?" Newman asked.

"He'll be here in a few, I guess," she said. "What do you need my Gary for? He ain't done nothin' wrong."

"Are you his wife?" DeLong asked.

"Yeah, sorta...I'm his girl."

"We have questions for Mr. Parrish," Newman said. "Mind if we hang around until he comes back?"

She shrugged and led them inside the trailer. A distinct odor hit DeLong's nostrils as his scanned the cramped room.

"All I got is some beer." The woman opened the refrigerator. "You want one?"

"Uh, no," DeLong said, "We're on duty. What's your name?"

"Suzette," she answered, grabbing the neck of a beer bottle from the fridge. She made her way to the playpen and set her son down. "This here's Scotty."

"How old is he?" Newman asked with a slight smile.

"Two. My Gary went to jail after I got knocked up. Thank the lucky stars when he got out, he wanted nothing more than to take care of us!" Suzette let out a hackneyed laugh.

"That's a good thing," DeLong agreed. "Does Mr. Parrish work?"

"Yeah, manages the Dollar General." Using the tail of her shirt, she twisted the top of her beer to open it, then took a sip.

"He seems to have come a long way," Newman said. "From the kid he used to be, I mean. He recently was released from prison, right?"

Suzette scoffed, then cursed. "He didn't belong in prison. All my baby wanted was to get noticed. Instead, he gets locked up by that witch who claimed to want to help him."

"What witch?" DeLong asked although he knew the answer.

"That Miss Goody Two Shoes. The one they found dead." She shook her head, her stringy brown hair swaying in the air. "Saw that coming a mile away."

"You mean Bree DeLong?"

"Yeah, her." Suzette took another long swig from her beer. "If you ask me, someone was bound to pound her perfect little face in."

Before DeLong could respond, he heard tires spinning over the rocks. A few seconds later, a car door slammed shut and the door to the trailer opened.

"Hey, babe, whose car—" the man stopped speaking when he noticed DeLong and Newman. "Who are you?"

"I'm Detective DeLong of the Piedmont County Sheriff's Department. This is Jeff Newman. I presume you're Gary Parrish?"

"Yeah."

"We have a few questions to ask you. About Bree DeLong, in fact. Your girlfriend here was telling us someone was bound to kill her. Would you care to elaborate?"

"You're talking to the cops?" Parrish exclaimed. He tossed his keys on the counter with a curse. The baby began to cry. "How many times do I have to tell you to quit running your mouth? And shut that kid up! I'm getting a headache."

"Calm down, sir," Newman said, holding his hand up.

"You think I killed her, is that it? Guess I'm the perfect suspect since I've been to prison."

"No one's pointing fingers, Mr. Parrish," DeLong protested. "All we need is for you to answer our questions, then we'll leave."

"He ain't saying nothing without our lawyer." Suzette set the baby back in his crib. She folded her arms across her chest and stuck her chin out.

Parrish glared at his girlfriend but remained silent.

Exchanging glances with Newman, DeLong said, "That's your right. However, you're not under arrest. We're hoping you may shed some light as to who may have wanted to hurt her."

Parrish glanced between DeLong and Newman. The baby continued to whimper as Suzette tried to console him. Parrish sighed and rubbed his temples.

"Keep that kid quiet," Parrish said again.

DeLong looked at Suzette, who pulled the baby up by his arms. "How well did you know her?"

"Me?" Suzette scoffed. "I didn't."

"You referred to her as 'Miss Goody Two Shoes,'" Newman reminded her.

"I've mentioned her a few times," Parrish said. "I may have given her that impression." He turned to his wife. "Why don't you let me talk to these officers alone?"

"But—" she protested.

"I didn't do nothing wrong," he interrupted. "If I don't talk to them, it'll look suspicious. Please, baby, just take the kid and go."

"Fine," she spat. She smiled and leaned into his ear. Suzette whispered something, but DeLong couldn't catch the words. Before turning to leave, she kissed Parrish's cheek, glared at their company, and sashayed out the door.

Parrish moved clothing and dishes from the fold-up chairs.

"That woman was too nosy for her own good," he muttered, lowering himself to the chair.

"Bree?" DeLong asked.

"Always checking up on me, never letting up, even when I told her to get lost." He scoffed, shaking his head. "Instead of doing what I asked her, she told me she saw something more than a broken little kid."

"You sound like you admired her," DeLong said, choosing to take a seat. He rested his elbows on his knees.

"Yeah, but I just wanted her to leave me alone. I came to her screwed up, and I left jail screwed up." He looked over at the crib. "It wasn't until Scotty was born that I got my life together."

"When was the last time you saw her?"

"About a month ago," Parrish said. "I called her and asked her to come to my workplace. I wanted her to see in person that I'd become a new man. One my son can grow proud of." He leaned back in his chair and sighed. "She was happy for me."

"Bree always saw the best in people," DeLong said.

"You knew her?"

DeLong nodded. "She was married to my brother."

"Of course. Your last name," Parrish murmured. "I didn't put it together."

"Did she mention anything to you?" Newman asked.

"About what?"

"We're hoping she may have confided in you about something that may have bothered her. Maybe someone threatening her?"

Parrish shook his head. "No, she didn't say nothing. My girl came by and after I introduced her, Bree had to go."

"So Suzette met her?"

"Only that one time," Parrish said. "Bree didn't stay long. Suzette only knows her by what I told her a long time ago." Parrish laughed and ran a hand through his hair. "Back then, I was high and angry, all I did was complain. Right now, I'm going to church. Suzette won't come with me. Says it's a waste of time." He frowned.

"I disagree with her," DeLong assured him.

"I'm sorry about what happened to her, Detective DeLong," Parrish said. "She ain't done nothing but try to help people. I hope you catch whoever took that good woman from this earth."

"That's my intention." He retrieved his card and handed it to Parrish. "If something else comes to mind, please give us a call."

Chapter 34

I T WAS LUNCHTIME WHEN DeLong and Newman parted ways, agreeing to resume Monday morning.

Although he agreed to take the weekend off, DeLong didn't intend on putting the investigation to rest. After lunch, he spent the time reviewing his notes, trying to fit the pieces together. Dr. Maxine Kendricks wouldn't be in her office until Monday, so there was little he could do to move that part of the investigation forward. While he checked in on Sullivan and Ally, he gave them their space. He also warned him not to avoid their mother for too long.

His brother had confided in him about what had happened late in the night. DeLong found himself concerned, but Sullivan assured him he needed it to happen. He left the conversation, telling him to call the second he needed something—anything at all. Sullivan agreed.

His mother continued to ask questions about the case. Since he couldn't comment on certain aspects of it, DeLong spent most his time away from the house.

It was late afternoon when DeLong sat on a bench, overlooking the vast river, not too far from where Bree had been murdered. It was a beautiful area, full of luscious trees with the river going along its way. It was a shame the beauty of the area entwined with the ugliness of a murder four days ago.

He hadn't received messages from Bree, so he hoped she'd appear to him at the scene of the crime. Part of him felt inane for hoping his dead sister-in-law would pop out of thin air and help him solve her murder. The other part wanted to embrace the idea that he might see something most normal people wouldn't. However, he'd been sitting on the bench for two hours and nothing happened.

DeLong retrieved a cigarette from his shirt pocket and lit it, inhaling the tobacco.

The Georgia heat was in full force today, climbing its way into the triple digits.

"There you are."

DeLong looked to see Samantha walking his way.

She wore short tan shorts, revealing her long, toned legs. Her mesh top fit loosely on her, the left sleeve sliding down her shoulder. She had wrapped her black hair in a messy bun. The only makeup Samantha wore was a pale pink lip gloss.

"How d'you know where to find me?" he asked as she sat next to him. He wrapped an arm around her and kissed her bare shoulder.

"Easy. I followed the smell of tobacco." A smile played on her lips.

"I see," DeLong chuckled.

"How are you doing? I haven't seen much of you the last few days to ask."

"Hmm," DeLong muttered. "Let's see. I went to work and discovered my sister-in-law was brutally murdered. I've had to spend almost every second with my brother who spent most of his life hating me." He shrugged. "At least, I'm thinking maybe he doesn't hate me like he used to."

"I know he doesn't," Samantha said, resting her head on his shoulder.

DeLong fell into a deep silence as he reflected.

"What are you thinking?" Samantha asked.

"Nothing," DeLong said. "I'm just...thinking."

She lifted her head and gazed at him. "Do you love me, Jim?"

He gaped at her and snickered. "You know I do. More than anything."

"Well..." she hesitated and looked across the water as though she was considering whether or not she wanted to continue.

DeLong draped his arm over her shoulder. "Tell me what's on your mind."

Samantha frowned but continued to look into the distance. "I know there are things you keep to yourself. I've always known, since the day I met you. I try not to ask about it because I feel if it's something I need to know, you'd tell me. But...sometimes Russ would let something slip. Then he'd change the subject when he realized what he'd almost said." She sighed and turned toward him. "He knew something about you that I don't, didn't he? Does it have to do with you and Sullivan?"

DeLong remained silent for a few minutes.

"Yes." He surprised even himself that he was admitting to it. Still looking across the river, he explained everything: from the time Sullivan climbed out the bedroom window until Russ Calhoun exonerated him.

"Being in juvie was the worse time in our lives," DeLong mumbled. "We were...assaulted. In more ways than one. Especially by this one kid named Corey Black."

DeLong paused and leaned forward, resting his elbows on his knees and putting his head in his hands. He felt Samantha's calming hand on his back.

"Corey grabbed me one day. I still remember the feel of the ground when I fell. He got on top of me and I couldn't move. The guards were laughing. Cheering him on. He tried to pull my clothes off. But Sully pulled him off of me. Corey tried to shank him, but Sully was too quick. He grabbed the shank and stabbed him." DeLong rubbed his hands over his face with a heavy sigh. "Sullivan was sent to the hole for a week after that."

He paused, watching as birds flitted across the river.

"I was in that place for two months before I met Russ. Every day, it was the same ordeal. We were assaulted in ways I never thought were possible. Sullivan kept trying to protect me, and as a result, he'd be tossed in solitary so he couldn't protect me."

"I'm so sorry," Samantha said. "I can't imagine."

"When I got out, Sully made me promise never to tell anyone. And I never did." DeLong looked over as tears stung his eyes. "Until now."

Samantha's face streaked with tears and her eyes clouded with a mixture of anger and concern.

"I once asked Russ why he helped me when no one else would."

"What was his answer?"

"He said he looked at me and saw a hopeless kid who had more in life to give." DeLong scoffed. "Even back then I thought he was a lunatic."

"But he was a good man."

"Yeah," DeLong whispered, "He was."

"I'm so sorry, honey. I wish I could take the pain away."

"You do," DeLong assured her. "And Bella does too. Every day, I wake up and I want to be better than I was the day before because you and our daughter deserve better."

DeLong looked into his wife's eyes. They glistened with tears. He put his finger underneath her chin and lowered his lips to hers. He kissed her, tasting the hint of cherry from her lip gloss.

When they broke apart, Samantha rested her head on his shoulder with a sigh.

"It'll be okay. Everything will work out in the end," Samantha reminded him. "It's a given."

"Is that you talking or Jesus?"

"It's both of us."

"Sullivan's right about one thing," DeLong said as he pulled her closer to him.

"Hmm?"

"You are too good for me."

Samantha smiled at him and kissed his cheek. "Don't you forget that, either."

DeLong pivoted so he could get a better look at her, taking in the beauty only Samantha could give.

He leaned in to rub his lips against hers.

"I love you," he muttered. He kissed her as she welcomed his advances. "Thank you for putting up with me."

When they broke apart, Samantha laid her head on his shoulder again. Together, they watched the activities going on around the Augusta Canal.

Chapter 35

DeLong entered his house with bags of groceries loaded on his arms to find his mother cleaning the inside of the stove. He noticed the kitchen floor had been swept, mopped and waxed.

He rolled his eyes.

"Mom, what are you doing?" He set the bags on the counter and linked his arms over his chest.

A muffled sound came from the inside the oven.

"What?"

Felicity pulled herself out of the oven and smiled, her face flushed and sweaty.

"I said I'm not doing anything," she said. She tilted her head toward the other room. "Samantha's in the living room. Bella is on a playdate. You go watch television with your wife. I'll put your groceries up."

"Mom, you don't have to—"

"What did I just say, James Lee DeLong?"

"Yes ma'am," he said, finding himself amused. "I'm headed there right now."

Entering the other room, he found Samantha multitasking by reading a book during the commercials.

"Hey," DeLong said.

She looked up and smiled, then set the book on the end table.

"Hey, you. Did the rest of your solitary day do much for your psyche?"

"Yeah, I guess it did." DeLong motioned toward the kitchen. "What's my mother doing?"

"Cleaning," Samantha said with a smile. "I told her not to, but she insisted, saying I deserved a day off from house management. Who am I to argue with that logic?"

He sat next to her, and she leaned into his chest.

"You know, I've been so busy trying to figure out what happened to Bree and worrying about Sullivan," DeLong began, "that I haven't asked how you're handling all of this. You two were pretty close."

"I'll miss her," Samantha answered. "I'll never understand how people can do these things to someone like her."

"Me either," DeLong said.

She sat up to look into his eyes.

"But you see it just about every day. I don't know how you can handle it. And I have to say, I admire you for your dedication and pizzazz."

DeLong raised an eyebrow. "Pizzazz?"

"Yes, pizzazz." She smiled and kissed his cheek.

"Sometimes I don't know how to handle it," DeLong admitted with a heavy sigh. "Sometimes I think it's going to get the better of me."

"It doesn't show," Samantha said.

"That's good," DeLong said.

"Hey, what do you think about adopting?"

DeLong's eyebrow rose again. "What did you just ask me?"

"I want another baby," Samantha said. "I don't care how we get one. But I want another child. Don't you?"

"Samantha, we can barely handle the one we have."

Her face fell, and she sat back with a frown.

"I just don't think we're ready for another baby, Sam," DeLong said, trying to ease the tension. "We've got a lot going on now, with both home life and work life. It's hectic."

Samantha remained quiet for a few more minutes. DeLong released an inward groan and placed a hand on her back.

"I need some more time, okay?"

"It's fine," Samantha said with a weak smile. "I mean, yeah, you're right. Things are crazy." She toyed with the pillow she'd set on her lap. "I just thought you wanted another baby. That's all."

"Sam, I do," he assured her. "I really do. I just don't think we're in the place where we can adopt. Plus, it's expensive."

"Fine," she said. "It's out of the question."

"Not out of the question," he said. "It's just not something I want to be thinking about right now. That doesn't mean never."

He tried to read her eyes as she gazed at him, but they wouldn't tell him anything. DeLong leaned into her and offered a chaste kiss. She responded halfheartedly.

When he pulled away, he sighed and rose.

"I'm going to have a shower," he said. "Care to join me?"

Samantha looked toward the kitchen. "What about your mother?"

DeLong grimaced. "I don't know about that. I love her and all, but...you know. That'd be a bit freaky, don't you think?"

Samantha tilted her head back with laughter and swatted his leg with the pillow. He held his hand out for hers. She accepted it and allowed him to lead her upstairs.

Chapter 36

AFTER CHURCH ON SUNDAY morning, DeLong waited for Samantha to collect Bella from her Sunday school class. He sat on a bench underneath the elm tree having a smoke when an elderly woman made her way toward him.

"Good morning, Jim," she said as she neared, her words filled with cheerfulness. "May I sit next to you?"

"Certainly, Mrs. Kirk." He motioned with his hand and said, "How are you doing?"

"I'm getting there," she said with a sigh. "Sometimes I have my hard days; others, I'm at peace knowing Carolyn and Phil are in a better place than us."

Mrs. Kirk's daughter- and son-in-law had been killed the month before in a car accident. A teenager and his friend had taken his parents' vehicle out for a joyride. He'd run a red light and t-boned the other car. The teenager now faced three counts of vehicular manslaughter and one count of reckless driving.

"I heard about your sister-in-law," she said, her voice lowering an octave. She twisted on the bench to shield herself from the afternoon sun. "It's such horrible news. I'm so sorry."

DeLong gave her a halfhearted smile. "Thanks. It's still a lot to process."

"Are you the investigator?" she asked. "Or did you have to pass it along to someone else?"

"My captain's allowing me to lead the investigation," DeLong said simply.

"Are you making progress?"

He let his shoulders rise and fall. "It's the same old story. With answers, we get more questions. But I'm not giving up yet."

Mrs. Kirk smiled and patted his knee. "I'm sure you're not. And I want you to know I'm praying for you and your family."

"We appreciate it, Mrs. Kirk," DeLong said, placing a hand on her bony shoulder.

"Daddy! Look what I made!" Bella flew across the courtyard, stopping short at the bench. Samantha and Felicity strolled behind her, arms linked.

Bella handed DeLong a card and said, "We're supposed to give this to someone who needs encouragement. I thought about Uncle Sully."

"That's very sweet of you," Mrs. Kirk said.

Bella didn't respond but offered a shy smile to the older woman.

DeLong read the card. Bella had drawn stick figures of her family and Sullivan's. She wrote, "I love you, Uncle Sully and Ally."

He pointed to two stick figures that looked like they were standing on a cloud. "Who are they?"

"That one's Aunt Bree, and that one's Jesus. They're watching us from Heaven."

DeLong closed the card with a smile. "I think your uncle will love it, baby."

"I'm going to give it to him today when we see him at lunch," Bella said. "So he won't feel sad anymore."

"That's a great idea," DeLong said as his wife and mother approached.

"You are raising such a wonderful child," Mrs. Kirk beamed, glancing between DeLong and his wife.

"Thank you." Samantha put her hands on Bella's shoulders.

"She certainly can be a handful at times, though," Felicity said with a light laugh. "But she's a delightful handful."

"She reminds me of my own daughter when she was little," Mrs. Kirk said. She leaned over to pull Bella in for a kiss on the cheek. "Keep doing what you're doing, and she'll turn into a wonderful lady."

"I don't want to be a lady," Bella said with a frown. "I want to be a detective like Daddy."

Felicity scolded her, her tone light. "One policeman in the family is enough."

"But it's what I want to be," Bella insisted, looking up at her grandmother.

Felicity smiled at Mrs. Kirk. "We're hoping it's a phase."

"I wouldn't count on it, my dear," Mrs. Kirk said as she rose. "But if she turns out anything like your son, she'll be an excellent policewoman."

After saying goodbye to Mrs. Kirk and a few of the other church attendees, the DeLongs left the church for lunch.

When DeLong finished eating lunch with his family, he informed his brother he'd check in with him in a few hours. Sundays were his Alcoholics Anonymous meetings, and he hated the idea of missing even one. Especially with all that had been going on, he felt he needed some encouragement.

DeLong entered the building and spotted Harry, his sponsor. As Harry filled a paper plate with doughnut holes, DeLong grabbed a cup of coffee.

"Hey, man," he said, patting Harry on his back. "How you've been?"

"Good, good," Harry muttered. He jammed a doughnut hole into his mouth and chewed. "I've been meaning to call you. Were you related to that woman found at the canal Wednesday morning?"

"Wednesday. Has it been that long?" DeLong frowned. "Yeah, she was my brother's wife."

"Man, I'm so sorry to hear about that," Harry said as he swallowed. "How are you holding up?"

DeLong shrugged. "It's been...weird. Stressful. Inconceivable. So many things, I can't put a feeling to it. I haven't been on friendly terms with my brother in over fifteen years and now suddenly I see him every day."

"I remember you telling me about your brother," Harry said with another mouthful of doughnut. "I know you've wanted a second chance at a relationship. Look's like that day's here. How has it been going?"

DeLong grabbed a doughnut hole and led the way to a row of chairs facing the podium. The room buzzed with the arrival of more attendees. "It isn't exactly the reunion I wanted. But we're in a good place now. Sort of. I think."

Harry put a hand on DeLong's shoulder and squeezed. "Just hang in there, Jim. We've got your back."

"I know," DeLong said, lowering himself to a seat. He glanced over at Harry and studied him. "You're wondering if I had the desire to drink again, aren't you?"

"I wasn't going to say anything," Harry said. "But since you've brought it up, well, let's just say it's easy falling back into temptation when you're dealing with deep-rooted personal problems that led you to drink to begin with."

DeLong shook his head. "You've got it wrong. My brother was never the reason. Not in any direct way, at least. And besides, we're doing good now. We're killing each other a little less each day."

Harry nodded. "I'm glad to hear that, Jim. Maybe one day you'll feel comfortable enough to talk about the reason. Anything that's said here never leaves this room. Remember, we're all recovering. We all have issues that lead us to alcohol or drugs. We're the all the same. No judgments."

DeLong frowned with apprehension. He had to admit it. His confession to Samantha about the juvenile detention center lifted a major burden from his shoulders.

But was he ready to tell the world?

Even in this group of men and women trying to beat an addiction, just like him?

The leader of the group stepped up to the podium. DeLong breathed a sigh of relief for the ending of the conversation.

As the meeting began, DeLong felt Harry's gaze. It had been hard enough telling Samantha, but if he told these people, then he'd have to face the truth in a new way.

He wasn't ready for that.

Chapter 37

M ONDAY MORNING, NEWMAN AND DeLong headed to the Psychiatry and Behavioral Health office. It was a small building tucked in
the middle of downtown, next to a large bank.

When they opened the door, a bell announced their arrival. There was
no one at the reception desk, so DeLong rang the bell sitting on the
counter. Minutes later, an elderly woman appeared around the corner with
a frown playing on her lips. DeLong assumed either she wasn't a morning
person, or her day had already begun roughly.

"Can I help you?" she asked, her voice matching her expression.

"I hope so. I'm Detective Jim DeLong from the Piedmont County Sheriff's office. I was hoping Dr. Maxine Kendricks is available this morning."

The woman sized him up with small eyes before speaking.

"Let me see if she's available."

She snatched the phone from the receiver, punched in a few numbers.
She informed the doctor she had company. When the receptionist ended
the call, she informed them that the doctor would be right with them, and
to take a seat.

Newman grabbed a copy of *People* and flipped the pages until he settled
on an article about Angelina Jolie and Brad Pitt. DeLong grabbed a *Na-
tional Geographic* and skimmed an article on sharks.

Ten minutes ticked by before the lobby door opened and a woman
stepped through.

"I'm sorry for your wait, Detective DeLong. I'm Dr. Maxine
Kendricks." She extended her hand toward the detective.

Dr. Kendricks was a tall, slim, toned woman with short, feathered black
hair. She had a birthmark on the left side of her chin she attempted to hide

with thick foundation. When DeLong shook her hand, she squeezed tight, full of confidence and authority.

"Come on back, gentlemen."

As they followed her through the door leading to an array of offices, he introduced Newman. She led them to a small office, making DeLong feel a little cramped with three people squeezed inside. Dr. Kendricks offered them a seat and lowered herself into the chair behind her desk.

"Are you kin to Bree DeLong? The woman who was found at the Savannah Rapids last week?" Dr. Kendricks narrowed her eyes with a mixture of curiosity and concern.

"She was my sister-in-law," DeLong admitted.

"Oh, I'm so sorry for your loss," she said with a frown.

"Thank you," DeLong said. "The reason we're here is that we found a voicemail on her phone. Bree tried contacting you, and you had returned her call?"

Dr. Kendricks nodded. "I remember. I'm afraid I never had the opportunity to speak to her, though. She did call back, and we made an appointment for her to come by last Thursday. But as you know, she was already..."

DeLong nodded in response.

"Do you know what she wanted to talk to you about?"

Dr. Kendricks hesitated, then said, "Unfortunately, it falls under doctor-patient confidentiality. You'll need to show me a warrant."

"How long has Bree been a patient of yours?" Newman asked.

Dr. Kendricks looked at them and sighed.

"No, it wasn't like that. She wasn't my patient. Mrs. DeLong only wanted information. Even if I had the chance to meet her, I wouldn't have been able to tell her anything much. She was insistent though. I guess she wanted to see if she could find a loophole to get me talking."

"If it wasn't about her, then who did she want to talk about?" DeLong pressed.

"Doctor-patient," the psychiatrist reminded him. "If you bring me a warrant, I'll tell you all I can. Until then, my hands are tied."

"Okay," DeLong said. "I understand. We'll be back."

They rose, and before leaving the claustrophobic office, DeLong turned back, a thought playing in his mind. "Do you have reason to believe Bree was murdered because she was going to meet with you?"

Dr. Kendricks leaned back in her chair and considered the question. "Honestly, I'm not sure, Detective. But I suppose it's possible, bearing in mind the reason she was so desperate to talk to me. That's the only thing I can tell you."

"Thank you, Doctor," DeLong said. "We'll be back with that warrant."

As they returned to Newman's car, DeLong said, "So Bree came here for another reason, other than herself. But why?"

Newman let his shoulders rise and fall.

Climbing in the car, DeLong said, "Let's call in a request for our warrant."

As promised, Rhonda returned to the police department so she could talk to the sketch artist. She'd spent half the morning considering pretending she forgot about it until her conscience reminded her it was the right thing to do and once it was done, it'd be a distant memory.

She hated her conscience. Always forcing her to perform her civic duties.

When she walked to the window, she saw the desk sergeant crunching into a Granny Smith apple. She had a small bag of potato chips sitting at arm's length. It must have been calling out to her because the sergeant glanced at it with longing eyes.

"I'll save you from those chips if you save me from the sketch artist person," Rhonda said, trying to joke in order to ease her mind.

The desk sergeant frowned at her.

"Dieting ain't never easy. Can I hep you?"

"I was here on Friday..."

"Ah, right," the sergeant said. "Captain Lowell's waitin' for ya."

She tossed her apple on its plate and waddled toward the door to exit her work home. She led Rhonda to Captain Lowell's office, who took her to a small room that seemed a lot like an interrogation spot.

"I'm not in trouble, am I?" she asked with a dry swallow. She'd seen enough cop shows to know the mirror she was looking through was a two-way mirror and not just something to check her reflection. "I mean, I didn't expect an interrogation."

"No," Captain Lowell assured her. "I wanted to give you some privacy while you describe the man you saw to our sketch artist. It can get noisy out there as my officers begin their shift changes. If you will, just wait here and once the artist gets arrives, I'll bring her back. She called and said she was running late."

"Um, okay." Rhonda swallowed again as she lowered her wobbly knees to sit in a chair. She continued to look at herself in the mirror, all the while wondering who was looking back at her.

She attempted to take her mind away from the interrogation room and thought about the day of her best friend's wedding—the day she saw a man arguing with the dead woman.

Was he young or old?

Black hair or brown?

Did he have a hat or no hat?

Rhonda swallowed again as her heart raced. Sometimes, she wished she didn't always try to do the right thing. Doing the right thing now and again had a way of biting her. She wondered whether or not she should leave. Should she slip out the door and hide where the police wouldn't be able to find her? Slip away so she wasn't forced to describe the man that may have already killed one woman and who may go after her?

She shook the thoughts from her head, scolding herself. "No, Rhonda, get a grip. It won't be all that bad. You'll see."

She reminded herself that the murdered woman had a family. She had a child. And for that child, Rhonda would force herself to remember all she could.

Still, the fears invaded her mind, and she wasn't sure why. Her eyes skirted around the bland interrogation room.

Maybe it was the room.

Maybe that was why her heart rate was climbing why her skin felt clammy.

Until she dialed the number at the bottom of the television screen, she never had dealings with the police. Not even a speeding ticket.

It seemed as though hours crawled by before a woman with crewcut red hair entered the room with a smile.

"Good morning, Miss McIntosh. I'm Jules O'Reilly. Are we ready?"

Chapter 38

WITH THE WARRANT IN hand, DeLong and Newman returned to Dr. Kendrick's office and again sat in the cramped space. The doctor studied the contents of the warrant before reaching across her desk to hand it back.

"Okay." She folded her hands together. "What do you want to know?"

"You said Bree wanted to meet with you last Thursday," DeLong began, "Why?"

Dr. Kendricks leaned back in her chair, a frown cresting her features. DeLong couldn't tell whether she was still hesitant to hand over her patient's information, or if something else was on her mind.

Regardless, she spoke carefully. "She first contacted me because she was concerned about a friend of hers." The doctor paused. "And I use the term 'friend' very loosely."

"Who was it?" Newman pressed.

"His name's Benjamin Beaumont."

DeLong narrowed his eyes in thought.

"Benjamin Beaumont?" DeLong echoed.

"Yes," Dr. Kendricks confirmed. "Mr. Beaumont is a long-time psychiatric patient. He'd been seeing a therapist for, let's see..."

Dr. Kendricks trailed off as she turned to her computer, tapping on the keys.

They waited with patience until she spoke again.

"He's been receiving therapy for fifteen years. He saw me for three. Mr. Beaumont is being treated for manic-depressive disorder."

"Okay," DeLong said slowly. At the corner of his eye, he saw Newman write fervently on his pad. "Doctor, do you think manic-depressive patients are more likely to kill? Even if it's not intended?"

"The thing with manic-depressive disorder—or any disorder for that matter—is anything can happen. It's impossible to discern whether or not it causes one person to kill another. Are their actions more erratic? Sometimes. They can switch from angry to sad to happy in matter of seconds. It can be unpredictable in some, while it's controllable in others."

"Was he taking medication?" Newman asked.

"Yes, I've prescribed Lithium."

"What was Bree concerned about?" DeLong asked.

"I don't know," Dr. Kendricks admitted. "She passed away before I had the chance to meet with her. Her voicemail only informed me she needed to talk about Mr. Beaumont. She didn't say the reasoning. Just that it was urgent. She wanted information. Unfortunately, I wouldn't have been able to give her the information because policy forbids me."

She scanned her desk until pulling a thick folder from underneath a stack of papers.

"I figured you'd return," she said, "so I pulled Mr. Beaumont's file. There you will see the extent of his disorder and notes of all his sessions since day one."

DeLong reached into his pocket to pull out a business card. He handed it to the doctor and accepted the folder. "Thank you. If you think of anything else that may help, please call me."

"I'll do that."

When they settled in the truck, DeLong opened the folder to see a photo of Benjamin Beaumont. The pages contained dates and times of counseling sessions, how he reacted in each session, and how he reacted toward certain medications.

"I wonder whether or not Sylvia knows about his disorder," Newman muttered. "I find it curious she never mentioned it."

"Yeah," DeLong slipped deep into thought. He closed the folder and handed it to Newman as he pulled out of the parking lot. "We'll pay her another visit later and ask. I want to check in with his parents before we go to her again. But first, let's eat. You hungry?"

"Starved."

"Okay, me too. And we'll pour over Benjamin's file so we'll know what we're getting ourselves into."

While eating their lunch at McDonald's, DeLong and Newman spread Benjamin Beaumont's file along the table and looked through the contents.

"Wow," Newman said, his mouth full. "The guy threw a pocketknife at some guy who cut in front of him at the store? And punched a former employee?" He shook his head as he swallowed. "I don't get why Bree would want to get involved with this guy. He seems a little dangerous."

"She's always helping people like him." DeLong took a sip of his Coke. "It was her nature."

He considered the hate emails sent to Bree by the skullz4 address.

Was Benjamin the sender of those messages?

He had a psychological problem...that went without saying. And the idea Benjamin fell in love with her—at the very least *thought* he fell for her—was still at the forefront of his mind.

And with him diagnosed as manic-depressive, he could have hit someone in anger. Beat her until she was on the brink of death.

It'd make sense with the remorse aspect.

Sullivan admitted the handkerchief found over her face once belonged to Bree, but Sullivan hadn't seen it in a long while. Did she give it to Benamin?

DeLong chewed his food in silence, reflecting on his thoughts.

"Earth to Jim." Newman waved a fry in front of DeLong's eyes. Newman bunched his eyebrows together.

DeLong focused in on the investigator. "I'm sorry, Jeff. Did you say something?"

"You kind of left me here," he frowned. "Wanna tell me what you're thinking?"

DeLong shook his head to focus. "I'm trying to figure things out. Maybe Benjamin's the one who has been following and threatening Bree."

"He does seem like a viable person of interest," Newman agreed. "According to the files, if he wasn't on his meds, it's possible he lost it."

Newman jammed the final bit of his burger in his mouth. He folded the wrapper his burger came in and placed it on the tray.

"Have you seen any more of Bree's ghost?"

As he noisily sucked his cup dry of Coke, DeLong wavered his head to say he hadn't.

Not wanting to talk about seeing ghosts, DeLong closed the file and pushed back his chair.

"Let's get out of here."

They tossed their trash in the bin. When his cell rang, DeLong answered to find it was Sullivan wanting an update. DeLong heard the edge in his voice and could tell his brother was becoming impatient.

"We're moving along," DeLong said. He listened to the steady breathing on the other end of the line. "We're on our way to Austin Beaumont's to ask him more about his son."

"You think Benjamin did it? Could we be living in a neighborhood—"

DeLong cut him off. "We found a new development about his character. Something Benjamin and his parents failed to clue us in on. We're going to find out why."

"I take it you aren't going to tell me?"

"No," DeLong said. "Sorry, I can't do that right now. Listen, Newman and I are about to leave McDonald's. Since we're headed in your direction, do you and Ally want anything?"

When Sullivan said they didn't, DeLong ended the call and waited by the door for Newman.

A text came through from Captain Lowell that the sketch artist finished with the witness. He included the photocopy in the message. DeLong studied it, his heart sinking. He motioned for Newman, who was busy refilling his drink, to come over.

"We've got a sketch," DeLong started. With hesitation, he passed his cell to Newman, who gazed at the photo.

Newman cursed underneath his breath.

"Let's go," DeLong mumbled.

Chapter 39

DeLong stepped inside Sullivan's house and decided the soft chatter came from the living area. Before he continued to the room, Newman placed his hand on DeLong's shoulder.

"Are you sure you don't want someone else to do this?" he asked. "Because we can call for backup."

DeLong shook his head. "It should be me."

Without another word, he made a beeline for the living room to find his brother, mother, and wife hovering over a stack of papers.

Felicity was the first to notice they'd arrived. She offered a sad, yet warm smile.

"Jim! Come on in, son."

She rose and offered her youngest son a tight hug. "We're finishing the final touches on the funeral arrangements. Have a seat."

DeLong hesitated until Newman urged him by clearing his throat.

"I'm afraid we're here on business," DeLong said. He looked past his mother at Sullivan. "Newman and I need to have a word with you. In private."

It was obvious Felicity's motherly instinct was kicking in. She narrowed her eyes. "Is something wrong? Tell us."

DeLong put a hand on his mother's shoulder. "We need to talk with Sully in private, okay?"

"It's fine, Mom," Sullivan said, rising from the couch. "I could take a break from this, anyway."

He led the way to the backyard. Once the door was closed behind them, Sullivan lowered himself to the bistro chair. "Got a smoke?"

With hesitation, DeLong handed him the pack, saying, "I didn't realize you smoked."

"I don't usually," Sullivan admitted. "It's more of a..."

"Nervous tactic?"

DeLong lowered himself into the chair next to his brother.

"Something like that."

"Sam keeps telling me to quit," DeLong said as he lit Sullivan's, then one for himself. He knew he was delaying the inevitable. Newman leaned against the side of the house, hands in his pockets, allowing DeLong leeway.

"She's right. It's not a healthy habit," Sullivan shrugged. "But I suppose there are worse ones out there."

"I suppose," DeLong echoed.

They sat in silence, listening to the birds chirping.

"So, what's going on, Jim?" Sullivan said after minutes ticked by.

"You still haven't given us a good alibi," DeLong said. He stared across the vast yard. "Where were you when Bree was killed?"

"I told you. I was home," Sullivan insisted. "I was alone. Ally was at a sleepover and I was home."

"How convenient," DeLong muttered, blowing out smoke.

"What's that's supposed to mean?" Sullivan snapped. He glared through his glasses.

"It means you and your wife were having problems," DeLong said, now looking sidelong at him. "And your daughter happened to be at a sleepover on the very night her mother was murdered. And you have no one to collaborate your alibi."

Sullivan cursed his brother as he pushed to his feet. He turned to face DeLong, arms linked across his chest. "So we're back to this, now, huh? You think I killed my wife."

"Did you?" DeLong asked, trying to remain collected. He placed the cigarette in his mouth and inhaled.

His heart drummed against his chest faster, faster.

In his head, DeLong counted to ten and focused on steadying his breathing.

"I've got to know because all you've been doing throughout this investigation is lie to me. I'm trying to help you, Sully, but..."

"But what?" Sullivan hissed. He scoffed. "Sam told me you've been trying to get pregnant again, but can't. I don't know, Jim. Maybe you're trying to do away with me so you can adopt my daughter."

"Hey!" Newman interjected. "That's way out of line."

"Newman," DeLong warned as he rose. He kept his focus on his brother. "It's fine. Why don't you go inside and let us talk?"

"Jim—"

"Please," DeLong said. He broke the glance and looked at his friend. "Let me handle this."

A sigh.

"Fine. Let me know if you need me."

DeLong waited until the investigator stepped inside the house and closed the door.

"Listen to me, Sullivan," DeLong began. "You need to stop bringing my family into your mess. I asked to stay on this investigation because I *didn't* think you killed Bree. I wanted to be certain whoever did...is brought to justice. But now...now...I don't know. I can't help you if you're going to continue to lie to me."

Sullivan narrowed his eyes at DeLong but remained silent.

"Were you with Bree at the pavilion? Did you argue with her and hit her? C'mon, Sully. If you tell me the truth now, I can still help you."

Sullivan rubbed the nape of his neck, then without warning spat in his brother's face. He cursed him, grabbing DeLong by his shirt collar.

"She meant everything to me!" he hissed.

Sullivan pulled DeLong to the ground. He kicked him, but DeLong blocked the impact and force his brother to lose balance. He fell, his head snapping to the ground.

DeLong straddled him and laid a punch to Sullivan's face, once, twice, three times.

Sullivan blocked the fourth punch and struggled with him. He connected his fist to DeLong's cheek, knocking him sideways.

Sullivan pulled himself up so one knee held him close to the ground, almost touching the dirt. His back foot was on his toes, ready for any needed defense.

DeLong remained on his back, breath rising and falling in a mixture of anger and exhaustion. They continued to stare at each other, eyes burning with anger.

"Yeah," Sullivan said. He allowed his other knee to fall to the ground so he could lean forward, covering his head. When he lifted his head and peered at his younger brother, his eyes were moist. The fight had left him. "I was there. But I didn't kill her. I swear I didn't kill her."

"Why didn't you tell me to begin with?" DeLong breathed.

Sullivan pushed to his feet and held a hand out for his brother. DeLong accepted it and rose to meet his eyes.

"Would it have changed anything?" Sullivan asked. "Because I knew how it'd look. They *always* look at the husband."

DeLong paused, not taking his eyes off his brother.

"I have to take you in."

"I know," Sullivan said with a nod. His chest heaved with exertion. "I know. Can I see Ally first?"

DeLong didn't answer. He watched as Sullivan turned to disappear into the house. Feeling anger bubbling within him, he brushed himself off and followed.

"What's going on?" Felicity demanded.

With a sigh, DeLong told her the answer he never wanted to give. "We've got to take Sully in for questioning."

"You've got to *what*?" Felicity exclaimed. "You're arresting your own brother?"

DeLong saw Samantha lower her face to her hands. Felicity stepped close to her son and looked up into his eyes.

"You can't honestly think your brother is capable of killing his own *wife*?"

DeLong wanted to tell her. He wanted to say of course, he didn't think Sullivan would commit murder. Not under *any* circumstance. But he couldn't. Instead, he put a hand on her shoulder and sighed. "We're going to question him. What happens then is up to Sullivan."

"If you put my son in jail, I'll never speak to you again for as long as I live," Felicity threatened. Her eyes burned with fury and pain. "Your brother has already been through too much."

"I'm only doing my job," DeLong said. He swallowed, feeling a lump form in his throat. "And I'll continue to do my job, whatever happens."

"I'm ready," Sullivan said from the doorway.

DeLong glanced toward Samantha, whose lips quivered. A single tear slipped from her eyes.

Felicity grasped Sullivan's arm.

He put a hand on her cheek, offering a chaste kiss. "It's okay, Mom." Sullivan looked at DeLong. "Let's go."

With a quick nod, DeLong guided Newman and his brother to the car.

Chapter 40

"I'M GOING TO HANDLE this interrogation." Captain Lowell leaned back in his chair.

"You don't trust my judgment?" DeLong folded his arms against his chest.

"That's not the case and you know it, Detective." The captain rubbed his face with his hand. "I've given you enough flexibility. Anybody else, I would have reassigned them. But this is you—"

"It *is* me," DeLong interrupted. "I caught the case. You let me work it. I'm not going to blow my whole investigation just because my brother is being questioned."

Lowell studied him as he thought. Minutes seemed to crawl until he released a heavy sigh, shaking his head.

"I'm sorry, Detective, but I'm afraid I have to say no to this. I've already spoken to Mr. Newman. He's in agreement that you should step back." The captain held up a palm when DeLong opened his mouth to protest. "I'm not removing you from this investigation. It's still yours. But I'm going to be the one to interrogate your brother."

"I can be objective, Captain," DeLong insisted. "I'll do what I need—"

"I've already made my decision, Detective DeLong," Lowell said with an edge in his voice. He pushed to his feet. "You can watch. But you can't question him. You have a problem with that, then it's desk duty. Is that understood?"

DeLong squared his jaw, knowing he was fighting a losing battle. He nodded and followed his captain out of the office.

While Captain Lowell entered the interrogation room, DeLong stood behind the two-way glass. Newman appeared next to him.

"You told the captain I can't be objective?" DeLong asked, crossing his arms over his chest.

"After what happened at his house earlier, do *you* think you can be objective?" Newman questioned. "You look like crap, by the way."

"I know how to do my job," DeLong grumbled.

He'd spent years coming to terms that his brother hated him. They were finally in a good place, only to be sucked back to where they began.

And now it looked like the game was changing, and he wasn't just battling his sister-in-law's killer—no, he was battling his entire family. What would happen if his brother wound up incarcerated for Bree's murder? Would their mother follow through with her threat and never speak to him again?

DeLong forced himself to focus on the interrogation.

Captain Lowell sat in the chair across from Sullivan. He had spread evidence and photos along the table. He'd already spoken into the tape recorder of the event that was about to take place.

"Thank you for coming in, Mr. DeLong," Captain Lowell began.

"It wasn't like I had much of a choice," Sullivan grumbled, his arms resting on the surface of the table.

The bruising on his face had already turned bright purple.

"In the beginning, you told my investigators you were home from five o'clock the evening of May 20 until the next morning, correct?"

"Yeah," Sullivan muttered. "I did."

"Is that the truth?"

Sullivan hesitated before shaking his head. "No. I went to find my wife. I wanted to talk to her."

"And did you find her?"

"Yes," Sullivan said. "I knew she'd be at the pavilion. She goes there sometimes to clear her mind. It's her way of meditating."

"So you were the last person to see her alive?"

"No," Sullivan said through clenched teeth. "Whoever killed my wife was the last person."

"Fair enough," Lowell acknowledged. "I'll rephrase. You were the last person...that we know of."

"I didn't kill my wife," Sullivan protested. "I'd never hurt her like that. I wouldn't hurt her—or anyone for that matter—period."

Lowell paused before continuing. "Have you ever been in jail, Mr. De-Long?"

Sullivan narrowed his eyes. "Yes. I spent twelve months inside a juvenile detention center."

"Right," Lowell said. "I read your record before I came in. You and your friends attempted to rob a gas station when you were a teenager."

Sullivan ran a hand through his hair.

DeLong turned to Newman. "That has nothing to do with Bree. He doesn't need to throw that in his face."

"Let the captain do his job," Newman said.

DeLong shook his head, feeling the heat of anger rising to his cheeks. He knew where his captain was going, and he wanted him to stop this line of questioning.

"We were kids. We made a mistake," Sullivan said. "If I could turn back the time, it never would have happened."

"I'm sure it wouldn't," Captain Lowell continued. "Do you know a young man by the name of Corey Black?"

DeLong shook his head again. Before he realized what he was doing, he stepped into the interrogation room.

"Captain, a word, please?"

Lowell turned to face DeLong, an annoyed expression overcoming his features. He turned back to Sullivan, excused himself and met the detective in the hall.

"What is this about, Detective?" Lowell asked.

"You don't need to go into detail about his time in juvie," DeLong said. "That has nothing to do with what's happening now."

"Detective, I've been in law enforcement since before you were born," Lowell said, showing his teeth. "I think I know how to interrogate a person of interest. If you don't want to handle this investigation my way, then I'll hand it over to Lieutenant Kane and assign you to something else. Your choice."

DeLong watched Lowell watch him before he nodded.

"Good. Don't interrupt me again."

Lowell stepped back into the room and DeLong continued to watch through the two-way mirror, well aware his heart was beating against his rib cage.

"Sorry about that," Lowell said to Sullivan. He reclaimed his place in the chair. "Now, do you remember Corey Black?"

"Yeah," Sullivan admitted.

"What happened to him?"

"He was sent to the infirmary a few weeks after I arrived."

"Why was that?" Lowell pressed.

Sullivan frowned. "Because I put him there. It was self-defense. He was trying to..."

DeLong swallowed hard as his brother trailed off. Sullivan's face grew white, and he looked away from the captain, fighting back tears.

"You created a shank, then shanked him, correct? He almost died."

Sullivan shook his head with fervor.

"It was his sha-it was a long time ago. I wasn't trying to hurt him. I really wasn't. It just happened."

"Like you weren't trying to hurt your wife?"

Sullivan lifted his head. Tears escaped the corner of his eyes. "I told you I never would hurt her. I loved my wife."

"But someone did," Lowell reminded him. "Someone hurt her. You claimed to have been home alone during the time of her murder. Then later, a witness put *you* at the scene." He pushed a sheet of paper toward Sullivan. DeLong assumed it was the sketch. The captain continued: "A witness places you at the scene. According to her, you were arguing. Your wife's friends stated you were having marital problems."

"So what? I never said our marriage was perfect," Sullivan scoffed. "That doesn't mean I killed her."

Lowell pushed the evidence bag containing the red handkerchief across the table. "Do you recognize this?"

"Like I told my brother," Sullivan began through clenched teeth. "I haven't seen that in a while."

"It covered the victim's head," Lowell said, "Usually that's a sign of remorse. The assailant can't stand to look at his victim's face after they kill them, so they cover their faces. Maybe they reminded them of someone they loved. Or maybe they realized what had occurred, but knew it was too late to change anything. Is that what happened, Mr. DeLong? Was this in the heat of the moment? Did you kill her by mistake?"

"No," Sullivan insisted. "I went there to talk to her. That's all. Yes, we got into an argument, but when I left, she was still alive."

"What was the disagreement about?"

"That morning, we argued about her...*friendship*...with Benjamin Beaumont. I didn't trust him to be around her." Sullivan scoffed. "She was so set on saving the world. Ben was becoming more attached to her. He thought he was in love with her and she returned the feeling. When I left her, she was alive. You have to believe me."

"All right, Mr. DeLong," Lowell said. He gathered his files and the evidence and made his way to the door. "I'll be just a second."

DeLong waited as his boss opened and shut the door.

"What do you think?" Lowell asked.

"What he said is consistent with what he's said before," DeLong said.

"Yeah," Lowell said with a sigh. "But he's the last person to see his wife alive. I have no choice but to book him."

"Captain—" DeLong stopped speaking when Lowell held up his palm.

"I want you to question Benjamin Beaumont again. Ask him about the messages Bree received via text and email. Make him believe we know he's the one that sent him. Maybe something will slip enough to take the heat off your brother."

"Yes, Captain," DeLong said.

Lowell reentered the room. He informed Sullivan that he had the right to remain silent and he had the right to an attorney. The captain led DeLong's brother out of the interrogation room.

For a second, Sullivan gazed at DeLong. He opened his mouth to speak, but instead, closed it and hung his head with a sigh.

DeLong watched as his older brother was led to the holding cells.

Chapter 41

DeLong stopped by a Chinese restaurant to order takeout, then dropped it off to Amanda Schilling as he promised the week before. He found her in the break room drawing a picture of a barn with stallions in the background.

Today, her lips were dark green, and she wore a Bon Jovi hoodie, although it was nearing a hundred degrees outside. She had painted her short fingernails ten different colors.

"I've come to pay up," DeLong said, holding the takeout bag.

"Well, it's about time," she frowned. "Thought you've forgotten all about me."

She accepted the bag and opened the plastic container.

"Forget you?" DeLong said. "Never."

"Smells delicious," Amanda said. She removed the fork from its plastic and stabbed her sesame chicken. After tasting the first bite, she smiled. "Tastes delicious too. I forgive your lateness."

"That's a relief," DeLong said. "Especially since I may need to call on your services sometime in the future."

She chewed as she studied DeLong. "Something's on your mind, LT. Wanna talk about it?"

"Not really," DeLong mumbled.

"How's your investigation going?"

"Oh, you know the drill," DeLong sighed as he leaned against a table. He crossed his legs and jammed his hands in his pocket. "We get answers, but it still leads nowhere."

"I could never do what you do," Amanda said.

"And I could never do what you do," DeLong echoed. "Computers scare me."

Amanda laughed.

"Not as scary as seeing a dead body." Realizing what she said, her eyes grew. "I mean...I'm sorry. I shouldn't have said that."

DeLong lifted the corner of his lips to a smile and put a hand on her shoulder. "It's okay, Amanda. I know what you mean. When I first started, I almost passed out," he assured her. "All right, well, now that I've gotten you taken care of, I've got to get back to work. Enjoy your lunch."

"Thanks, man," she said. "I appreciate it. If you need me, you know where to find me. Oh, and Detective..."

DeLong turned back.

"Whatever's on your mind, it'll work itself out."

DeLong chuckled. "You sound like my wife."

She tapped her fork in his direction as she chewed another bite of sesame chicken. "We women know everything. The sooner you men realize that, the better we'll all be." She winked at him.

"Is that so?" DeLong said. "I'll try to remember that."

"See that you do. Later, dude."

DeLong thanked her and turned to leave.

He'd felt even more apprehensive about the investigation than before. Samantha called him earlier to inform him his mother packed her things to stay at Sullivan's, claiming it was to stay with Ally. Although DeLong knew that was part of the reason, he also knew the biggest was because her youngest son had arrested his brother.

Samantha urged him to talk to Felicity. He promised he would before the day ended, but felt nothing much would come of it.

When he arrived at Newman's office, he knocked on the door and slipped inside.

"Hey," Newman acknowledged without lifting his head. "Give me one second."

Keeping silent, DeLong looked around the vast office.

Newman had shelves of odd collectibles including a Chucky doll pillow, a stuffed *Hellraiser* bear and a masked Jason goblet from the *Friday the 13*th films. It was apparent, his friend not only lived out horror while at work, but he seemed obsessed with it on his days off. DeLong realized he'd never been inside Newman's office.

He picked up a full-sized plush doll from the *Saw* movies and studied it. He once tried to watch the first film but turned it off after deciding he already saw too much of the goriness in real life.

He turned to see Newman smirking at him.

"You actually collect this junk?"

"What are you calling junk?" Newman gasped. "Those are totally cool."

DeLong set the doll where he found it with a shake of his head. "Those are totally creepy and you are totally weird."

"I'm sure you have your own quirks." Newman linked his fingers behind his head.

"Um, no," DeLong insisted. "I don't."

"So if I called Sam right now, she'd say you are one hundred percent normal?" Newman asked, his eyes on his friend.

DeLong lowered himself in a chair with a pillow oddly resembling Freddy Krueger's shirt.

Newman's deep blue eyes shined with amusement as he continued. "Not even a tiny quirk."

"No," DeLong stated.

"Well, let's find out for sure." Newman picked up his cell phone and dialed.

"Fine. I might enjoy reading Bella's Disney books," DeLong rolled his eyes to the ceiling.

"That's nothing," Newman laughed. "I enjoy reading to my daughter, too."

"Yeah, but do you read them to yourself?" DeLong asked. "When there is no wife around, no kid?"

"Well." Newman set the phone on the desk. "Looks like you're a strange one, after all."

"Looks like," DeLong said. "Anyway, I'm on my way to visit the Beaumonts. Want to come along or are you wanting to stay here and rib me some more?"

"The thing about ribbing," Newman said as he rose, "is they come travel-sized."

"I hate you."

"If only that were the case," Newman retorted.

"You have to admit, though," DeLong said as they exited the office, "your quirks are a bit out there."

"So's reading a six-year-old's Disney princess books when she's not around," Newman shot back.

When they reached DeLong's truck, Newman paused.

"Tell me something, Detective. Do you play dress up too?"

"I hope Freddie visits you in your dreams tonight," DeLong muttered.

"Freddie's my homeboy," Newman said as DeLong turned the ignition.

DeLong shook his head in disbelief as he pulled out of the parking lot. "You need serious counseling, man."

Chapter 42

WHEN THEY ARRIVED AT the Beaumont home, Newman knocked on the door to announce their presence. They waited until Camille Beaumont answered.

She knitted her eyebrows with curiosity. "Is there something else I can help you with, Mr. Newman?"

"Mrs. Beaumont, I'm Detective DeLong. I'm the lead in charge of the investigation. We have a few questions for your family. Is your son home by any chance?"

"No," Camille said. "He's out with a friend, I believe."

"Would you mind contacting him to come home?"

"Uh, sure, I can do that." She opened the door to allow DeLong and Newman inside.

"We'd appreciate that," DeLong said as he entered the living room.

They found Austin Beaumont sitting on the couch, reading the paper. Seeing his visitors, he set the paper to the side with a frown.

"Detective DeLong. Mr. Newman."

"They want to talk to Ben again," Camille said as she grabbed her phone from the end table to make the call.

"Why Ben?" Austin asked. "I noticed you took Sullivan away earlier. Is he in jail?"

"We're not obligated to answer that," Newman said.

DeLong looked around the house and had a thought.

As Camille ended her conversation with Benjamin, DeLong requested to use the bathroom. Heading in the direction Austin pointed out, he gave Newman the "keep them busy look." Newman acknowledged in silence as he sat in a chair, making light conversation.

The door to the back was closed, and the one next to it was open and inviting. DeLong slipped inside, taking in the messy room.

It was obvious the room belonged to Benjamin.

Clothes strewn across the bed and along the floor, a guitar sat in the corner, sheet music scattered around. The bed was unmade, and the door to the closet stood ajar, clothes spilling out of it. DeLong wouldn't be surprised to see a litter of rats running around the dirty dishes.

Benjamin had a laptop on the bed, so DeLong opened it, only to find it was password protected. Next, he rummaged through the drawers but found nothing of interest.

He looked in the closet, only to see a replicate of the mess in the rest of the room.

DeLong considered where he'd put evidence if he were Benjamin. He checked underneath the mattress, found nothing. He knew it'd have to be where no one would think to look. His eyes rested on the guitar, realizing it had no strings.

He picked it up and peered inside the sound hole to find a thick mailing envelope taped to the back.

DeLong reached in to pull the envelope out and looked through it. There were several cutout photos of Bree's face posing with Benjamin.

By the hum of voices in the other room, Benjamin must have returned home. DeLong hurried to slip the evidence back in the envelope and into the hole of the guitar.

He slipped out of the bedroom and into the bathroom, flushed the toilet, then reentered the living room.

"Thank you for coming home, Mr. Beaumont," DeLong said.

"Mom said you have more questions for me?"

"Yes, we do. Over the last few months—beginning in February—Bree was in contact with someone via email. The address was…" he skimmed through his notepad, "skullz4@yahoo.com. I don't suppose you have an idea who belonged to that address, do you?"

"Nope," Benjamin said.

"According to a few witnesses," Newman interjected, "You had a crush on Bree. Witnesses say she didn't feel the same way. Is there any truth to that?"

"Like I said before," Benjamin said through his teeth, "Bree and I were good friends. She helped me when no one wanted to be near me." Speaking the last sentence, he glared at his father, who sat in silence in his chair.

DeLong considered mentioning the photos he found but decided it was best to keep quiet for now.

"Are you implying my son murdered Bree?" Beaumont asked, rising. "Because he wouldn't kill anyone. He couldn't have."

"Of course not," Benjamin said with a scoff.

"Have you ever been angry with her? Maybe thrown something like a book at her?" DeLong pressed.

They watched Benjamin closely. He crossed his arms, then uncrossed them.

"A couple times," he admitted. "But I wasn't in the right mind and I just…" Benjamin sighed and scratched his head, then closed his eyes.

"Are you on medication for your manic depression?"

"How did you find out about that?" Benjamin eyes flew open with surprise. "That's not public knowledge."

"We found Dr. Kendricks," DeLong informed him. He turned back to Benjamin. "Answer my question, please."

"Yeah, I am," Benjamin said, his eyes narrowed. "If I wasn't, a knife would be jammed in your throat."

"Benjamin!" Camille explained, with a gasp.

"Are you threatening us?" Newman shot back. "We could throw you in jail just for that, Mr. Beaumont."

"All right, that's enough," DeLong said, placing a hand on his friend's shoulder. "Mind if we take a look around your room?"

"Yes," the Beaumont men said in unison.

"You're not going anywhere except to the front door without a warrant," the elder Beaumont said. "I've opened my home to you enough. I won't stand for you threatening my son."

Newman opened his mouth to retort, but DeLong motioned for him to remain quiet.

"Fair enough," DeLong said. "That'll be all for now. Just don't leave town. We'll be back with that warrant."

Beaumont walked DeLong and Newman out.

"My son didn't kill Bree," he reiterated.

"For his sake," DeLong said, "I hope not."

After the door closed, DeLong and Newman headed for the truck.

"Did you find anything in Benjamin's room?" Newman asked.

When they slid into their respective sides in the truck, DeLong told him about the photos. "It looks like he was trying to live out some kind of sick fantasy about Bree."

"Interesting," Newman muttered. "That's proof he was infatuated with her. But it's still not enough to say he killed her."

"Yeah," DeLong said. He retrieved his cell phone. "I'm calling the ADA now. I think we have enough to go through his room to confiscate the photos and to have a look at his laptop."

As he placed the phone against his ear and pulled out of the driveway, DeLong noticed the blinds opening in the window. Because of the glare of the sun, he was unable to see who it was.

Chapter 43

WHILE THEY WAITED FOR the warrant, DeLong stopped at his brother's house to see about repairing the damage with his mother. He used his key to enter and called out for her, then found her in the kitchen, preparing supper. Felicity turned when he announced himself and turned back without speaking.

"Look, Mom, I had no choice," DeLong said with a sigh. "I didn't want to but, if it wasn't me, then it would have been someone else."

Felicity remained quiet. He could hear her sniffle away at her tears.

"Your brother wouldn't kill anyone. You know this."

DeLong nodded. "I do know this. And that's why I'm not giving up. I need to follow this by the book if I'm going to remain on this case." He leaned on the counter. "My men are good investigators, but I'm not so sure I'd trust them with Sully's life."

Felicity turned to face her son.

"What's going to happen to him?"

"Well, he's going to have to stay in jail overnight. He already called his lawyer. Newman and I are following another lead. We're waiting for the warrant now."

"You'll take care of him?"

DeLong stared at a family photo hung on the fridge by a magnet. "You know I will. He took care of me when we were kids. I plan on returning the favor."

"As long as the law allows you?"

He nodded.

She hooked her arms around his neck to bring him close for a hug. "Okay, then."

"We're good?" DeLong asked when they parted.

"I know you have a job to do, son. I won't stand in your way."

"Thank you. I'm going upstairs to check on Ally," DeLong said.

He turned to make his way upstairs. Before reaching his niece's room, he paused by his brother's. The door was open, so he checked his closet and see if he owned anything with a hood.

When he opened Sullivan's closet, he searched his clothing, and Bree's, but found nothing resembling the hood he saw in his visions.

He reminded himself it was possible he either threw it out or hid it. Or his mind had been playing tricks on him after all. But something inside him told him that out of the choices, the most likely was the former.

"Uncle Jim?"

DeLong turned to the sound of the small voice and smiled at his niece. He kneeled so he could be eye level.

"Hey, honey, how are you doing?"

"I'm okay," she said. She held her bunny tight by the neck. "When's Daddy coming back home?"

"Soon," he promised with a silent prayer that he wasn't telling a lie. "Don't worry about a thing, okay? Your dad's in good hands and so are you." He tapped the tip of her nose with his index finger, making her smile.

His cell phone pinged, and when DeLong looked at it, he saw it was a text from the assistant district attorney. The warrant was ready. "I've got to go, okay?"

She nodded, reaching around his neck for a tight hug. After they broke the embrace, he hurried down the steps and told his mother goodbye. He placed a quick kiss on her cheek.

"Listen, I want you to know how proud I am of you, son," Felicity said, grasping his hands. "Nothing you do will ever change that."

"I know," he said. "I'll see you later."

DeLong left the house to retrieve the warrant, satisfied he'd been able to clear the air. For now, anyway.

This time, DeLong enlisted Lieutenant Kane and Sergeant John for backup in case there was a need.

It was Austin Beaumont who answered the door, and he did so with a frown. "You're getting dangerously close to harassment, Detective De-Long."

"I believe you wanted us to show you a warrant," DeLong said, passing it on.

Austin looked it over, then let out a heavy sigh. "All right, come on in."

"Thank you," DeLong said as they entered the premises. He headed straight for Benjamin's room while Kane and John searched other rooms. Newman followed behind.

"This place is a pigsty," Newman muttered from the doorway.

"I know, right?" DeLong answered, picking the guitar up. He noticed the strings were now in place. His heart took a dive, and he was filled with dread.

No.

Removing the strings, he cursed when he saw the sound hole was empty.

"He moved it," DeLong groaned. He let out another round of curses. "Where'd he put the pictures? Help me with this."

He and Newman tore the sheets from the bed and turned the mattress over, then the box spring.

Nothing.

DeLong emptied the drawers of the dresser and looked underneath the bottom, in case Benjamin taped the envelope out of sight.

Still nothing.

After scouring the closet and the boxes stuffed on the shelves, he was forced to realize the evidence was no longer in the room.

Neither was Benjamin's laptop.

DeLong stepped out of Benjamin's room as Kane exited the master bedroom.

"Find anything?" DeLong asked.

"No," Kane answered. "Everything appears clean."

With an inward groan, DeLong returned to the living room where Sergeant John was making sure Benjamin's father didn't interfere with the search.

"Where's your son?" DeLong demanded of Beaumont.

As if on cue, the front door opened and Benjamin stepped into the living room. He had his books on one arm and his laptop in the other.

When he saw his house swarmed with police officers, he cursed under his breath.

"Now what?"

"We have a warrant," DeLong stated, waving the court document in front of him. "Which includes that laptop."

"Dad—" Benjamin looked wide-eyed at his father.

"Give it to him, son," Beaumont urged.

Benjamin groaned, passing his laptop over to DeLong. "This is an invasion of privacy. Surely there's a rule against that."

"Surely there is," DeLong agreed. "But no rule surpasses a court order. What's your password?"

He set the laptop on the coffee table and lowered himself to the couch. DeLong looked up at Benjamin, who had crossed his arms over his chest with frustration.

"Mr. Beaumont, if you don't answer my questions, I'll arrest you for impeding on my investigation."

Benjamin sighed. "It's 'skullz4.' All lowercase."

"Imagine that," Newman said, taking a seat next to DeLong. "The same skullz4 as the email address you never sent Bree?"

Benjamin remained silent as DeLong went through the laptop. The recycle bins were empty, and the documents contained files from Benjamin's classes. It wasn't until DeLong checked the email that he found a countless number of photos of Bree, and email exchanges between them.

"That's a lot of pictures," DeLong breathed. He looked up at Benjamin. "Why don't I give you a quick rundown, Mr. Beaumont? You were infatuated with Bree, but she told you she wasn't interested, right? A few tantrums later, her husband intervened." He watched the young man's expression. "Did you go to see Bree at the pavilion last Tuesday night? Maybe you offered her a chance to see things your way. Or maybe even to apologize for what you've put her through. But whatever the situation entailed, you lost control of your temper and beat her with the first thing you could get your hands on until she was dead."

"Son, maybe it's time you tell them."

Benjamin shook his head. "N-no. I don't want people to be looking at me any different than they do now. I can't help who I am. I just can't help it! I—"

Camille placed a hand on Benjamin's shoulder. "It's all right, son. It's nothing to be ashamed of." She looked over at DeLong, her eyes filled with sadness. "My son was in Atlanta on the evening Bree was killed. He was being treated for depression. He-he tried to kill himself."

Benjamin hung his head, closing his eyes tight.

"So now you know," he said.

"Why would you do that?" DeLong asked. "Try to kill yourself?"

"I loved her, okay?" Benjamin answered, his words so soft, DeLong had to strain to hear. "I wanted her to love me back, but she wouldn't."

"Bree?" Newman asked.

Benjamin nodded.

"I tried to kiss her. I just thought she..." Benjamin made his way to a chair and sat. "She pushed me away. I just lost it. I kept throwing things, screaming. It was like I stood outside my body, watching myself lose all sense of control. Then she said it. She told me I was insane. That did it."

"When was this?" DeLong asked.

"Two weeks ago." A tear slipped from his eyes. "After that, I swallowed the entire bottle of my medication. I only wanted the pain to go away. I passed out. The next thing I remember was my parents were taking me to a psychiatric hospital in Atlanta."

"Ben," Newman said, keeping his voice even, "were you taking your medication? On the day you and Bree had that...encounter?"

Benjamin shook his head. "I wanted to be normal. I didn't want to have to be on medication for the rest of my life. She wouldn't have loved me, otherwise. No one would. I wanted to show her I could do it. But...I guess I couldn't."

"Ben," Camille said, "your father and I love you no matter what. Just because you have psychological issues doesn't mean you aren't normal."

Benjamin glanced at the consoling face of his mother, then over at the stern, disapproving face of his father. He shook his head and rubbed his neck.

"All my life, people have looked at me funny. They treat me like I'm from outer space. Then I met Bree."

"She showed you that you were more than that," DeLong presumed.

Benjamin nodded, wiping his tears.

"When did you get back from Atlanta?" DeLong asked.

"Thursday afternoon." His voice sounded, for the first time since De-Long met him, lonely and defeated.

"The doctor who helped him was Davis Garrique," Camille offered. "I'll get you his number so you can call for an alibi."

"You must think I'm weak or something," Benjamin said when his mother left the room.

"Not at all," DeLong assured him. "Bree never gave up helping you. That's saying something."

"What's going to happen now?" Benjamin asked.

"Well, we're going to leave, confirm your alibi, then move on from there."

DeLong empathized with Benjamin, but his stomach churned. With the young Beaumont's alibi, his brother was number one on the suspect list.

"I'm taking my medication now," Benjamin said to no one in particular.

"Good," DeLong said as Camille reentered the room. He accepted the card with the Atlanta doctor's information.

"Thank you both for your time," DeLong said. He looked over at the two officers standing in the doorway. "Come on. Let's move out."

"I'm not sure what to say about all this," Newman said when they were out of earshot.

"Me either," DeLong agreed. "With Benjamin no longer a suspect, we have little to go on."

Newman slapped DeLong on the back. "It's not over for Sullivan yet."

"Why do I feel like it is?" DeLong asked. "He admitted to being there, and he was seen there. My brother was the last person to see his wife alive."

"Why don't we call it a night? Let's go home to our families and meet in your office tomorrow morning."

DeLong only nodded as he climbed into the truck.

After dropping Newman off to get his car, DeLong drove by Protecting the Lord's Children. The sun hid behind thick, dark clouds, threatening rain.

He spotted Zoe, the girl who babysat for Ally every occasionally. She sat on a bench by a bed of flowers, scribbling in her notebook.

He pushed his door open and stepped out of his car, making a beeline in her direction.

"Hey, Zoe."

Startled, she looked up, but soon, a smile spread across her face.

"Hi, Detective DeLong," she said.

"Mind if I have a seat?"

"Sure."

She bookmarked her notebook using her pen and watched as he lowered himself to the bench.

"How are you doing?" DeLong asked.

"Good. How about you?"

"I'm managing," he said. "What are you writing?"

Zoe showed him her notebook. "Miss Bree used to tell us to write our feelings on paper when we can't express them. She said it might help us feel better." She looked at her notebook as though it were something she cherished. "I hadn't been doing that for a little while. I just started back, and I kinda do feel better now."

"I'm glad it helps," DeLong said.

She shrugged. "Guess it's better than moping around or coping with drugs, huh?"

"You may have a point there." DeLong watched as a small group of kids played tag. He looked back at her. "How old are you, Zoe?"

"Thirteen."

"What happened to your parents? If you don't mind me being too personal."

"My mom's doing life in prison. My dad died when I was six."

"I'm sorry," DeLong said. "If you ask me, they're missing out on something special."

Zoe's cheeks reddened.

"Thanks. Do you know anything yet?" she asked as she toyed with the corner of her journal. "About who killed Miss Bree?"

DeLong frowned. "Not yet, Zoe. But we'll get there." He put his arm around her and gave her a quick hug. "Good talking to you. I'll see you soon."

She nodded and opened her journal to write some more.

Chapter 44

DELONG STEPPED INTO HIS bedroom and found Samantha brushing her hair in the bathroom. He watched as she put her hair in a ponytail. She smiled at him in the mirror, then frowned when she saw he didn't reciprocate.

"You okay?"

"Yeah," DeLong said. "I'm just tired."

"Your expression is telling me otherwise," Samantha said.

He moved behind her to wrap his arms around her waist. She melted into him with a content sigh.

"Did you make things okay with your mom?"

"Yeah, I think so," he said. "It's Sullivan I'm more concerned about. For a second, I thought I got my brother back. Now he's the prime suspect in a murder."

"It'll be okay, honey," Samantha said. "Just keep doing what you're doing. You're an excellent cop. Your brother couldn't be in better hands."

He leaned close to trail kisses on her neck. Samantha let out a soft moan.

"You know, I've been thinking about what we were talking about earlier," he said into her ear. "About adopting."

"Yeah?"

"I think we should do it. If you still want to."

She spun in his arms, her eyes wide with hope. "Really?"

"Bree took care of a lot of children who didn't have anyone," DeLong said. "Most of them seem happy and content, despite being unwanted. But they deserve a family to love them and provide for them."

Samantha smiled. "Yes, they do."

"Those kids, you know, most of them are older. And people don't always want to adopt older children."

"What are you saying?" Samantha asked. "You want to take in an older child?"

"Maybe," DeLong said. "I'd like to keep the option open. If you're willing. We'd also have to include Bella in our decision. I don't want her to feel threatened, especially if we go for an older child."

"You've thought about this, haven't you?"

"I have," he said. "So, what do you think?"

"I'm willing," Samantha squealed. "I'm most definitely, absolutely, completely willing."

She kissed him in eager, leading him to the bed. He climbed on top of her, willing to forgo sleep a little longer to be with his wife.

After Samantha fell asleep, DeLong watched her. Her breathing was steady, her black hair feathered across her face. He brushed it out of the way so he could take in her face. Memorize every aspect. He'd been studying her a lot the past year.

It was his way of reminding himself he was lucky.

He didn't deserve it.

DeLong brushed his lips against hers. She didn't reciprocate. She'd fallen into a deep, restful sleep. He wished he could, but he decided he wouldn't trade the chance of watching his wife sleep next to him for anything.

Help me.

DeLong sat upright in his bed, heart pounding.

Help me.

When he heard the words again, he looked at Samantha to see she was still sound asleep. DeLong swung his legs to the side of his bed. He got to his feet, grabbed a robe from the bathroom and went to check on Bella.

His daughter sat upright in her bed, the covers pulled up to her chin.

"Bella? What's wrong, baby?"

"I heard something, Daddy. There's a monster in my room."

"There's no monster in your room," DeLong said.

"Yes, there is. His face was dark from the shadow of his hood."

DeLong narrowed his eyes. "What did you say? This monster of yours wore a hood?"

She nodded.

"What was he doing?"

"Hurting Aunt Bree."

DeLong's heart sank, and he swallowed hard.

Now his daughter was seeing the same things he was?

It was impossible, right?

DeLong shook his head. "I'm sure you just had a bad dream, baby." He flicked on the lights. Bella squinted at the brightness of the room. To appease her, he opened the closet door, then checked underneath the bed. "No monster anywhere."

DeLong sat on the edge of her bed and leaned over to kiss her cheek. "That'll keep the monsters away. They can't hurt those that have been kissed."

Bella giggled. "Thanks, Daddy."

"Anytime. Now get back to sleep."

DeLong waited until he was sure Bella had drifted to sleep before he left the room. But he was more awake now than he had been a few minutes ago.

He went down the steps, grabbed a Coke from the refrigerator and made a beeline for the living room. Lying on the couch, he switched on the television, making sure the volume was low to keep from waking up the house.

He channel surfed until he found a rerun of *The A-Team* and hoped it'd help him fall back asleep.

Chapter 45

"Okay, so, Benjamin Beaumont is no longer a suspect," Newman reiterated the next morning. He ticked off his list with each finger, pacing in DeLong's office as he thought. "We still don't have a solid alibi for Sylvia. Gary Parrish was working. Blake and Dawn Parsons were at a party with fifty other people. Your brother was the last person to see his wife alive. Bree keeps telling you to trust—"

"Hold on," DeLong muttered. He leaned forward and linked his hands together. He yawned as he tried to forget about the incident with Bella the night before. "Let's forget about the whole Bree ghost thing right now, all right?"

Newman looked over with a frown, then sighed. "You're right. That won't exactly hold up in court. But she is trying to help you—"

"Jeff," DeLong groaned. "It's bad enough I'm hearing and seeing things." He frowned and narrowed his eyes, shaking his head. "I shouldn't have even told you."

"Yes, you should have." Newman plopped onto a chair across the desk. "That's what friends do. They talk. But we'll move on from that one for now."

"Thanks," DeLong said.

"Let's have a look at the evidence," Newman suggested. "There's the red handkerchief the killer leftover Bree's face. Sullivan said it used to belong to her, right?"

"Yeah. But he hadn't seen it in a long time."

DeLong ran his fingers through his hair as he swiveled his chair to look out the window. Rain had fallen early in the morning and didn't appear to be letting up anytime soon.

The darkened clouds seemed to match his mood.

"We're running around in circles. There's something we're not seeing," DeLong murmured. "Bree was a friend to everyone. On the outside looking in, there's no reason to kill her, right? So we need to start looking from the inside out. Let's list any and all reasons."

"Okay," Newman said, lowering to a chair. He crossed his legs and narrowed his eyes in thought. "Maybe she had competition for that ministry she was running. Or someone didn't like what she was doing to begin with."

"It doesn't seem likely someone would want to kill her for doing a service for orphaned and unwanted kids."

"A lot of them were taken from their families," Newman mused. "A disgruntled parent may stop at nothing to get their child back."

"Possible," DeLong agreed. "Worth checking out, anyway. Let's first narrow down the list. Some of those children don't have families, so they can be ruled out."

"What about past kids?" Newman suggested. "The ones that committed suicide? We should question their parents. Maybe they blamed Bree for their deaths."

DeLong remembered seeing the faces of the twelve children who had given up on life. He agreed it was worth it to look into those cases.

"You track down those families. I'll have Kane work with you. In the meantime, Hunt and I will take the parents who lost custody."

DeLong reached for his desk phone, dialed Kane's extension, and requested he find Hunt and join them in the office. Next, he called the assistant district attorney to request a warrant for all the parents' names. He decided it was better to be prepared, just in case.

After he ended the call, DeLong rubbed his eyelids.

"So how are things going with you and your brother these days?" Newman asked as they waited. "Aside from him being in jail?"

DeLong opened the case file and stared at the crime scene photo of Bree's body.

"I stopped by to see Sullivan this morning before he got released," DeLong said with a frown. "But he's not interested in speaking to me. Not that I blame him."

"Sorry, man," Newman said. "But don't give up on him. I'm still rooting for you guys. After you clear his name, maybe you guys will *love always*."

DeLong looked at his friend, eyebrow raised. "What did you say?"

"I said you guys probably will become friends again."

"No," DeLong said, shaking his head. "That's not what you said. You said, 'love always'."

Newman let out a scoff. "No, I didn't."

Narrowing his eyes, DeLong gazed at his friend, whose light laughter subsided. Newman's expression changed to one of interest.

"Did Bree speak to you again?"

DeLong opened his mouth to reply and closed it again. His mind was reeling, but he forced himself to laugh.

"Gotcha," he said.

"Not nice," the investigator said, his lips curving into a slight smile. "Not nice at all."

"Sorry," DeLong muttered. To keep his hands busy, he rummaged through the files.

When the knock sounded at the door, DeLong told them to come in. Hunt and Kane stepped over the threshold.

"You wanted to see us?" Kane asked.

"Yeah, you guys aren't busy, are you? Because I've got a job for you."

"Well, we were going to play a few rounds of poker, but what's up?" Hunt said with a smirk.

DeLong informed them of what he and Newman had discussed. After he finished talking, Newman and Kane went on their way. He told Hunt to wait for him, then they'd head over to Protecting the Lord's Children Ministry.

After Hunt shut the door behind him and he was alone, DeLong dropped the file he held and put his head in his hands.

He knew he heard the words "love always" when Newman was speaking. But what did it mean, exactly? It was the same words written on the red handkerchief that covered Bree's face.

DeLong considered why he kept hearing and seeing ghosts.

Maybe Bree *was* trying to tell him something, or maybe he was finally going crazy on the job. All DeLong knew was that he had never heard or seen ghosts or spirits until the murder of Manny Grimes.

Pushing back in his chair, DeLong rose. He wanted to ignore the callings from the grave. He tried putting the pieces of the puzzle back together, but it was nothing but a tangled mess.

Chapter 46

Sergeant Hunt pulled up the driveway at Protecting the Lord's Children. It had sprinkled, and if the new report was correct, the rest of the day was going to end horribly.

DeLong climbed out of the passenger side and hurried to the door, Hunt following behind. He pushed the door open and stepped inside. Sylvia Richardson was heading for another room when she stopped to gaze at him.

"Detective DeLong," she said. "Didn't Ben and I already answer your questions?"

"Miss Richardson, how are you? Is it possible for you to give us a list of the children's parents? We have a few questions."

"I'm afraid you'll have to get a warrant. It's for our kids' privacy."

DeLong passed it over. "I figured you'd want it."

After scanning the document, she ushered them inside. "Okay, I'll have to go up to the office. It'll take a few minutes to compile everything."

"Thank you," DeLong said.

As Sylvia went up the stairs, he followed the sound of a soft voice carrying from the living room. He stood in the doorway, watching as the children sat in the dark and on the floor. Zoe positioned her legs Indian style, holding a flashlight to her chin. She spoke slowly, scanning the eager faces which formed the circle.

"And then, the werewolf crept behind her..."

"What happens next?" one of the younger boys pressed.

"Be quiet!" another younger girl hissed. "Let her tell the story!"

While they were arguing, a boy about Zoe's age rose to his feet and grabbed something from a nearby table. The children, except for Zoe, were oblivious.

"Do you want me to tell you what happened or not?" Zoe scolded, putting a hand on her hip.

"Yes!" they exclaimed in unison.

"Okay," she said. "Then let me finish. Where was I? Oh, yes." She positioned the flashlight back underneath her chin and leaned forward. She spoke in a hushed tone. "Anyway, the werewolf crept behind the cheerleader and *ripped* her head off!"

As she said the word *ripped*, the older boy screamed, grabbing two of the children from behind. There were screams, each ending in laughter.

"Gotcha!" the older boy beamed. "Man, they're too gullible."

"No, we're not!"

Zoe glanced toward the doorway and realized they were being watched. "Detective DeLong, you're back!"

"Yes, I am. Sylvia's helping with something we need."

"To find Miss Bree's killer?"

The room had grown quiet as all eyes fell on the detective. He stepped into the room, lowering himself on the couch.

"Possibly. We'll see if anything pans out."

Sylvia reappeared. "I have what you asked for."

DeLong told the children goodbye and left the room. He took the sheet of paper as Sylvia explained the twelve names notated with stars were the parents of the deceased.

"Thank you for your help," he said.

Sylvia only nodded as she led them to the door. She stuffed her hands into her back pocket.

"If there's anything else I can do to help, let me know."

DeLong said he would and climbed into the passenger side. After they buckled, Hunt turned the ignition and pulled away from the house.

"I'll text Newman his list." DeLong used his camera option to snap a photo, then messaged it to Newman. "It's getting close to lunchtime, so why don't we grab some fast food. We'll work as we eat."

The nearest fast food restaurant was Wendy's. Hunt pulled into the parking lot and they ordered.

Waiting for their food to arrive, they stepped aside huddled over the list.

"I know Zoe's mother is doing life, and her father passed away when she was six. She doesn't have any other relatives around," DeLong said. He crossed out her name, then drew a line, dividing the list in half. "You take the top, I'll go to the bottom."

After receiving their food, they took a seat in the corner of the restaurant by the windows.

"Okay," Hunt said a few minutes later searching through the database on his iPad. "Charles Beauregard died three years ago of a drug overdose. His wife, Jessie, is in jail now, so they didn't do it."

"And I struck out on Thomas and Laura Jameson," DeLong said, his mouth full. "They both died four years ago in a car accident."

Over the next few minutes, DeLong and Hunt narrowed down the list to four possible suspects. After they finished their lunch, they left Wendy's and Hunt steered the car toward their first destination.

"I don't know what else I can do to prove to you people I'm fit to raise my own daughter," Clara Howard grumbled as she led them to the living area. "Maybe I wasn't a year ago, but I am now."

Clara brushed a thick strand of her curly red hair from her dark eyes.

"It must upset you," DeLong surmised, "that you can't take your daughter back."

"You better believe it," Clara said. She let out a hacking cough, then reached over for her bottled water. "I got a job and all."

"Have you been able to see your daughter lately?" Hunt asked.

"No, that woman at the ministry refused to let me see my own kid. Can you believe that?"

"You mean Bree DeLong?"

"Yeah, guess that's her name. She had the nerve to slam the door in my face and call my parole officer."

"That had to make you angry," DeLong said. "You must have wanted to hurt her for keeping you from your daughter."

Clara glared at him. "I heard about her death. If you wonderin' did I kilt her, the answer's no. But I'd love to thank whoever did, mind you." Her lips curved into a thin smile.

"Where were you last Tuesday night?" Hunt asked.

"With my beau. He and me were having a party if you know what I mean." Clara winked at DeLong. "You mighty cute. Maybe you'd like to be beau for a night."

"What is his name? Where does he live?" DeLong asked, ignoring her statement.

She shrugged. "Haven't a clue."

"You don't know his name?" Hunt inquired.

"Jason, Jamie, something or other." She rose to drop her water bottle in the trash by the table where DeLong stood. She took a sniff and smiled. "Is that your cologne or your natural scent?"

She put her hand on his chest and purred.

"Your heart's pounding like crazy," she whispered.

DeLong took hold of her hand and put it by her side. "Do you have an alibi or not?"

"Yeah, that neighbor of mine kept pounding the door, telling us to quiet down." She continued to smile at him. "Are you quiet or do you prefer loud?"

"I prefer your hands behind your back," DeLong said with a smile. "You're under arrest."

"Wh-what?" Clara exclaimed.

"Prostituting or escorting or whatever you prefer to call it is illegal," DeLong informed her. "You have the right to remain silent."

"This is ludicrous!"

"You have the right to an attorney."

"I demand you to let me go!"

"Anything you say or do can and will be used against you in the court of law. Do you understand your rights as I've said them to you?"

Clara groaned, which turned into a shrill scream.

"Let's get you to my house, honey," DeLong said as he guided her toward the hallway. "I'll be much more comfortable with you there."

Hunt flashed an amused look toward DeLong as they walked to the car.

Chapter 47

"JULIANA WAS THE LIGHT of my life." Heather Cork stared into the photo frame she held. She smiled, though her eyes shined with sadness. With a sigh, she passed the photo to Newman. "When she was three, her biggest worry was failing at being an actress." Heather snickered. "She wanted to be an actress so badly."

"How did she kill herself?" Newman asked.

"Her friends started experimenting with drugs when she was only thirteen. Eventually, she spiraled out of control and overdosed."

"She joined the Protecting the Lord's Children project, didn't she? How did things go there?"

Heather shook her head. "She didn't want to be there at all. She fought hard against all of us. But Mrs. DeLong refused to give up on her. She had all those other kids to take care of, but she never showed favoritism. She was always there, always trying to help heal whatever brokenness that was inside them. Juliana was no different."

When her eyes filled with fresh tears, Kane handed her a box of tissues from the table next to him.

"Thanks," she forced out as she dabbed the corner of her eyes. "I keep thinking there was something more I could have done to save my daughter. After her death, I had a lot of conversations with Mrs. DeLong. She tried to convince me it wasn't my fault that the drugs were controlling my baby's mind. I wanted to believe it, but I just couldn't. Eventually, my marriage fell apart and my husband left me."

"I'm sorry," Newman said. His throat felt raw. The one thing that frightened him the most was bringing his own children in a world where the innocent are lured into the snare of drugs and murder. He could only hope both his children would grow up away from it all.

"I'm sorry to break on you," Heather said. She tore her tissues into small pieces. "I get emotional when I talk about Juliana. No one else will let me mention her. It's like she never existed. Mrs. DeLong was the only one who would listen."

Newman exchanged glances with Kane.

"Mrs. Cork, have you seen the news lately?" Kane asked.

She shook her head. "I don't own a TV anymore. And I pretty much stay home. I have a nephew who brings me groceries."

"There's something you should know," Newman said, "about Bree De-Long."

Heather studied Newman, then Kane.

"Last week, on Tuesday night, someone murdered her. She wasn't found until the next morning."

"What—how can that be?" Heather stammered. "Who would kill her?"

"That's what we're trying to figure out," Newman said. "When was the last time you saw her?"

"Um, I don't know," she answered. "It's been awhile. She called me a few weeks ago, but I didn't talk to her. I kept meaning to call her back. She's really dead?"

"I'm afraid so."

Heather leaned forward, dropping her head in her hands. "Another good person was taken from us. I just can't understand it. I sit here, day after day, shameful because of this world we live in."

"Where were you Tuesday night from seven to nine-thirty?" Kane asked.

Heather looked up at him and blinked twice. She rubbed her eyes and let out a heavy sigh. "I was here as usual. My nephew came by."

"What's his name and information?" Kane asked. "We're going to have to check your alibi. Policy"

Heather recited the requested information.

"Can you think of anyone who may have wanted to harm her? Maybe you know of someone who threatened her?"

Heather shook her head. "I'm sorry, but she never said anything. She only cared about how I felt, or how I was doing. I was too wrapped in my own emotions to reciprocate."

"I'm sure she didn't see it that way," Newman assured her.

"If something comes to you, call us." Kane handed her a business card.

She accepted the card, glanced at it, then nodded. "Of course, Lieutenant."

"Thank you for your time," Newman said. "We're sorry for your loss."

She led them to the front door and let them out. Newman and Kane made their way to Kane's car and climbed in.

"The nephew doesn't live too far away. We'll check on him, then pay a visit to Leo Hart."

What he was saying didn't register in Newman's mind as his thoughts drifted to the world he was bringing his children into. Heather Cork seemed like she did a good job with mothering her daughter. But along the way, Juliana had fallen off the wayside. He didn't want that to happen to his children.

"Earth to Newman," Kane said. He switched off the radio that pulsed Toby Keith.

"What?" Newman said, blinking. "Did you say something?"

"I was asking what you thought about Sullivan DeLong? So far, he's the most likely suspect. Do you think he killed his wife?"

"I don't know," Newman said. "I hope not. But I'm not certain."

"If it turns out he did, DeLong won't handle it well," Kane continued. "I know it's rough having to arrest your own blood. I know he'll do what it takes to give the vict—his sister-in-law—justice. But what do you think that'll do to him?"

Newman pivoted his head to gaze at Kane. "Are you asking me if I think he'll start drinking again?"

"Well, it's no secret he's got an addiction," Kane said. "And it's no secret he's only been sober *again* for a little more than a year. Don't get me wrong, Mr. Newman. I'm not saying anything against him. I respect Lieutenant DeLong. He's an excellent investigator—one of the best, in fact. But I don't want him to lose his cool if his brother is incarcerated."

"You're right," Newman said, "He is an excellent investigator. Yes, he did slip up. But he's come a long way since then. If there's one thing that matters to him most, it's his wife and daughter. He's not going to do anything to ruin that."

"Certainly a point in his favor," Kane said.

Newman frowned but didn't reply. Kane parked at the curb in front of Heather Cork's sister's townhouse and pushed his door open. They walked to the door, knocked, and waited for someone to answer.

After Kane introduced himself and Newman, he explained why he was there. Heather's brother-in-law, Zac Pine, invited them inside and called for his son to come to the living room.

A second later, a teenager appeared, wearing earbuds. He removed them from his ears.

"You called me, Dad?"

"Yes, Daniel, I did," he said. "This is the police. They have a question for you about your aunt."

"My name's Lieutenant Kane, this is Jeff Newman. We're investigating the death of a woman your Aunt Heather knew. She claims that last Tuesday night, you went to her house. What time was that?"

"Around six thirty," he answered.

"What time did you leave?" Newman asked.

"I dunno. Maybe around nine thirty. Who died?"

"Was it that woman from the ministry my niece used to go to?" Pine asked. "We heard about it on the news."

"Yes, sir," Kane answered.

Pine cursed underneath his breath, shaking his head. "That's a shame. She was a good woman."

"You knew her?" Newman said.

"I've met her a few times when I went to visit Juliana. She seemed like a kind, caring woman. Her heart certainly was in the right place." Pine narrowed his eyes with curiosity. "You don't think Heather would hurt her, do you?"

Newman offered him a smile. "On the contrary. We need to be sure we've cleared all possible suspects."

"Thank you both for your time," Kane said.

When they headed for the car, Kane hesitated before getting in.

"Something on your mind, Lieutenant?" Newman opened the passenger door.

"Naw," Kane said, "Well, it's this world. It seems to be getting more dangerous than ever before. Good, sheltered girls turn to drugs and overdose, good people who want to help are dying."

"Like my wife likes to say: it'll get worse before it gets better."

"That doesn't help my pessimism," Kane said.

"But it's true," Newman said, climbing in.

Kane didn't respond as he pulled away from the Pine household to head for the next name on their list.

Chapter 48

"I AIN'T SAYING NOTHING to you," Clara said, her arms across her chest. She glared at DeLong as he led her to the cells. "You've got no cause to arrest me."

"Like I said back at your place—hooking is illegal."

"A woman's gotta do what a woman's gotta do," Clara protested. "I want my kid back. Can't do that 'less I have a job. Ain't no employers hiring me."

"Tough break," DeLong said. "Plenty of people are out of jobs. Welcome to the economy. They make do with what they've got. They rarely resort to breaking the law to make ends meet."

"Listen, I din't kill that woman," Clara protested. "Check with the landlord."

"Already did, and he cleared you." He pushed her into the cell.

"Then what am I doing in here?" she threw her arms out with exasperation.

"Your landlord claims you have a new...what did you call them...beau every night. I'm sorry to tell you that's going to be over for a while."

He left the woman cursing him as he made his way to the office.

The day was ending, and they weren't close to finding anyone with motive or opportunity to murder Bree.

DeLong stopped by the break room to pour himself a cup of coffee, then returned to his office, closing the door behind him.

He fell into his chair with a sigh as he sipped his drink and pressed the button to turn on the monitor.

His desk phone rang, and he answered.

"Detective DeLong."

"You've got a visitor."

DeLong let out an inward groan. "Who is it, and what do they want?"

"Benjamin Beaumont, Detective. He wants information or something. I told him you couldn't tell him anything—"

"Send him back," he interjected. "I'll talk to him."

He replaced the phone on its cradle, then rose. He parted the blinds with his fingers and looked across the vast parking lot.

When the knock came, he told them to enter.

"Thanks for seeing me, Detective DeLong," Benjamin said.

DeLong turned to look at the young man. His eyes were tired as though he hadn't been sleeping. His hair was disheveled and clothes wrinkled.

"Have a seat, Mr. Beaumont. Tell me what I can do for you."

"I want to know if you had any leads."

"I'm afraid I can't go into details about the investigation. Whatever we're able to share, we'll release it on the news."

Benjamin slapped his hand on the surface of the desk with such force, DeLong's cup quivered. "You owe me information after everything you put me through, Detective."

"Benjamin, look," DeLong said, trying to keep his voice even. "I understand what you're going through. But you need to be patient and let me do my job."

"You don't know anything," Benjamin muttered. "Someone murdered the only person who ever loved me for who I was. They need to pay."

"And they will," DeLong promised. He leaned forward, lacing his hands together. "Listen, maybe it would help if you went back to speak with your therapist, Dr. Kendricks."

"I don't need therapy!" Benjamin pushed his chair back. "I'm sick of everyone treating me like I'm crazy. Like it's all in my head."

"No one thinks that way," DeLong said, hoping to diffuse the situation. "I don't think that way. What I think is you've suffered a tremendous loss. A woman you cared about—a woman who cared about you—was killed. And now you feel lost. Right?"

He nodded. "I spoke to her every day. When I went for treatment in Atlanta, she was the only one who bothered to call. Not my parents, not even Sylvia." He turned back to face DeLong. "I have so many thoughts going on in my head. She was the only one who could quiet them. But it's so loud now. I can't hear myself think."

DeLong went around his desk and put his hands on Benjamin's shoulder. "I know it's difficult for you to see it right now. But you will be okay. You're right. Bree cared about you. And she cared about a lot of people. She wouldn't want you to lose everything you've been working for."

"I don't understand," Benjamin mumbled, a tear falling. "I wanted to be with her forever."

"In time, you'll move on. I promise you that. It takes time."

He nodded, searched his pockets and pulled out a pill bottle. He stuffed one into his mouth and swallowed.

"I'm sorry to bother you," he muttered.

"It's no bother, Benjamin. I'll let you know something as soon as I can. Okay? In the meantime, go talk to your therapist. That's what she's there for."

DeLong watched as Benjamin stumbled out of the office. When he was out of eyeshot, he shut the door and resumed his work.

Chapter 49

Zoe sat in the kitchen, writing in her diary about Miss Bree. She wanted to confide in her how much she missed her and that she wished Miss Bree was still around. She wasn't sure what would happen to her now she was gone.

Zoe felt lost.

Alone.

She paused, set her pencil down and glanced out the window. Most of her foster brothers and sisters were out playing. Two were upstairs.

Anna, who was taking care of them right now, stood in the doorway watching the kids play.

The deafening silence enveloped her.

It unnerved her.

But then somewhere on the second landing, she heard a loud crash.

With a gasp, Zoe hurried up the stairs. "J.J.? Petey? Are you guys okay?"

When she made it to the top, she searched the rooms until she found the one the boys were in. Petey was lying next to the wooden dresser, eyes closed. His glasses were broken and blood oozed out of the deep wound on his forehead.

"Petey!" she ran to his side and checked for his pulse.

"We were just playing," J.J. said. "Jumping on the bed. He lost his balance. Is he okay?"

"Go get Miss Anna," Zoe said as Petey let out a soft murmur. When J.J. didn't move, she added, "Quickly!"

Petey's eyes opened, and he moaned, attempting to sit up. Zoe pressed her hand to his shoulders.

"Stay down," she instructed. "You could have a concussion."

He spoke, but his words slurred.

"What?" Zoe said, leaning forward. "I didn't hear you."

"He pushed me," Petey forced out.

Her eyes wide, Zoe stared at the young boy. Petey passed out again. Zoe heard footsteps pounding on the steps. Anna pulled her back to get close to Petey. The rest of the children crowded in the doorway.

Anna was already on her cell phone calling for an ambulance.

Zoe saw J.J. watching them along with the others.

He pushed him?

"Miss Anna?" Zoe said.

"Not now, Zoe," Anna snapped. "Petey, Petey, can you hear me? Open your eyes for me, buddy.

Petey groaned but didn't open his eyes.

"I want everyone to leave this room," Anna instructed. "Zoe, when the paramedics get here, send them to us."

"Okay'" Zoe still watched J.J. She guided her foster brothers and sisters out of the room and downstairs.

Once they piled into the living room, Shane, who was the same age as her, tried to assure them everything would be fine. They waited in a harsh silence. Zoe could hear the muffled voices of Anna and Sylvia floating down the stairs.

Zoe grasped J.J.'s arm and pulled him into the kitchen.

"What happened?"

"I told you," he said. "He fell off the bed."

"He says you pushed him," Zoe said.

"And you believe him?" J.J. said, his eyes wide. "Why would I push him?"

"I don't know." Zoe folded her arms and narrowed her eyes at the younger boy. "That's something I'll have to ask him."

Zoe heard the sirens outside, announcing the ambulances. She pulled him back into the living room and hurried to open the front door. She watched as the EMT grabbed a stretcher from the back and their supplies.

"He's upstairs, hurry!" Zoe exclaimed. "Second room on the left."

The paramedics piled into the house, making their way to the front door. A police car pulled against the curb and two officers climbed out.

"I'm Sergeant Oglethorpe," one of the policemen said as he neared. "What's your name?"

"Zoe."

"Can you tell us what happened?"

She hesitated. She wasn't exactly sure what happened.

"I don't know," Zoe said. "I heard a loud noise, and when I ran up there, I saw Petey hurt really bad. J.J. says he fell off the bed, but..."

"But what?"

"But when Petey opened his eyes, he told me J.J. pushed him."

"Which one is J.J.?" Oglethorpe asked.

Zoe pointed. "The kid in the blue and white striped shirt."

"Okay, noted," Oglethorpe said. He scribbled on his notepad as he made his way into the living room. He looked up at the children, most of whom were huddled on the couch.

"Is Petey going to be okay?"

"I'm sure the doctors will do everything they can, Zoe," Shane assured her.

"I'm going to need to question each of you, okay?" Oglethorpe said. "So we can have different vantage points and figure out what happened."

Zoe watched as the paramedics went down the stairs, Petey on the stretcher.

Anna followed close behind, tears streaming from her face. She held her cell phone to her ear, and from what Zoe could tell, she was speaking to Sylvia.

Chapter 50

After DeLong was informed one of the children from Bree's ministry was in the hospital, he decided to see for himself what happened.

DeLong parked in the parking deck, and before climbing out of his truck, he called Newman to see what his status was. The investigator informed him all but one of the parents had been questioned. So far, it appeared none of them seemed to blame Bree for their children's suicides.

DeLong finished the conversation after informing him of what happened to Petey.

He made his way to the main hospital, then took the elevator to the floor where Petey was located.

When he arrived, he found Oglethorpe in the room, arms crossed. The doctor had placed a bandage on the side of his forehead, and the nurse was checking Petey's IV.

Oglethorpe acknowledged DeLong when he entered the room with a nod.

The nurse turned to leave and frowned at Oglethorpe and DeLong. "He's not in the state to answer questions."

"We understand," Oglethorpe said, "but the sooner we talk to the boy, the better."

The nurse sighed. "Fine, but make it quick." She turned to Petey. "If you need anything, press this button on the side of your bed, okay?"

Petey nodded.

"Hey, Petey," DeLong said. He studied the young boy. His eyes were dark and glassy, his skin pale. "How are you feeling? Heard you got a nasty bump on the head."

"I'm okay," he said.

"Do you remember me, Petey?"

He nodded. "You're that cop trying to find who killed Miss Bree."

"That's right," DeLong said.

"Did you know anything yet?"

"We're working on it, buddy," DeLong assured him. He turned to Oglethorpe. "What do we know so far?"

"Petey claims another boy pushed him," he stated. "The other kid's name is James Jordan. Goes by J.J."

"Is that right?" DeLong said to Petey. "Do you know why he pushed you? Was it an accident?"

He shook his head and bit his bottom lip.

DeLong took a step toward him. "We want to make sure it doesn't happen again. I promise, whatever happens, you'll be safe, okay? We need you to answer our questions. Did J.J. push you on purpose?"

With hesitation, Petey nodded.

"Why would he want to hurt you?"

"Will he go to jail?" Petey asked.

"He may not go to jail, but he could be in for a lot of trouble. Depending on what you tell us, we'll be able to decide the best course of action to take."

Petey lifted his hand to his forehead and winced at the obvious pain he felt. "I don't want to get into trouble."

Oglethorpe stepped next to DeLong. "You don't have to worry about anything, son. You're the victim here. We take assault very seriously. But we need you to tell us the truth."

Petey hesitated for a second more, then released a sigh.

"We were playing at first. Kind of horsing around, you know? Then I said something about Miss Bree. It made him angry."

"What was it?" DeLong asked.

"I just said I hoped you'd catch whoever killed her."

"He laughed and called her a name. He said he killed Miss Bree and no one will think he did it because he's only a kid."

DeLong exchanged glances with Oglethorpe. "J.J. said he killed her?"

"Yeah. I said I was going to tell. That's when he pushed me."

DeLong searched Petey's face, unsure of what he'd heard. Before he could say anything more, the doctor arrived, ushering Petey's visitors out of the room.

"He needs rest."

With hesitation, DeLong nodded in agreement.

"Wow," Oglethorpe muttered as they left the room.

DeLong looked back toward the room, deep in thought. He glanced at his watch to see it was almost five o'clock. "Let's take another trip to PLC. I want to question those children and the staff members. Let's not say anything yet to J.J. that Petey talked. I want to get a feel for him."

"I'll meet you there," Oglethorpe agreed as they walked down the hall toward the parking deck.

DeLong used his phone first to call Newman and update him. Next, he called Samantha to let her know he was going to be late getting home, so she and Bella could eat dinner without him.

By the time he finished talking to his wife, he'd returned to his truck. DeLong climbed in and headed back to Protecting the Lord's Children.

Chapter 51

DeLong told Oglethorpe to question Sylvia while he took Anna. He wanted to be sure Sylvia would cooperate with the investigation, so he decided a change of investigators might do the trick.

DeLong sat with Anna in the kitchen where she could be in sight of the children, but their conversation was still private.

"How was Bree when it came to the kids?"

"She was good with them. They liked her a lot. Bree had a way of making you feel special. Needed."

"Had anyone ever become aggressive with her? Maybe they threatened to hurt her if she continued the ministry?"

"No. This is the problem with everyone on the outside. They think because most of these kids come from drugged up families, they're troublemakers. That's not the truth at all."

DeLong put a hand on the table and leaned over so he could catch her full attention. "I don't think that way at all. I don't think anyone does. The problem is that Petey's in the hospital. He's claiming one of your kids confided that he killed Bree."

Anna narrowed her eyes. "What? That's crazy. Why would he say a thing like that?"

"That's what I'm trying to find out. Now, I want you to think, okay? Think about a time where one of them would become aggressive. Something that didn't seem normal."

"I don't know," Anna said. "For the most part, they've behaved. They come from troubled families, Detective DeLong. Sure, they'll act out from time to time. But that's normal. We try to provide a safe, happy environment. They're good kids."

"What did J.J. tell you about what happened with Petey?"

"Just that Petey fell off the bed."

"That's all he told you?"

Anna leaned forward. "What are you trying to say, Detective?"

"After hearing Petey had an accident, I went to the hospital to see how he was doing. He told us that when he mentioned something about Bree, J.J. became angry. Eventually, J.J. let it slip that he was the one who killed her. When Petey told him he was going to tell that's when J.J. pushed him off the bed."

Anna shook her head with fervor. "Impossible. J.J. could never do that. He would never. He's not a killer."

"Then why would Petey say that?" DeLong cornered.

He opened the folder he had set on the table and handed Anna a photo of Bree at the crime scene. When she closed her eyes and turned away, DeLong instructed her to look at the picture.

She did.

"I could say this was an accident, but I can't. Whoever did this to her did it in anger. Hatred." He let his words sink in. "Whoever murdered Bree DeLong wanted her dead. She had a husband. A daughter. Her family loved her."

Anna wiped a tear from her eyes.

"Has J.J. ever shown violent behavior? With Bree or anyone? I need your help with this, Anna. You and Sylvia are the only ones around who can speak for your friend. You know what the kids are capable of."

"It was a long time ago," Anna said after a few minutes of silence. "But he came a long way since then. That's not the boy he is now."

"Tell me what happened," DeLong pressed.

"Before he was sent to us, he'd spent two years living on the street. He'd run away from a bad home situation and two gang members found him. They took him in as their own. Trained him to take care of himself on the street. But they also taught him how to lie, steal and..."

Anna trailed off, her eyes staring at the surface of the table.

"And what? Kill?"

She nodded. "He never hurt anyone, but on the night he was caught, he was holding a gun on a rival gang member's temple. J.J. was taken into custody. When Bree heard about it on the news, she advocated for him to stay here."

"What happened to the gang members?" DeLong inquired.

"One was arrested. He's in prison now. The other one escaped." She scratched her head, then played with her ponytail. "The first year J.J. was here wasn't ideal, but that was expected. He'd tried to run away, he threatened and cursed all of us. But I guess you know Bree. She was so patient with him. She did everything right, and eventually, he calmed down."

"Has he ever been in contact with his old gang since being here?"

"Of course not," Anna said. "We don't allow contacts like that. Bree always believed it was too risky for the kids."

"What about Petey? What's his story?"

"He's usually quiet. Keeps to himself mostly, but he became friendlier with J.J. Petey's parents died a year ago. He has an aunt, but she's a model in southern California and doesn't want kids. So Bree took him in."

"Okay, thank you. Send J.J. in for me to talk to him."

Anna frowned, but nodded as she pushed her chair back. "I know what you said, Petey told you, but I don't think J.J. would hurt Bree. He loved her."

"Noted," DeLong said.

Anna disappeared from the kitchen and DeLong entered the new information in his pad.

When J.J. appeared, DeLong closed his pad and set the pen on the table.

"Hey, J.J. How are you doing?"

He shrugged as he took Anna's place in the chair. "Okay, I guess. Is Petey okay?"

DeLong offered him a smile. "He'll be fine. The doctors want to keep him overnight, but he should be released sometime tomorrow."

J.J. set his arms on the table, scanning DeLong's face.

"So, do you want to give me your version of what happened?"

"I already told that other cop," he said.

"I know, but I'd like to hear from you. You were playing in the room?"

"Yeah. Jumping on the bed. We were kinda bored. But then he fell and hit his head."

"That must have been scary, seeing your friend fall like that," DeLong surmised. "I remember when I was about your age, maybe a little bit younger. My grandparents had a farm. My older brother dared me to walk on the wooden fence without falling. I almost made it, then fell, hitting the back of my head."

"That had to hurt."

"It did. I could hear my brother freaking out, asking if I was okay. All I could see were stars flashing in my eyes. Head injuries aren't fun. They can be dangerous, even."

J.J. leaned back in his chair, popping his knuckles, but he didn't reply.

"Anna was telling me you used to be in a gang," DeLong continued.

J.J. let his shoulders rise and fall. "I never got to make it in. They were initiating me, but the cops arrested us."

"How did that make you feel?"

"I don't know," he admitted. "I wanted to be a part of them, but I was kinda scared of having to shoot someone."

"I've had to shoot people before in the line of duty," DeLong said. "It's rare, but I hated it each time. It actually made me physically sick."

"Did you kill anyone?"

DeLong considered whether he wanted to lie or tell the truth.

The fact was, he did kill someone. The only person who ever knew about it was his friend, Russ Calhoun. He was off duty, and it was in self-defense, but it haunted him nonetheless.

"Yeah," he said. "I did kill someone. He was a very bad man. He would have killed me if I didn't fire my gun."

"What was it like for you? Taking his life?"

"Well, I never wanted to hurt him. But he forced my hand."

"You're lying," J.J. observed. "You were happy he was dead."

DeLong narrowed his eyes. "No, I wasn't. Killing another person is never easy. No matter what they've done to you or others." He shook his head as if to clear the conversation from his mind. "But we're here to talk about you. Have you been in contact with any of your friends in the gang?"

"Nope," J.J. answered.

"Did Petey say anything to you before he fell?"

"No, why?"

"Maybe he upset you."

"Are you accusing me of pushing him?" J.J. scoffed. "I didn't."

"He said you did," DeLong said.

DeLong studied the young boy. He wanted to ease into the subject of Bree, but he wanted to be careful about how he said it.

"That's stupid. I didn't do nothing to that whiney baby." He pushed his chair back in anger and rose to his feet. He stalked out of the room until DeLong called out to him.

"We're not finished here."

"I didn't do nothing!" J.J. protested. He pushed at the table and it moved with a loud creak against the tile floor. His breath rose and fell in steady movements, but eyes were wide with anxiety. J.J. unleashed his grip on the edge of the table. He muttered something inaudible.

DeLong watched him. He saw the young boy's knuckles were turning sheet white. J.J. fell into his seat and rocked his body.

"J.J. if you tell me the truth about what happened, I'll do all I can to help you," DeLong said. "Did you push Petey off the bed?"

"Am I under arrest or something?" J.J. leaned back in his chair and folded his arms.

"Listen, son," DeLong began.

"I'm not your son," J.J. hissed. He shot his eyes toward DeLong and narrowed them.

"Right," DeLong started again. "Listen, I'm sure you didn't mean to hurt him. Maybe you were roughhousing, and it got out of control faster than you realized."

J.J. looked away again with a frown.

"Fine," DeLong spat at him. "Petey said you pushed him. He had to end up in the hospital somehow. And to top it off, he also mentioned you confessed to killing Bree DeLong."

"What?" J.J. gasped. "That no-good two-bit scum. He's a liar!"

"Were you with her when she died?"

J.J. frowned, shaking his head. He jumped from the chair again, pushing it back to the kitchen floor. He charged at DeLong, screaming. "He's the one who killed her! He told me! That's why I pushed him! I should have bashed *his* skull in!"

J.J. stood nose-to-nose with him, but DeLong didn't flinch.

"Now you're saying *Petey* killed Bree?"

"That's what I said," J.J. snapped. He righted his body and crossed his arms. Before he turned around, DeLong noticed the tears sliding down the corner of his eyes.

Anna and Sylvia, along with a few of the other kids, crowded in the kitchen doorway. Quick footsteps descended the stairs, and Oglethorpe appeared behind the crowd.

"Is everything okay, Detective?" Oglethorpe pulled a few of the spectators away and pushed his way into the kitchen.

"We're fine," DeLong answered, keeping his gaze set on J.J. "I'm going to take you in."

"What?" Anna exclaimed.

"Why?" Sylvia asked. "On what grounds? Detective DeLong, he's just a kid."

"He admitted to pushing Petey off the bed out of anger. And we need to question him about the murder of Bree. I suggest you get him a lawyer."

"You're kidding me!" J.J. threw a round of curses at DeLong. "He had it coming! I didn't do nothing!"

"Sergeant Oglethorpe?"

The sergeant offered a quick nod as he took the boy's arm. "Let's go, son."

As the sergeant led J.J. to the car, DeLong turned back to Sylvia and Anna.

"Will you take me to the boy's things? Please?"

Sylvia frowned but nodded and motioned for him to follow her. As they went up the stairs, DeLong heard Anna telling the younger children not to worry, but things would be okay.

"This is the boys' room," Sylvia said when they reached the room. He could detect the hint of resentment in her voice.

DeLong noticed the blood stain from Petey's wound had been cleaned. However, that wasn't what he was after.

He went into the closets and searched through the boys' clothing in search of the hood.

But nothing was to be found.

He turned to Sylvia.

"Is there any other place where the boys would store their things?"

"No," she said. "Not unless they've found a hiding place I don't know about. Which wouldn't surprise me since they're young and they're boys. What are you looking for?"

"A hoodie," DeLong said. "Or at least something with a hood."

Sylvia shrugged. "I don't know anything about that."

"Okay," DeLong said with a sigh. "Thanks for your help. I'll touch base with you sometime tomorrow."

As DeLong made his way out of the bedroom, a sound caught his attention. He turned in time to see something fall off the bedside table with a crash.

Sylvia noticed it too. "That's weird."

Jim.

"Did you hear that?" DeLong asked.

"It's just a picture," Sylvia answered with a shake of her head. "I'll clean it up later."

"No, this was something else."

DeLong stepped over to the small walkway and bent to retrieve the small frame, now broken. Glass scattered along the floor. He noticed a thick red material sticking out from underneath the bed.

No.

It wasn't red material.

The material was a light green but had a dark red stain on the sleeve. Using the broken picture frame, DeLong dragged it out from underneath the bed.

A hoodie.

He turned to Sylvia. "Have you seen this before?"

"I can't be sure."

"Interesting," DeLong muttered. "I'm going to hold on to it."

Without waiting for an answer, he made his way to meet Oglethorpe at the car. He'd already gotten J.J. settled in the backseat.

"This is becoming more of a mess," DeLong muttered as he neared the car. "We have two children pointing their fingers at each other. One of which is in the hospital. But I found this."

He held the hoodie for the sergeant to see, then opened the backseat of the car.

"Have you seen this before?" DeLong asked J.J.

J.J. glanced at the hoodie and then up at DeLong. "It's Petey's."

"All right," DeLong said. "Let's get on out of here." He pushed the back door shut and opened the passenger's side to climb in.

Chapter 52

INSTEAD OF GOING STRAIGHT home, DeLong dropped the hoodie off at the lab. Newman wasn't there, so he instructed the lab technician to process the evidence and call as soon as he found something.

While he waited for results, DeLong went to the gym for a workout session. He had a lot of pent-up frustration and wanted release.

DeLong rested his back against the bench and pushed fifty-pound weights into the air. He lowered it to his chest.

With a soft grunt, he lifted the weight once more.

And then again.

And again.

After a few more reps, his muscles grew tired, and he set the weight bar in its holder.

Sitting up, DeLong swiped at the sweat he'd earned for the hour.

The banging around the large gym gave him a headache, but he didn't want to leave yet. He didn't trust himself to.

Instead, he chose an empty treadmill and cooled down with a slow jog.

DeLong reflected on the visions he saw. Two of them had hoods on—the vision on his computer screen and the one in his own backyard. It made sense whoever killed Bree would wear a hood.

But the visions weren't clear enough for him to tell how tall the culprit was.

He also kept hearing the words "love always."

But what did that mean, exactly?

"You must be deep in thought."

DeLong glanced over to see his sponsor, Harry, stepping on the treadmill to his left.

"Hey," DeLong acknowledged. "Yeah, I'm thinking about my investigation. I'm trying to piece together what I've learned, but I'm turning in circles."

"Be careful not to get dizzy," Harry said. "Especially while on the treadmill."

DeLong chuckled as he set the machine to stop. "Don't worry about that. How are you doing?"

He stretched his arms to loosen his muscles.

"Good," Harry said. "I've been seeing someone. I think it might actually go somewhere."

"That's great, man," DeLong said, slapping his old friend's shoulder. "How d'you convince her to go out with you?"

"Easy," Harry said with a wry smile. "I played the prince in distress. She ran into my bumper at a grocery store."

"Really," DeLong laughed. "You've got to be kidding me."

"Not at all. We were backing out at the same time and ran into each other," Harry explained. "She was very beautiful and apologetic. Did I mention she was beautiful?"

"I think you may have," DeLong answered. "Well, it was good seeing you. I better get home and take a shower. If this investigation taught me anything, it's that I need to see my wife more often." He cursed. "Anything can happen."

"Amen to that," Harry agreed. He extended his hand. "Nice running into you, Jim."

"You too." DeLong grasped Harry's hand and shook it. "When am I going to meet this girl of yours?"

"Soon would be good. We can have a double date."

"Sounds like a plan. Talk it over with her and give me the details. Sam and I will be there."

DeLong left the gym, feeling more energized, but his mind wouldn't let go of the investigation. He drove until he realized he was headed toward his brother's house.

When he arrived, he parked at the curb but didn't get out. The house was dark, so he figured his mother, Ally, and Sullivan were asleep. It was just as well, because he wasn't exactly sure what he wanted to say to his brother. The last time they'd spoken was before his release, and it wasn't exactly cordial.

DeLong rolled the window halfway and retrieved a cigarette from his pocket. He lit the tip and sucked in the tobacco, holding it for a second before blowing it out.

"Mind if I have one?"

Startled, DeLong looked out the window to see his brother leaning in.

"Uh, sure," he said, handing him the pack. He pushed the door open and stepped out as Sullivan put the lighter to his cigarette. After a few puffs of smoke, he passed it back to his brother.

"Thanks."

"Sure," DeLong said.

They leaned against the car in silence, staring at the starless sky. The clouds were thick, the moon full and bright. To DeLong, it seemed to be closer to the earth than normal.

"How you been?" DeLong asked, trying to break the awkwardness.

"Oh, you know," Sullivan said, his voice dry. "I'm a widower, my brother arrests me for a crime I didn't commit, I'm out on bail...I'm peachy."

DeLong cursed. "Are we really going to get into this again, Sullivan? I had no choice."

"Yeah, you did," Sullivan insisted. "You're my brother. We're blood. And I didn't kill my wife. You know that."

"I know that now," DeLong admitted. He turned to face Sullivan. "But when you sucker punched me off my feet, I had reservations. My concern—my *only* concern—is to find out who murdered my sister-in-law. I didn't want to believe you did it. Actually, I *didn't* believe it. But I had to follow the evidence. A witness put you at the scene of the crime."

"I admitted I was there."

"Yeah, eventually you did," DeLong reminded him, "But for a while, you lied to me. You said you didn't know where she was."

He took another drag from his cigarette and blew out the smoke. He watched as the stick between his fingers dissolved.

"We've got two other suspects. We're holding one and the other is in the hospital."

Sullivan turned to gape at him. "I'm in the clear now?"

"Not completely, but I'm working on it."

"Oh. I see. Well, who are your suspects?" Sullivan asked.

DeLong told him about the day's events and what happened between the two boys. His brother watched him, his eyes filling with interest and pain.

Sullivan cursed underneath his breath and scratched the back of his head. "I always told Bree she needed to be careful. She was so busy with saving the world by taking in troubled kids. She never thought about the consequences."

"I think she did," DeLong said. "She saw the best in everybody. And those kids, most of them aren't troubled. They need to be shown they're worthy."

"And your two suspects—what's your excuse for them?"

DeLong pushed out a breath.

"I don't have one—yet. I can't even say either one of them killed her. They're pointing their fingers at each other. But one's dealing with a head injury and the doctor doesn't want us to talk to him until tomorrow. The other one is angry. And he looked scared."

"Of course he's scared," Sullivan said, his words laced with anger. "He murdered someone in cold blood and he got caught."

DeLong chose not to reply. Instead, he chucked the remaining cigarette to the tar, putting it out with the toe of his shoe.

"I should be getting home," DeLong said. "I don't want Sam to worry."

Sullivan nodded. "Yeah, it has gotten pretty late."

DeLong hesitated for a second, then opened his door. "I'll talk to you soon."

"Listen, Jim." Sullivan kicked at the tar so he wouldn't have to look into his brother's gaze. "Whatever's gone on between us, I want to fix it. I don't know how, but I want us to try. It's what Bree would have wanted, and Mom won't shut up about it."

"Me too," DeLong agreed.

"But that can't happen until you find somebody to arrest for murdering my wife. Somebody other than me."

DeLong nodded. "Understood."

"Good." Sullivan tapped the hood. "Be careful getting home. You look like you're about to fall asleep."

"I feel like it," DeLong said. He climbed into the truck and pulled away. As he left, he glanced in the rearview, watching his brother watch him.

Chapter 53

DELONG'S EYES OPENED, AND he stared into the darkness. He had his right hand stuffed underneath his pillow and his left gripped the edge of the bed.

His breathing heavy, he remembered the dream he'd woken from. He had returned to the heart of the juvenile detention center that was once his home for two long months. He'd once again become a target of harassment and pain. The laughter of the inmates and guards rang loud in his ears. Corey Black's was the most vibrant of them all.

He released his grip on the covers and rolled onto his back.

It's okay, Jim. It was only a dream.

When he reopened his eyes, he glanced at where Samantha slept in peace. It wasn't until he sat up that he noticed Bella standing in the doorway.

"What's wrong, honey?" DeLong asked.

Bella didn't reply.

She looked behind her, then back at her dad.

DeLong rose from the bed and kneeled in front of her. Bella's eyes were tired and bloodshot. It looked like she'd been crying.

"Did you have a bad dream?" he asked, putting a consoling hand on his daughter's cheek. "Want to talk about it?"

"I saw Aunt Bree," Bella said. "And I saw the one who killed her."

DeLong sighed. "Come on, let's get you some warm milk, okay? Then we'll get you tucked back into bed."

"You don't believe me, do you?" Bella asked.

"Let's go in the kitchen," DeLong insisted. He held his hand out for her to take it. "I don't want to wake your mother."

When she took his hand, they walked down the stairs. Bella sat at the kitchen table, watching her father move with high interest.

DeLong busied himself by pouring two mugs of milk and placing them in the microwave. He waited for a minute until the two mugs were heated before he retrieved them. He set Bella's drink in front of her and sat next to her.

"Aunt Bree needs help," Bella said. "The one in the hood is going to get away."

"No, he's not," DeLong said. "I've got good men working to find him. We'll get him."

Bella sipped her milk and when she set the mug on the table, she licked the white mustache on her upper lip.

"So you think you saw your aunt?" DeLong asked.

She nodded. "At first, she scared me."

"Now she doesn't?"

"No. She's trying to get away from the one in the hood. But he keeps trying to kill her."

DeLong listened to his daughter's tired voice, still amazed she was seeing and hearing ghosts, just like he'd been. Could it be a genetic trait? Or was he transferring his thoughts to her somehow?

"So, the one in the hood," DeLong started. "You haven't seen his face yet, have you?"

Bella shook her head. "It's too dark."

DeLong rubbed his eyes as sleep again came for him. He tried to fight it, but he knew it was a fruitless effort. He didn't want to return to the detention center and face Corey Black and his pals.

Bella had rested her head on the table and fallen asleep.

Leaving the mugs on the table, he pulled Bella into his arms and carried her to her bedroom. When she was underneath the covers, he kissed her forehead and slipped out of the room.

Instead of returning to his own bed, DeLong opted to sit at the bistro table outside. He poured himself a fresh cup of milk and snatched the cigarette pack from the dish on the counter.

He also brought his case file with him, but knew he'd looked them over enough in the past few weeks. He'd more or less memorized the contents.

As the seconds crawled by, he became more agitated.

DeLong's mind swirled in a colorless mural of the past, the present and the uncertainties of the future. The more he tried to think about the investigation, the more his blood pulsed through his veins.

With shaky hands, DeLong removed a cigarette from the pack and slipped it between his lips. He lit the end and breathed in the smoke, his eyes closed.

His short days in juvenile detention snaked his way into his thoughts. He could smell the blood coming from Corey Black after Sullivan shanked him.

The cold tension between the brothers chilled DeLong's body.

The screams pounded against his head.

The laughter seemed to match.

He kept so much anger in him that it seemed to heighten everything. He couldn't quiet his mind, and he couldn't focus. Everything seemed to muddle him. He may as well have been shut in a small room with no windows with all the bad memories of his past.

When the noise in his head became too much, he swung his arm across the table, knocking the drink and files to the cemented patio. The cup crashed, breaking into five small pieces.

DeLong sighed and put his head in his hands, his cigarette burning between his fingers.

Little by little, the screams and voices subsided.

All but one.

"Jim?"

He hesitated before turning to see his wife stepping out the back door. She'd put on a thick robe, her black hair hanging unkempt over her shoulders.

"Why aren't you in bed?" She put a hand on his shoulder, gazing his eyes with deep concern.

Pulling her into his lap, he put his hand on her neck and brought her face to his for a kiss.

"Jim," she said again.

"Shh," he whispered. "Please don't say anything."

He kissed her again, longing for the memories of the past to go away. She allowed him to hold her until a few more minutes passed and she pulled away.

"What's wrong?" she asked.

"Nothing," he said. "Or everything. I don't know."

She leaned her head against his shoulder with a sigh. DeLong could smell the coconut shampoo she used.

When Samantha peeled herself from him again, she took her husband's hand and tugged. "It's four-thirty in the morning. You need some rest. Let's get back to bed."

DeLong shook his head, kissed her hand.

"I don't want to go to bed. My mind's too wired to sleep."

Samantha frowned, but nodded. "Fine. Just come up when you want to."

He told her he would. When the door closed behind her, he gathered the notes from the ground and set them on the table.

He drew in tobacco and pushed it back out as he prepared to go over his investigation again.

Petey or J.J.? Or were they in on it together? And why did they kill Bree?

DeLong began at the beginning, when he first arrived at the Augusta Canal.

The moment when his life collapsed.

Chapter 54

WHEN DELONG OPENED HIS eyes, he realized he'd fallen asleep with his head on the bistro table and his arms dangling toward the cement. He gathered his files and stepped into the house, glad Samantha and Bella were still asleep.

Getting the coffee ready, DeLong crept up the stairs for fresh clothes and a shower.

He let the hot water wash away some of the leftover anguish for a few long minutes. When he turned the faucet off, he pulled the shower curtain back and let out a startled curse.

Samantha stood in the doorway, her long hair in a bun, arms draped across her chest. She frowned, her eyes clouded with worry.

"You startled me," he said, wrapping the towel around his waist. He stepped out of the tub.

"Sorry," Samantha said. She paused. "You never came to bed."

"I know, I'm sorry." He ran the comb through his hair. "I fell asleep outside."

"Jim, I'm worried," Samantha confessed. "I'm getting more worried the longer you don't talk to me."

He scoffed. "What's that supposed to mean? I talk to you."

"Not lately. You've been muttering in your sleep every night and when I ask you about it, you wave it off. One minute you and Sullivan are finally getting along, then the next, you arrest him."

"Seriously? Samantha, I was doing my job. If it wasn't me, then it would have been someone else. I can't be seen as biased. Captain Lowell will take me off the investigation before you know it."

"Maybe that's not such a bad idea."

DeLong turned to stare at her. "You're kidding me, right? I've come way too far in this investigation. I need—"

"Right now, I don't care what you need," Samantha hissed. "Your brother lost his wife. He's depressed, he's angry, and you're not making things any better." She put her hand on her forehead, sighed, and put them on her husband's shoulders. "Look. I'm not telling you that you're the cause of this bad blood between the two of you. But, Jim, he needs you. And whether or not you want to admit it, you need him."

"Give me one more week," he compromised. "We're onto something right now. We have two persons of interest. If, after a week, we don't figure out what happened to Bree, then I'll give Kane the reign. Deal?"

"Guess that'll have to do. As long as you don't keep sleeping outside."

"Deal," he said. He didn't want to get into the dreams he had when he first woke. "Guess in that case I should get into work."

"Okay, honey," Samantha said. She lifted herself on her toes to brush her lips against his. "Love you."

Samantha left the bathroom so he could finish dressing. When he pulled on his clothes for the day, DeLong went downstairs to find Samantha pouring Bella a bowl of cereal. He kissed his family goodbye and hurried out the door.

DeLong sat in his office, again scanning over his notes and the photos of the crime scene. He pushed all unrelated thoughts from his mind and focus on the investigation, but as usual, he was still missing a piece of the puzzle.

DeLong studied the evidence until his eyes blurred, trying to imagine if either boy could have done the deed. He concluded it wasn't *impossible*.

But if one of the boys did kill Bree, then one question remained.

Which of them was telling the truth?

Or were they both telling the truth?

J.J. pushed Petey off the bed. He admitted it. On the other hand, J.J. said the hoodie he found belonged to Petey. However, the boys had both been blaming the other.

DeLong frowned.

When his cell phone rang, he retrieved it to find it was the lab.

"What d'ya get?"

"The red substance tested positive for blood," the tech said. "I ran a sample, and it was a match to your sister-in-law's."

DeLong hesitated.

"Thanks."

He ended the phone call, set it on the desk, and flipped the file closed. DeLong put his elbows on his desk and lowered his head to his hands, pushing out a long, heavy sigh.

A knock sounded at the door and he muttered for the person to enter.

"Detective."

DeLong looked up at his captain.

"Hey, what's up, Cap?"

"Just checking in," he answered. Captain Lowell slid into the office and took a seat in the chair across from the desk. He crossed his legs, eyeing DeLong. "From the look on your face, things aren't going so well."

DeLong scoffed, then let out a curse.

"This investigation has been nothing but giving me a headache, Captain. But the good news is I found a green hoodie with her blood on it. J.J. says it belonged to Petey." He shook his head. "But with both boys pointing fingers, who knows? If I don't solve it in a week, then I promised my wife I'd withdraw from the investigation."

Captain Lowell arched his eyebrow. "You did?"

DeLong nodded. "She's afraid it's getting to me and that it'll draw a bigger wedge between my brother and me."

"I see," Lowell answered. "Well, I have to admit, I am concerned myself. I have been ever since you and Newman brought your brother in for questioning. I'd be a foolish leader if I didn't voice my own concerns."

"I'm fine, Captain."

"I hope so," Lowell said. "Well, why don't you tell me your opinion on these kids' confessions, Detective?"

DeLong leaned back in his chair and folded his hands behind his head. "Honestly? I don't have an opinion at this time."

"That's a first," Lowell said with a smirk.

DeLong lifted the corner of his lips in a brief smile. Once again flipping open his file, he stared at a photo of the lifeless body that used to be his sister-in-law.

"She never did anything wrong, Captain. Never in her entire life," De-Long pushed out a heavy breath. "She didn't have a selfish bone in her body. I mean, if you needed her, she'd be there. No questions asked." He looked through his eyelashes at his captain. "But I spent most of her marriage avoiding her. Because if I got close to her, then I'd have to get close to my brother. And at the time, neither of us were ready."

"I'm sure she knew you cared about her," Captain Lowell said. He reached across the desk to pick up the crime scene photo and studied it. "But times like these are what makes us wonder, what's the point? We wake to a new morning, we attempt to serve and protect, then a good woman dies. We're left with nothing but anger and regret. It can eat you alive." He set the picture back on the desk, rising to his feet. "I have a meeting with the mayor this morning. He wants an update. Wish I could say it gets easier, but I'd only be lying."

"Well, Cap, if I can manage to survive this, then I'll be able to survive anything that comes my way."

As Captain Lowell turned to walk away, he acknowledged Newman, who rapped his knuckles on the doorframe. They shook hands and Newman stepped into the office, setting two large coffees from McDonald's on the desk.

"I took the liberty of bringing you some coffee," Newman said.

"Thanks," DeLong muttered. "I need all the caffeine I can get."

"I know," Newman said. "I got an interesting call from your wife."

"Sam?" DeLong narrowed his eyes.

"No, your other one," Newman answered, hiding his smirk by taking a sip. "Yeah, Sam. She's worried about you. I'm supposed to watch you and make sure you stay in check."

"Are you my wife-appointed sponsor now?" DeLong grumbled, wrapping his hands around the cup.

"I'm your friend who is also worried about you," Newman commented. "This investigation is bound to get to you. I haven't said anything because you haven't given me a reason to, but you're in danger of falling down a dark road."

DeLong cursed underneath his breath. "Listen, Newman, I know all about dark roads. I invented them. You don't get to tell me I'm falling down one. My whole life is a dark road."

"So you're second-guessing your decision?" Newman asked, leaning back in his chair. "Because you were only doing your job. And your brother knows that. But we've got two more suspects, so your brother is likely cleared."

"Right," DeLong snapped. "We've got two troubled teenagers pointing their fingers at each other. What am I supposed to do? Charge both of them for murder?"

"Do you think both of them did it?"

DeLong held his friend's gaze in silence before he broke it to stare through the blinds at the parking lot.

"I don't know," DeLong said.

"Yeah, you do," Newman answered. "You've got a sixth sense about these things. In more ways than one. And I'm not even thinking about ghosts telling you where to look. When your gut is telling you something's off, well, ninety-nine percent of the time, something's off. So, I ask again: do you think both of them did it?"

DeLong turned to face his friend, who was still sitting in the chair.

"I'm not sure about that. Petey never showed a history of violence. Not like J.J. but both boys, when I looked in their eyes, they were scared."

"Of getting caught?"

DeLong lowered himself to the chair.

"I don't think so," he answered. "All the kids adored her. That's clear. But J.J. and Petey know something. Or one of them knows something."

"Why point the finger at each other, then?"

"Maybe they're protecting someone," DeLong suggested. "But the question is who."

"You said J.J. was being initiated into a gang before he got caught holding a gun to a rival gang member's head. Maybe he has kept in contact with him. After living a bad home life, he finds refuge in a gang. Their means may be unconventional, but they're like a family. Hurt one of them, they'll go after you with a vengeance. Then J.J. gets arrested and meets Bree. He was at the ministry for a little more than a year. So if one of the gang members came for him, maybe he's torn. We have a woman who shows her love and faith toward him, and the gang who became his family when he needed it most. If a member of his gang did kill her, it stands to reason he's reluctant to rat him out."

"Little boy lost," DeLong muttered.

"Well, let's have a chat with J.J."

Chapter 55

"HOW ARE YOU DOING, J.J.?" DeLong asked as he and Newman made their way to the holding cell.

J.J. was lying on his back, hands behind his head. His eyes were closed, but when he heard DeLong speaking, he blinked and swung his legs on the side of the bed.

"What do you want?"

DeLong opened the cell and he and Newman stepped inside. DeLong slid the bars shut.

"We want to talk to you if that's all right with you."

"Guess I don't have a choice, do I?"

"No, guess you don't," DeLong answered. He crossed his arms over his chest, uncrossed them and sighed as he sat on the bed next to the young boy. "You know, J.J., we all make mistakes. It's how we respond to those mistakes that define our lives."

"What's your point?" J.J. demanded.

"I'm going to cut to the chase and say I don't think Petey hurt Bree." J.J. lowered his eyes to the ground with a frown. He breathed heavy. "And I don't think you did either."

J.J. looked up at DeLong and watched as he made his way to the cot and sat.

"At least not in a direct way. Not intentionally."

"What are you trying to say?" J.J.'s voice grew soft. More hoarse. His eyes were wide and glassy. His lower lips quivered, and he quickly looked away in an attempt to hide how he was feeling.

"I know you cared about Bree," he continued. "She came along when you needed someone the most. She took you out of a situation which could have changed your life for the worse. Isn't that true?"

"Yeah," J.J. admitted, his voice soft.

"Do you want to tell us what really happened?"

J.J. swallowed hard, then coughed. He shook his head and jumped from the cot. He paced the floor, grabbing hold of his hair.

"It wasn't supposed to happen that way!"

"What wasn't?" Newman asked.

J.J. dropped to the cot and put his head in his hands. "I can't tell you."

"Whatever you think they'll do, I can assure you, we'll keep you safe, J.J.," DeLong urged him. "Think about what happened to her. Is it worth protecting someone else?"

"She wasn't supposed to die." J.J. held his head up but continued to avoid eye contact. Tears fell from the corner of his eyes. "She was mad at me. She found out I snuck out the window one night to see him."

"Who is he?" Newman asked.

No response.

"Listen, kid," DeLong pressed. "We want to help you. But you have got to start talking."

Another silence, and then, "Charlie Lewis. He is the leader of the Grey Wolves. He told me he would come and take me away. Miss Bree didn't like him."

"Did you want to go with him?"

J.J. shook his head. "I don't know. I liked it with Miss Bree and the others. But people always leave me. At least Charlie came back. Later, Petey told Miss Bree I was still in touch with Charlie. She was really upset. She'd punished me."

"Were you at the canal when she was killed?" Newman asked.

"Will I stay in jail?"

"Depends on whether or not you help us," DeLong said. "Were you at the canal?"

"Yeah. Miss Bree took me there once. She said walking helps clear her mind. I thought maybe it would help me. So I snuck out and went."

He paused as his voice shuddered.

"Charlie found me and was trying to get me to run away with him. I heard Miss Bree calling out to me."

"What happened next?" DeLong asked.

"I saw her running." J.J. sniffled. "Charlie called her a name. She screamed at him to leave. But he just laughed."

J.J. wiped the corner of his eyes as he struggled to compose himself.

"He pushed her and got on top of her and kept punching her. She was crying. Begging for him to stop. Begging for someone to help her. At first, I froze. I didn't know what to do."

J.J. blinked through his tears and drew in a shaky breath before continuing.

"Then I screamed at him to stop hitting her." J.J.'s voice became monotonic and angry as he reflected on that night. "He looked at me. He smiled and told me he was doing it for me. I begged him to leave her alone. But he told me 'no, James, it's too late for that now. We need to finish the job.'"

DeLong looked over at Newman, whose eyes were fixed on J.J. For a second, Newman met DeLong's gaze, then J.J. continued.

"Charlie climbed off her and she didn't move. I think she was in too much pain or something. I heard her groan. She was still crying. Charlie grabbed the biggest rock he could find. He looked around and got back on his knees. He looked over at me. 'Now we can stay together.' Then he hit her again and again until she didn't move anymore. She was so still and there was so much blood. He pushed her into the water and brushed his clothes off. I couldn't move."

"Did you put the handkerchief over her face?" DeLong asked.

J.J. bit his lower lip and nodded. "I didn't want her to be left like that. She gave it to me a long time ago. She told me it could be a reminder that someone would always love me."

"What happened next?" Newman asked.

"Charlie told me I couldn't tell anyone what happened. If I did, I'd be just as guilty." He sniffled. "I'm sorry. I never wanted anything to happen to her. She was nice to me."

DeLong didn't speak because he wasn't sure he'd be able to. Instead, he put a hand on the young boy's shoulder and squeezed.

"Where can we find Charlie?" Newman asked J.J.

J.J. hesitated with a frown. He looked at the ground, swinging his feet in the air.

"Son, we need you to help us," DeLong said. "We want to help you, but we can't if you're not willing to talk."

Again, J.J. remained quiet.

"You cared about Bree, right? You didn't want her to die. You loved her. She loved you, too. She helped you when no one else would."

J.J. sniffled, then wiped his eyes. He spoke softly but told them where to find the Grey Wolves.

"Thank you," DeLong said. "You did the right thing."

DeLong and Newman left the holding cell and made their way to Captain Lowell's office.

"You okay?" Newman asked, putting his hands on DeLong's shoulder.

"Yeah, I'll be fine," he said. He lifted his hand to the door and rapped his knuckles to announce their presence.

When Captain Lowell called for them to enter, DeLong opened the door and stepped into the office to brief him.

Chapter 56

DeLong and Newman waited until ADA Jablonski issued them the arrest warrant. Once they had it in hand, they arrived at Charlie Lewis' downtown loft. Lieutenant Kane and Sergeant Hunt went with them for backup.

DeLong knocked, and they waited until someone answered.

A young woman wearing a short leather skirt and a black half-top opened the door. She sported a belly button ring and two nose rings and had a tattoo of a rose. She'd dyed her long hair green and painted her lips orange.

"Yeah," she slurred. "What d'ya want?"

"We're looking for Charlie Lewis," DeLong answered. "He around?"

The girl's eyes grew as if she'd just realized who had come calling.

"Cops!" She swung the door and DeLong jammed his foot against the frame to prevent it from closing.

He heard scuffling and various shouts coming from the loft.

"Run!"

"Hurry!"

DeLong shouted for Kane to go around the back of the building and cut off any escape route. Next, he instructed Hunt to take the back room of the loft. Newman would contain the three girls hanging out in the living room while DeLong chased a white male attempting to climb out the window.

He threw his foot on the windowsill and tried to push himself through the large opening, but one of the girls grabbed his pants and pulled.

"Run, Charlie baby! I got ya!"

DeLong pushed the woman into Newman's arms and he flew out the fire escape.

Charlie Lewis knew his downtown territory like the back of his hands. He ran through the streets as fast as he could, but one of the cops was closing in on him.

"Police!" the cop shouted! "Stop or I'll shoot!"

Lewis turned his head enough to see the cop holding his weapon, but he didn't stop. Lewis knew the cop wouldn't shoot unless his life was threatened.

He turned the corner, leading the cop further downtown.

DeLong could see Kane on Lewis' tail, but he still seemed to be too far from their suspect to apprehend him. As he followed after the two men, he tried to guesstimate where Lewis was headed, so he could find a way to cut him off.

He saw Lewis in the distance. Their suspect turned a corner, followed by Kane.

"Lewis, don't do this to yourself any more than you have!"

The cop's voice was closer, then he felt something grab hold of his shirt collar. Lewis gasped and fell to his knees but make a quick recovery by grabbing the switchblade from his pocket. He swung his arm and sliced at the cop's ankle. The officer cried out in pain as he fell to his knees.

Lewis scrambled to his feet, but the cop grabbed his leg, forcing him to the ground.

He kicked the cop's face.

Lewis recoiled as the cop's fist connected with a jaw, but he recovered quickly, kneeing him in the stomach.

The cop took a few steps back, his breath heavy.

Both men eyed the weapon laying on the ground nearby.

They dove to claim it.

DeLong didn't see Kane or Lewis.

He cursed as he searched the neighboring vicinity, trying to pinpoint where they had gone.

He grabbed his radio.

"Kane! What's your location? Kane!"

There was no answer from the lieutenant.

Lewis held the cop's gun to his face.

"Son, you don't want to do this, okay? We can help you." The cop held his hands in front of him.

Lewis cursed him and spat on him.

"Ain't no pig's gonna help a gangbanger like me," Lewis hissed.

"Listen, we'll—"

Lewis cursed him, kicked his face in anger, and pulled the trigger.

Chapter 57

DeLong heard the gunshot echoing through the air. He felt his heart leap into his throat as he picked up his pace. His body drenched in sweat from the chase and the heat, but he didn't let it faze him.

Seconds later, he found Kane lying on the curb of the road. A man was leaning over him.

When DeLong came closer, he saw it wasn't Lewis, but an elderly, dark-skinned man. He was holding a towel to his neck.

"Kane!"

DeLong fell to his knees and placed his fingers to his veins.

Good. A pulse.

"He is good," the man said in a thick accent. "I hold wound. Ze man who shot 'im went there." He pointed west.

DeLong snatched his radio and spoke into it. "Man down Greene Street, by the Episcopalian church. Repeat, man down, need a bus. Suspect is Charlie Lewis, last seen wearing a black tank top, cap and a bandanna around his neck. He's considered armed and dangerous. I'm en route. Request immediate assistance."

After the information was received and copied, DeLong looked again at the man.

"Go," he said before DeLong had the chance to speak. "I will look out for him." He tossed DeLong his keys and pointed to a hunter green jeep. "This may get you to go faster."

"Thank you," DeLong said. Without another word, he unlocked the jeep, jumped in, and turned on the ignition. The tires squealed against the tar as he maneuvered the jeep around parked vehicles.

He drove through the streets, keeping his eyes open for Lewis. It seemed as though he'd vanished.

When his cell phone rang, glancing at the caller ID, he answered, seeing it was Captain Lowell.

"Yeah," DeLong muttered.

"I sent additional men to Lewis' loft," the captain informed him. "We've apprehended the three girls and two men who were with him. Did you find him?"

"No," DeLong grumbled, still looking from street to street. "He's in the wind. How's Kane?"

"The bullet grazed his neck. If that Jamaican hadn't held his towel to the wound, we would have lost him."

DeLong pushed out a breath. "We'll get him, Cap."

"Yes, we will," Lowell agreed. "But later. I need you here."

"But Captain—"

"We need you to question these witnesses. If anyone knows where Lewis is headed, they will."

"Yes, sir," DeLong acknowledged. "I'll be there soon. Where's Newman?"

"He's in the loft, processing the apartment. The Jamaican man is here, giving his account of what happened. You can return his jeep."

"All right," DeLong said. "I'll see you soon."

Letting the jeep idle for a few minutes, he scanned downtown, hoping he'd get a glimpse of Lewis.

Just enough of a glimpse to follow him.

But he didn't appear.

Behind him, someone laid on a horn, so DeLong pressed the gas pedal and headed for the sheriff's station.

Newman fingered through a stack of *Playboy*s and loose paper scattered along the tables and floor.

"There are enough drugs in here to put these guys away for a long time." Hunt looked through a large wooden box that appeared to have been used as a coffee table. He snapped a photo. "Prescription and illegal."

"I'd rather have them for murder and attempted murder," Newman muttered as Hunt's cell phone rang.

The sergeant answered the call, and as he spoke to Captain Lowell on the other end, Newman made his way to the kitchen.

He noticed a locked box sitting on the counter. After snapping the picture, he used his lock-picking tools to break in. He opened the case when he heard footsteps behind him. Newman glanced over his shoulder at Hunt. "Any word on Kane?"

"He'll be fine," Hunt said. "The bullet grazed his collarbone, enough for him to lose a lot of blood, but he had a guardian angel. Some Jamaican man was in his shop when Kane was shot. He contained the wound until the EMTs arrived. Then he gave DeLong his jeep. Imagine that. There are still good people in the world."

"Good to know," Newman agreed. He opened the latch on the case. Inside, he found a handgun. Newman reached for the weapon and studied it. "Check it out. The serial number's been scrubbed off."

"Probably unregistered," Hunt said, scanning the loft. He rested his eyes on Newman's. "Like I said: we've got enough evidence to put these guys up for a long time."

Newman placed the weapon in its spot. "This will all be moot unless we have Lewis in our custody."

"Yeah," Hunt agreed, his voice soft.

"So we know we have them for possession of illegal drugs," Newman began, "but do we have anything connecting Lewis to Bree DeLong's murder?"

"Negative." Hunt pulled open a drawer. "Sorry, man. I know you're close with the detective. How's he doing, by the way?"

"He'll be fine," Newman said. "As you can imagine, this investigation is weighing heavy on him. And when he was forced to arrest his own brother, that didn't help matters much. But he'll be fine."

Newman drummed his fingers on the table and scanned the room.

"You see, a key anywhere?" Newman asked. "If he has evidence connecting himself to Bree's murder, and it's not anywhere in the loft, maybe it's in his vehicle."

"Or the Grey Wolves have another hideout." Hunt lifted a newspaper, then held out a key ring. "Maybe this is it."

"Nice." Newman snatched the bundle from the sergeant's hands. "Let's see which of the cars belongs to Lewis."

Newman led the way to the parking lot. Using the key fob, he pressed the unlock button. The taillight of a beaten up gray Buick flashed.

They made their way to the car and checked the front, then the back seat, but nothing was of interest.

Newman popped the truck and Hunt pulled it open.

Again, it was clean, but Newman wanted to have the car impounded for a more detailed inspection. He used his cell phone to make a request as Hunt kneeled to look underneath the vehicle.

"Well, we're done here," Hunt said when Newman ended the call.

Newman nodded. "Tow truck's on the way. In the meantime, I'll leave you here with your officers and run the ballistics on the weapon. I'm curious to see if it matches any of my caseloads."

"You got a key to DeLong's truck?" Hunt asked.

"I know where he hides his spare. One time, Jim told me when Bella was a baby, Sam shut the door before getting her from the backseat. Unfortunately, it was locked. So Jim had to leave work to get her a spare key." Newman chuckled as he reached underneath the front passenger tire and found the magnetic key holder. "Ever since then, they hide a spare key in both of their vehicles, just in case."

"That must have been awful," Hunt said with a toothy smile.

"It happens when you're a new parent, I suppose. A few months ago, I was so tired from the nights having to feed Joanie, I made myself a cup of warm milk and put the carton in the cereal cabinet."

"The joys of parenthood," Hunt laughed, slapping Newman's shoulder.

"Well, I will see you in a bit," Newman said, unlocking the driver's side.

He set the evidence in the passenger seat and turned to shake Hunt's hand. Climbing behind the wheel, he turned the key, and the truck rumbled to life. Hunt returned to Lewis' loft and Newman pulled away, heading for his lab.

Chapter 58

DeLONG STARED ACROSS THE table at the man who leaned against the back of his chair, legs apart, one hand near his crotch, the other on the edge of the tabletop. He wore a hole-ridden shirt with an art print of a cobra, his wrists decorated with thick brown bracelets. Around his neck was a chain of teeth.

DeLong wondered whether they were real human teeth or fake.

His real name was Vin Diaz, but he preferred to go by "Snake."

Snake was Charlie Lewis' right-hand man, and it was becoming clear he wasn't interested in giving up his buddy.

Captain Lowell was in another interrogation room, interviewing one of the girls.

"Listen, Diaz," DeLong said. "I wouldn't be surprised if those girlfriends of yours were already giving up your friend. If you go ahead and tell me where to find Charlie, I will help both of you. But if you don't help me, I can't help you."

Snake chuckled. "Yeah, that ain't gonna fly, pig. I ain't no rat, and I certainly ain't ratting out my homey."

"Charlie murdered a woman in cold blood," DeLong said through his teeth. "She didn't deserve what he did to her. Not only that, he shot a cop. We don't take too kindly to cop killers. It's in your best interest—and his—if you tell me where he can be found."

"I told you, pig. I ain't a rat."

Snake curled his lips in a devilish smile. DeLong scratched the back of his head, pushing out a frustrated breath.

He pushed his chair back, walked out of the interrogation room to where Sergeant Oglethorpe was watching the scene.

"He needs a push," the sergeant said.

"Oh, he's going to get a push, all right." DeLong narrowed his eyes at Snake. He sat whistling in his chair, staring into the two-way as though he were listening to the exchange between the two officers.

DeLong switched off the camera.

"What are you planning, Detective?" Oglethorpe asked

"Do me a favor and knock on the glass the second you see Lowell."

DeLong returned to the interrogation room and Snake tilted his head to the side.

"I don't suppose I can get a drink while I'm here. Maybe a Coke?"

DeLong flexed his fingers as he stepped toward Snake and grabbed his shirt collar. He tore him from the chair, knocking it to the floor with a clatter. Snake grunted when DeLong pinned him to the wall.

"Guess not," Snake muttered.

"Where's Charlie Lewis?"

Snake cursed him and spat in his face.

DeLong threw an undercut to Snake's stomach. He keeled over with a gasp. Snake chuckled.

"Is that all you can do, pig?"

"Where's Charlie Lewis?" DeLong asked again.

"Riding your mother," Snake answered. "Hard."

Grabbing a fistful of hair, DeLong snapped Snake's head backward. He wrapped his hand around his throat.

"Listen, punk," DeLong growled. "Your buddy murdered my brother's wife. I'm going to find him with or without your help. It's up to you whether or not you want to help yourself."

"C'mon, man," Snake forced out. "Not like you're gonna kill me or nothing. You don't got it in you."

DeLong squeezed his neck tighter. Snake tried to release the hold on him, but to no avail. "Do you want to chance that? This is my family."

After a few minutes of gasping and failing to free himself, Snake forced out that he gave up. DeLong pushed him to the ground. Snake slid, hitting his head on the wall. He groaned, grabbing the sore spot.

"Where is he?" DeLong asked again.

"He's got a sister," Snake said with a series of coughs. "She lives in South Carolina. He probably went there."

DeLong stormed to the table, grabbed the pad and pen, and tossed it to Snake. "Write down the address. And I'm warning you, if you lie, I'm coming back for you."

Massaging his neck, Snake scribbled the address as a knock came from the window. Looking at DeLong, he curled his lips into a sideways smile and flung the pad to the ground.

"There ya go, pig."

DeLong kneeled to retrieve the pad as Captain Lowell entered the room.

"What's going on in here?" he demanded, one hand on the knob, the other on his hip. He glared between DeLong and Snake.

"Yo, man, he's crazy! I call police brutality." He cursed. "He gotta be locked up, man!"

"Got the address of a sister," DeLong muttered, pushing by his captain.

He headed for his office, trying to calm his nerves. When he entered the room, he shut the door and closed his blinds. DeLong shouted out an angry curse and found a book to throw to the floor.

Someone barged into his office, snapping the door shut.

Captain Lowell.

"You are way out of line, Detective," the captain hissed. He jabbed his finger in the air. "That man's going to press charges against you, you know that?"

"Captain, he wasn't talking," DeLong argued. "What was I supposed to do?"

"Not that!" Lowell shouted. He crossed his arms. "I know this has become personal to you. I am sorry. I should have given the case over to someone else. But I was under the impression you could control your feelings. Obviously, I was wrong."

"No, you weren't," DeLong said.

"Oh, so some imaginary force beat the crap out of him?" Lowell snapped.

DeLong fell into his chair, pressing his fingertips to his eyelids. "No," he answered. After seconds ticked by, he looked at his captain.

"Take a team and head to the sister's house. As of right now, you're on notice. Pull a stunt like that again, and you're done. For good."

DeLong watched as the captain opened the door and stalked out, pulling the door behind him.

DeLong cursed underneath his breath as he called a team to assist him at the sister's house. Next, he called Newman and learned he was running the ballistics from the weapon he found in the loft.

"You okay?" Newman asked.

"I'm fine," DeLong lied. He didn't want to get into what happened in the interrogation room right then. He wasn't sure if he ever wanted to. "Keep me updated and I'll see you soon."

"All right," Newman said. "Be careful out there. He already shot one of our guys. That's more than enough."

"Agreed," DeLong said. He ended the conversation and left for the weapons locker to grab a bulletproof vest. As he made his way to the front of the building, he saw Hunt, Oglethorpe, and John waiting for him. "You guys ready?"

"More than," Sergeant John said.

"Okay, then," DeLong said, latching his vest over his chest. "Let's do this."

Chapter 59

Charlotte Lewis-Grayson lived in a small, two-story brick house out in North Augusta with her husband, two girls both under the age of five and one teenage son. Her husband worked at an insurance company while she maintained the house and took care of their children. She used to work as the secretary at the same insurance before she fell in love and married her husband.

Neither Charlotte nor her husband had a criminal record.

Sergeant John pulled to a stop at the curb a few feet away from the Grayson house.

DeLong studied the yard before he stepped out of the car.

It was one thirty, so he guessed the children would be at school, and Charlotte's husband at work.

That meant Charlotte was likely at home.

DeLong hoped she was running whatever errands she normally did, but wondered if Charlie would ever harm his own sister.

When Hunt rapped his knuckles on the window, John used the motorized button to slide it down so they could speak.

"How do you want to do this?" Hunt asked, leaning over.

DeLong considered the options.

Lewis shot a police officer, meaning he was armed and dangerous.

If his sister was home—and to be on the safe side, DeLong assumed she was—then her life could be in danger.

And to top it off, Lewis would not go quietly.

"Hunt and John, you make your way to the back, cover all the windows. Oglethorpe and I will take the front. Remain in radio contact." His men muttered their acknowledgments. "If you see the sister, take her away from the house, out of harm's way."

DeLong opened his door and stepped into the muggy heat. He smelled rain in the air, but the clouds weren't dark, so he couldn't tell if it would rain anytime soon.

Hunt and John sneaked around the back of the house.

DeLong gripped his weapon and removed it from his holster.

"You know, this may not be the best time," DeLong started as they made their way to the front door, "but about what happened in the interrogation room..."

"Hey, man, don't worry," Oglethorpe said. His eyes were focused on the surrounding areas. "I'm surprised you held yourself back. It's no secret she was your sister-in-law. And I can tell there's history—bad history—between you and your brother. I'm not going to pry and ask what went on. Not any of my business. But I can tell you care about him. I commend you for how you've treated this investigation. If it were me, I'm not so sure I'd handle it well. Actually, I know I wouldn't."

"Thanks," DeLong said.

They stood at the front door, weapons in hand.

Oglethorpe knocked.

"Just know that Hunt, John, and I got your back. We take care of our own."

The door opened.

A young woman, appearing to be in her late twenties to early thirties, stood in the frame. Her eyes widened when she saw the guns.

DeLong put his finger to his lips and showed her his badge.

"Are you Charlotte Grayson?" DeLong asked.

She nodded, fear flashing in her eyes. "Wh-what's going on?"

"Is your brother here? Charlie Lewis?"

She shook her head. "He's out running some errands."

Oglethorpe took to his radio to announce to the others Lewis wasn't around, but to hold their position.

"Can we come in?" DeLong asked. "We'll explain everything. After you call your brother and get him back."

She opened the door to allow them entry. "He went to get soup for my daughter. She's got a fever today. She's staying home—did my brother do something wrong?"

DeLong asked her again to call him, promising he'd explain everything. She did as he asked, then dropped the phone in her lap.

"Listen, whatever you think my brother did," Charlotte began. She looked from DeLong to Oglethorpe and back again. "You're wrong. He's a good, caring guy."

DeLong leaned forward, resting his elbows on his knees. "Miss Grayson, have you heard on the news about a murder that happened at the Augusta Canal, near the Savannah Rapids Pavilion?"

"Yeah," she answered. "But what does this have to do with Charlie?"

"We have reasons to believe he was involved."

Charlotte scoffed, then laughed. When she realized he hadn't joined in, she widened her eyes again.

"You're not kidding, are you?"

"I'm afraid not," DeLong said. "We have a witness, and other evidence implicating him."

"No," she forced out. "That can't be true. He said he was done with all that stuff."

"I'm sorry," DeLong said. He heard the garage rumble open. A few seconds later, the kitchen door opened.

"Hey, Char, I'm back. Got the soup for the little kiddo. She feeling any better?"

DeLong motioned for Charlotte to remain quiet. He rose, making his way toward the kitchen.

"Charlie!" Charlotte exclaimed. "Run!"

"What?"

DeLong flew into the kitchen, his weapon at the ready. "Lewis, it's over. Lay on your stomach and put your hands behind your head."

Lewis froze for half a second.

Before DeLong realized what was happening, he tossed the bag of soup cans toward him and darted back into the garage.

"He's en route through the garage!" DeLong shouted into his radio as he chased after him.

Lewis ran through a bed of flowers and tripped. He fell face-first to the ground.

DeLong caught up with him, aiming his gun toward Lewis' head. "Don't make this any worse than—"

Lewis had hurled the garden gnome he'd fallen over toward DeLong. He ducked, the gnome grazing the top of his head. Lewis kicked him in the face and DeLong fell backward, but swept his legs to knock him over.

DeLong scrambled to his feet and attempted to kick Lewis' face.

Lewis blocked him with his hands and forced DeLong back to the ground. Lewis crawled on top of him and threw left and right punches.

DeLong blocked one of the fists coming at him and twisted his hand. Lewis cried out in pain when a bone popped. But that didn't give him much pause.

Lewis head butted DeLong, forcing him to fall back. He heard gunshot fire and once his vision cleared, he saw his suspect holding his weapon in front of him.

"Stay back or I'll kill him!" Lewis jammed the barrel of his gun against DeLong's throat.

"No one else has to get hurt!" It was Oglethorpe who'd spoken. "Just lay down your weapon!"

Lewis cursed him. "I put my weapon down, you'll hang me! That ain't happening."

"You don't have to do this," DeLong said. It wasn't easy trying to ignore the gun lodged against his throat. "You're trapped. You kill me, they'll kill you. You run, they shoot and kill you."

"So I'm a dead man, no matter, is that right?" Lewis chuckled.

"Unless you give me the gun," DeLong promised. "We'll take you in and you'll get a fair trial."

"Charlie, please," Charlotte stood from a distance. "Just tell them what happened. Please."

"It doesn't matter, Char," Lewis exclaimed. "I shot that cop in the neck. They ain't gonna let me go now. No matter what I tell them."

"Please!" Charlotte's voice had become more frantic. "I can't lose both my brothers. Not again."

DeLong watched as tears fell from the corner of Lewis' eyes.

"What is she talking about, Charlie?"

"I can't," Lewis whispered. He looked over at his sister, eyes narrow. His voice grew louder, more enraged. "It's my fault! I did this to him!"

DeLong watched as Lewis released the gun's pressure on his throat.

"Give me the gun, Charlie," DeLong said. "We'll go inside and talk it out."

Charlie shook his head, his lower lip quivering. "I'm sorry. Tell him I'm sorry for ruining his life."

"Charlie!"

DeLong's voice rang out, but before he'd grabbed the gun, it fired, echoing through the neighborhood.

Chapter 60

C HARLOTTE SCREAMED FROM BEHIND him.

Outlines of people filled the streets.

Voices were calling to him. Misty, faraway voices.

DeLong felt the sticky, wet blood clinging to his skin and clothes.

Through his blurry vision, he saw the outline of Charlotte falling to her brother's side. She picked his lifeless head and held him to her lap. She wailed, a high-pitched wailing, sounding inhuman.

"Detective, talk to me."

DeLong turned his head to see Oglethorpe kneeling next to him. As his vision cleared, he saw John and Hunt speaking into their radios, requesting backup and an ambulance. Neighbors piled out of their houses at the commotion.

He looked back to see Charlotte still weeping over her brother's body.

The image of him swinging his gun to his temple flashed before his eyes.

The sound of the gunshot when he pulled the trigger rang in his ears.

DeLong shook his head, trying to free himself from the memory. He looked back at Oglethorpe.

"I'm okay," he assured him.

The sergeant helped him to his feet.

Within minutes, police cars and ambulance sirens filled the air. The EMTs hurried to Lewis' body. A man urged Charlotte to let her brother go.

"Why don't you let the technicians look at you?" Oglethorpe suggested. "I'll talk to the girl."

"No," DeLong insisted with a shake of his head. "I'm fine."

He led the way to Charlotte, who sat on the bed of the ambulance. The man who coaxed her away from her brother's body had wrapped a brown towel around her shoulders. She held onto it, her body shaking.

"I'm sorry about your brother," DeLong said.

"How could he do this to me?" Charlotte's voice sounded small. "He promised he'd take care of everything."

"What did your brother mean when he said 'he did it to him'?"

Charlotte hesitated before speaking.

"He introduced him to his friends. When they were the Grey Wolves. Most of them split up when their leader was arrested." She closed her eyes and tears streamed down her cheek. "Charlie worked hard to clean up his act. But James was way out of control."

"Wait a second," DeLong said. He sat next to her. "James? As in J.J.?"

She nodded. "He's our brother. Well, half-brother. I'd already moved out of the house when he was born. I couldn't stand living with our parents. Especially our stepfather. He had these rules, where if you broke even a simple one, you were punished. Severely. He wasn't always like that, you know? Something happened that made him angry. And our mother was too weak to put a stop to it. So I left."

Charlotte wiped the tears from her eyes as she watched the EMT put her brother in the body bag.

"Charlie left next. So James had to deal with him alone. I told Charlie he had to get him away from there. So he collected a few of his closest friends. They went to the house and found that *man* beating him. Charlie jumped on his back and punched him until he was thrown off. James had found a gun in the desk drawer and held it to his head. I walked in the house just as he pulled the trigger." She paused. "He killed him. Right in front of us. And you know the worst thing? His eyes were different. They were cold. I didn't recognize my own brother."

"But the police reports say Charlie killed your dad."

"For a second, we froze." Charlotte's voice was becoming soft. "Then Charlie grabbed the gun. Told James he was never there. Charlie told him to run away."

"And that's when he showed up at Bree's," DeLong concluded.

She nodded. "She had approached Charlie at some point. He said she seemed like she'd actually care. But he thought he didn't deserve that kind of love and attention."

"But J.J. did," Oglethorpe put in.

"Yeah," she whispered. "J.J. did. After he left, Charlie wiped the prints off the gun and fired it again in case they checked for residue. By then, the police arrived. We scattered and found a place to lie low for a while."

"And J.J. was hidden at the ministry," DeLong muttered. "Who killed Bree?"

She didn't reply.

"Charlotte, did Charlie kill her?"

Charlotte shook her head.

"J.J. did," Charlotte said, her voice cracking. "Somehow she found out he killed our stepfather. She wanted him to turn himself in and take the responsibility."

"But he couldn't allow that to happen," DeLong concluded.

"No."

"Charlotte, I know this is hard for you, but we're going to need you to come with us and give us your statement."

"I can't," Charlotte whispered, her voice raw. Her eyes had become bloodshot from the tears she cried. "I don't want to lose the only brother I have left."

"Listen," DeLong said, his voice even. He put a hand on her shoulder. "With your statement, we can find a way to help him."

She whimpered and put her head in her hands. She nodded. "Okay."

After they arrived at the sheriff's office, DeLong had sent Oglethorpe with Charlotte to document her statement. He decided to pay J.J. a visit.

When he found him, he was chewing on a piece of bread.

"This food you give us is crap," he complained. "I need out."

"Your brother's dead," DeLong informed him.

J.J. hesitated, blinking his eyes twice. He shook his head. "I don't have a brother. I was an only child."

"We also found your sister, Charlotte," DeLong continued. "She's here now, writing her statement. Telling us exactly what happened on the night you killed your father. And when you murdered Bree."

J.J. frowned. "You're lying. You want me to confess to killing Miss Bree. Well, I ain't doing it! I didn't kill her!"

"How did she find out you killed your father?" DeLong asked. "Did she overhear your conversation with someone? Did you confide in her at one time, then realized later she was going to insist you turn yourself in?"

"No! That's not how it happened."

"Then tell me what happened," DeLong suggest. "If you tell the truth, we can help you."

"I ain't telling you nothing," J.J. spat as he crawled to the corner of the cot, hugging his knees.

DeLong's cell phone rang. He looked at the caller ID and saw it was his brother. He stepped out of earshot from J.J. and answered.

"We know who killed Bree," DeLong said. "But I'm trying to get more evidence. I'm trying to get him to confess why."

DeLong heard his brother sniffle on the other end of the line. "Who?"

"I'll tell you everything later, okay? For now, I've got to go."

After he ended the conversation, he returned to J.J.'s cell.

"That was my lab technician," DeLong lied. "You remember him? Mr. Newman. He finished processing the hoodie I found. The one you claimed belonged to Petey. It had hair all over it. Newman found a match." He watched J.J's expression. "To your DNA."

Anger burned in J.J.'s eyes as his chest rose and fell in quick movements.

"It was her fault!" J.J. jumped to his feet. His eyes went dark, and he glared at DeLong. "She was going to tell everyone. Then *I'd* be in trouble."

"How did she find out?"

"My stupid brother came by and told her. He fed her all that crap about how he was worried about me. He didn't care about me at all. She took me to the Safe Room and asked me about it. Asked me if it was true. She said she'd protect me if I told the truth." J.J. kicked the cot. "She lied to me. She wanted me to tell the truth myself, but I told her to forget it. She said 'fine. Then I'll do it myself.'" J.J. spoke the quote in imitation of Bree.

"What happened next?"

"I knew she would be at the pavilion. When I got there, she was arguing with her husband. So I waited until he left." He paced the cell. "She walked the trail, so I hid. When I saw her coming, I got the biggest rock I could find and hit her. Then I hit her again and again. I don't know what's wrong with me. I couldn't stop."

"So you left the handkerchief and walked away?"

"Yeah. I couldn't look at her like that," J.J. said with a half-smile. "You've killed before. You know how it feels."

"I know I didn't feel the same way you do," DeLong said. "I don't kill on purpose."

"It was her fault. And Charlie's. And Charlotte's."

"Of course," DeLong muttered, linking his arms across his chest. "It's everyone's fault but your own. Is that accurate?"

"My brother and sister left me with him, knowing how he treated us."

"What about Bree?" DeLong asked. "What did she do to you besides want to help you? It wasn't your fault your father was abusive. She would have helped you argue self-defense."

J.J. only stared back. His cold, dark eyes ran chills up DeLong's spine.

"Guess sometimes being helpful is too much of a good thing," DeLong observed. He turned to leave J.J. alone with his thoughts.

Chapter 61

DeLong sat at the bistro table, watching his brother pace the cement. After he showered to wash off Charlie Lewis' blood, he'd stopped by to fill his brother in on what had happened during the day, and now they were dealing with the aftermath.

Newman had called from the lab to confirm the hair sample matched J.J.'s DNA. He couldn't help but wonder how one kid in a bad situation could turn to murder while another grew to overcome all his obstacles. It was unnerving to think about it all.

DeLong removed a cigarette and offered the pack to Sullivan.

He shook his head to decline.

"So J.J. killed her because all she was trying to do was help him?" Sullivan cursed and fell into the seat. "I can't believe this."

"He was afraid of what would happen if she turned him in."

"But according to you, killing his father was self-defense," Sullivan said. "Nothing would have happened to him."

"We can't be so sure of that," DeLong reminded him, "You know the way the system is. J.J. is an angry kid with a lot of emotions running inside him. We don't know about his father, but I don't think he intended on actually killing Bree. Fear took its place. You understand that more than anyone."

Sullivan frowned and looked over at DeLong. "Yeah, I do."

They remained quiet, letting the tension build.

"Listen, I—"

"You know—"

They stopped speaking and laughed with discomfort.

DeLong told his brother to go first, and he pushed out a deep breath, staring off into the distance.

"I'm sorry," he said. "For everything I said or did over the years. For the things I *didn't* say or do. From that first day in juvie, until now, I was..." he trailed off, shaking his head.

"A jerk?" DeLong finished, drawing the tobacco smoke in his lungs, then pushing it out.

Sullivan laughed. "That's one way of putting it. In any case, I'm sorry. I blamed myself for everything. In one night, our whole life changed because I was mad at Dad and I wanted to rebel against him."

"The other day, you told me you were still there." DeLong tapped the edge of his cigarette. "Are you still?"

Sullivan hesitated before speaking. "No. You got me out."

DeLong stared at the ground, unable to find words to speak.

"Now that we got that awkwardness out," Sullivan said with a chuckle, "how's Lieutenant Kane?"

"He's doing better." DeLong set the cigarette between his lips. "The doctor said he should be ready for release tonight."

"That's great."

They fell into another awkward silence, then Sullivan pushed to his feet. DeLong followed suit.

Sullivan held his hand out. "Thanks, Jimmy, for all you did."

"It's my job," DeLong said, taking his hand. "But you're welcome, all the same."

Sullivan moved in and grabbed his brother in a hug. "I've always been proud of you, little brother. Always."

"Thanks," DeLong said.

They parted and Sullivan put a hand on his neck. "But if you tell anybody I said that, I'll deny it."

DeLong turned the corner of his lips into a smile. "You're all heart, brother. But your secret's safe with me."

DeLong opened the door and stepped into the house to see his wife and his mother busy at the stove fixing a late lunch. He didn't realize until that moment he was starving. He hadn't had the chance to eat all day.

"Something smells good," DeLong commented.

"How are you doing, son?" Felicity asked DeLong, her eyes narrowed in concern.

He leaned over to kiss her cheek. "Everything's good. Promise. Fix me some dinner. I haven't eaten all day."

"Now he's giving us orders." Felicity winked at Samantha, a smile playing on her lips. "I'm going to have a little talk with him about that."

"Why don't we let it slide for now," Samantha said. "After all, he hasn't eaten today. Hunger makes men crazy." She patted her husband's stomach and stood on her toes for a kiss.

"I guess you may be right, dear," Felicity agreed. She waved the spatula at him. "You're on warning."

"I'm used to that."

Bella and Ally appeared in the room, wearing princess costumes.

"You girls headed to a ball?" Sullivan asked, lowering himself to a chair. He pulled Ally into his lap.

"No, just playing," she said, putting her head on his shoulder. "I miss Mommy."

"I do too, honey," Sullivan said, wrapping his arms around Ally. He kissed her forehead.

"We all do," Felicity agreed, her voice soft.

She sniffled and DeLong wrapped his arm around her shoulder. Samantha leaned in close to him.

"Daddy," Bella said by the window. "Look."

While Felicity and Samantha continued to fix dinner, DeLong went to check on what his daughter wanted to show him.

"See?" she said.

He looked out the window but didn't see anything. "No. What are you talking about?"

"You don't see her?" Bella said with surprise. Her eyes glanced at their family, who weren't paying attention. "It's Aunt Bree. She's here."

"Bella," DeLong warned. "Don't do that. Please."

"But I saw her." She looked back out the window, then frowned. "She was there. I know it."

DeLong wasn't sure whether he wanted to believe his daughter was seeing ghosts or not. He was still having trouble wrapping his mind around that he'd been seeing and hearing things from beyond.

In any case, he kneeled, so he'd be at eye level.

"I saw her," she insisted.

"I believe you," he said. "I think she wanted you to tell your uncle and cousin something. Do you know what it could be?"

Bella frowned, then smiled. "I think so. Ally!"

When her cousin climbed off her dad's lap, she rubbed her moist eyes with her fingers.

"Your mom's here. I know it." She put her hands on her cousin's shoulder. "And she'll always be."

"Thanks," Ally whispered, rubbing her eyes again.

"C'mon." Bella grabbed her cousin's hand. "We need to get to a ball."

The girls darted out of the kitchen and pounded their feet up the staircase.

DeLong opened the door and scanned the yard.

There was no sign of his sister-in-law.

"What are you looking at?" Samantha asked, linking her arm around his waist.

"Nothing," he answered.

DeLong shut the door and felt a hand squeeze his shoulder. He looked where Samantha stood, only to find she had already moved back to the stove to help Felicity transfer the food into containers.

A chill crawled down his spine.

Love.

There was no denying he'd heard the words in the kitchen, amidst the chatter and banging pots.

"Sully," DeLong said.

Carrying two dishes to the table, Sullivan looked over at his brother.

"I think Bree would want to make sure you knew how much she loved you. No matter what went on. That's why she couldn't ever leave you."

"I know," Sullivan said with a brief pause. "But there are so many things I wished I'd said. The last time I ever saw her was when we were fighting."

DeLong put a hand on his shoulder. "Bella's right. She's here now. And she's not going anywhere."

"Thanks, man," Sullivan said.

After the table was set, DeLong went to the bottom of the staircase to call the girls to the table. Then he sat, said the blessing and ate.

"I think I'd like to finish what Bree started," Sullivan said as he stared out the windshield at the house. "She helped a lot of people. People like us."

DeLong turned the ignition off and dropped the keys in his lap.

"I think she'd be thrilled if you did, Sully," Samantha said from the backseat. She leaned forward with a smile. "She'd be proud."

"Agreed," DeLong said. "C'mon. Let's go see the kids."

DeLong climbed out of the car and helped Samantha to her feet. He shut the door and looked around.

He saw Zoe sitting on a bench with Petey. They looked over and waved.

DeLong waved back and took Samantha's hand. "Come with me. I want you to meet someone."

They made their way to the bench.

"Hey, Detective," Zoe said, her voice happier than when he first met her.

"How are you kids doing?"

They said they were good.

DeLong introduced Samantha to them. When another boy called for Petey to join them in a game, he took off, leaving the DeLongs alone with Zoe.

"What's going to happen to this place?" Zoe asked. Her eyes sparkled with concern. "What's going to happen to us? I mean, without Miss Bree, well..."

"I wouldn't worry, sweetheart. My brother said he wants to keep it running," DeLong said. "So I don't think it's going anywhere anytime soon."

"Good. Because I've been in the system before. I don't think I'd be able to take it again."

"What if you don't have to?" DeLong asked. "What if you became adopted?"

"What do you mean?"

"Sam and I want another kid," he explained. "We've tried over this past year, but it's impossible for us to get pregnant. And we'd like to have another kid."

Her eyes grew. "You want *me*?"

"We'd like to keep the option open," Samantha said. "Would you like to come over for dinner tonight? Meet our daughter?"

"Yes," Zoe exclaimed. "Thank you!"

She wrapped her arms around DeLong's neck and hugged him. Next, she moved over to Samantha.

When she pulled back, she wiped a tear from her eye. "I've seen others get adopted from under Miss Bree's care. But I never thought anybody would want me. I'm too old and already practically an adult."

"Zoe, you're thirteen," DeLong reminded her. "You've got some years to go before adulthood."

She smiled. "Will I still be able to help around here? I don't want to leave for good."

"We'd expect you to," Samantha said. "Sullivan will need help."

"Then he'll get it!" Zoe's head bobbed with excitement.

DeLong and Samantha rose to their feet. As they walked toward the front door, he put his arm around her waist.

She leaned into his ear. "This was a good idea, Jim DeLong. You've made me very happy."

"You make me happy just being here with me."

Zoe stepped inside, and before DeLong did, he took Samantha's face in her hands and kissed her. She moved further into the moment with a sigh.

He was satisfied with how things turned out. His brother was back in his life and they'd become friends. But he hated that Bree's death was the reason for it all.

Samantha pulled back from the kiss, smiled at him, and took his hand to lead him inside.

DeLong made a silent promise to Bree that her death wouldn't be in vain.

He stepped into the living room and watched as his brother spoke to Sylvia, Anna, and the children about the future o*f the ministry.

Books by Angela Kay

The Jim DeLong Mysteries
The Murder of Manny Grimes
Blood Runs Cold

The Aidan O'Reilly Serial Killer Thrillers
A Killer's Mark
A Killer's Vengeance
A Killer's Cell
A Killer's Web
A Killer's Edge
A Killer's Return

The Genevieve Steel FBI Mystery Series
The Daughter's Curse

Standalones
Whispers of the Dead
Kept in Silence
Gone Viral

Novellas
The Naked Eye: A Locked Room Mystery
A Killer's Trail (Part of the Aidan O'Reilly Series
and takes place after the events of *A Killer's Mark*, and right
before *A Killer's Vengeance*, however, this can be read at any time.)

About Angela Kay

Angela Kay delves into the darkest corners of the human mind, weaving tales of suspense and FBI thrillers that keep readers on the edge of their seats. Intrigued by the complexities of human nature, she explores themes of darkness and intrigue, creating stories that linger long after the last page is turned.

Every morning, she writes at her desk, accompanied by her loyal feline assistants, Loki and Nutmeg. When not immersed in writing, she enjoys watching crime shows or getting lost in a good book, always in search of the next spark of inspiration.

www.ingramcontent.com/pod-product-compliance
Lightning Source LLC
Chambersburg PA
CBHW052034240626
47153CB00006B/2079